Grey

The Balance: Book One

By

Nick Shamhart

Dedication

Once upon a time I fell in love with a girl. That girl became a woman, and I fell in love with her too. That woman became my wife, and I fell in love with her again. My wife became a mother and I fell in love with her once more. What will she become next? I don't know, but I'm sure I'll love her too. This book could not have been possible without that girl whom I love and loved so long ago. Love you Jen.

Acknowledgements

This book is for my family and friends who spent years telling me to write a book, so I did. I hope you enjoy it. A special thanks to "Omega Squadron" for all their last minute input.

Chapter 1

You ever wonder what happens to you when you die? I never did. It crossed my mind that I would die, but what happened after? I was always of the "we'll see what happens when we get there" mindset. Well sure enough I got there just like everybody does at some point; death don't discriminate. It comes for all of us, every man, woman, and child to walk this good earth has to pay their toll at the end. When my end came I was given a choice. Not by a god or the God, but by a cute little brunette in a blue cotton sundress, with a light sprinkling of freckles across her nose. She said her name was Harmony in a perky lilting country voice. She was the kind of pretty that had I met her while I was livin' she would've knocked my socks right off.

Sounds kind of strange I know. Y'all have certain ideas or concepts for what the afterlife should be like don't you? That is of course if you believe in one at all. Most of you were probably expecting me to say I was greeted by a warm light that beckoned me forward or some such; sorry not how it worked for me. No visions of loved ones who'd passed on offering an open armed welcome for me, no sir. I was shot and killed in a back alley, bang! I was dead but not gone, a collateral casualty in another man's war, so game over for me, or in retrospect I guess it was only round one. But

I didn't know that at the time. Then moments later I woke up in that same alley feelin' better than I had in years, and looked back to see my body lying flat out like a sack of grain. This pretty young girl with freckles was standing before me with a smile, and she said, "Jasper, your time has come, and you have to make a decision." That's my name by the way Jasper Reynolds, my momma used to call me "Jas," but over the generations somewhere people just started callin' me "Grey."

"Jasper," she continued, "the choice is yours. I cannot make it for you. You can stay here on this plane of existence choosing to become a force for good or evil depending on your actions. You could move on to the next phase of being, some call it moving back to the Source of all life. Please do not ask me what that means, because I do not fully know myself. My place is here among this world and the creatures that reside there in. Your final choice is that you could stay and work for me; to fight for the Balance. Life cannot exist without balance. We are the ones who keep existence from spinning into chaos. We are neither good nor evil. We are neutral. Will you join me?"...........

***

The beeps, hisses, and hums emitted from the monitors in the dying man's room served more as a funeral dirge than a measure of how the patient was doing. He had gone past the point where anything could be done for him other than to make him comfortable until the end came. The bloated body that once lived so vitally was shutting down. His lungs had started to slowly fill with fluid as his heart failed. What family he had wandered in and out over the last few days to say their "goodbyes," and make their peace. The man's name was Peter Malcolm Halberstein, but ever since elementary school when the other boys started in on phallic humor he insisted on being called Pete. Pete had been slowly and steadily dying in increments over the last few years.

Late in the night when visiting hours had long been over (the days when hospitals enforced such rules had past, especially in the cases of those who are close to death), Pete watched the shadows play along the door to his room as he tried to breathe. The oxygen being forced into his lungs made him feel queasy and nauseous, making it all but impossible for him to smell anything past its industrial plastic odor. Given the state of his fellow patients Pete thought that might actually be a blessing. There was a woman a couple rooms down who was suffering from the end stages of dementia. She ranted and raved with sundowner's syndrome every night. Pete had seen her with her grandchildren during the day when they came to visit, and he wondered what those grandchildren would think of Granny if they were here now to hear her shouting, "Fucknuts," at every passing employee. Pete laughed, and said to the empty room, "Gee Grandma these chocolate chip cookies sure are swell! What kind of nuts are these anyway? Walnuts?"

"No, they're-" Pete said in his imitation of the old lady's voice motioning toward the open door to his suite, where an angry voice could be heard calling out, "Fucknuts!"

Pete laughed causing his feeble body to shake. Spasms and cramps turned the old man's chuckles into sobs. When he caught his breath Pete muttered, "Indignity all around, man. Nobody should fall apart like this." He lifted up a bruised shaking hand to look at the discoloration left by the seemingly endless succession of IV lines that had now been taken away. The nurses told him his body was retaining too much fluid, and the swollen brown fingers of his right hand were a testament to that. "Call it tragically poetic, but dying ain't no way to die damn it!"

He fell into a light doze as the night lengthened. Nurses came and went quietly trying not to disturb him, but Pete wanted to be disturbed. He was happy that their constant prodding and poking woke him. He wanted to hear them. He wanted to hear any noise, even

Fucknuts down the hall, because that meant that he was still alive. That he was still there, and that he was not yet dead.

Death had scared Pete since he was a boy when he realized that death was for keeps, "no do overs" as the kids in his neighborhood used to say. There had not been any moments of sagacious epiphanies on the meaning of life and death for him as he aged. Pete did not find God, or a religion that gave him comfort. Death had terrified him more and more as the years passed. Instead of coming to terms with it through his deteriorating health, Pete started to actually see Death.

He had first noticed Death as a shadow of a man who lingered at the corner of his vision, but never appearing clearly when Pete would try to focus on him. Pete would see Death hovering around the frozen food section at the grocery store, standing in his kitchen in the middle of the night when Pete went for a snack, or sitting with his feet propped up in the back row during one of Pete's lectures. *It has to be Death*, Pete had thought to himself. *I'm too damn old to start believing in ghosts.*

Then Death hovered around him in longer stretches once he started this last hospital stay. It had silently checked in on him for hours at a time deep in the night, allowing him to conceive a more definitive shape for it. Death, to Pete, looked like a long limbed Caucasian man with salt and pepper hair wearing weathered jeans and a white tee-shirt. That made Pete chuckle ruefully to himself saying, "Wouldn't you know it, Pete, Death is going to come for you as a lean mean white boy! James Dean stars as Death in 'Rebel Without a Pulse.' The universe does have a sense of humor."

Pete had never given much thought to another man's ethnicity outside of how he could use it as a descriptive tool. He had been a professor of literature at Cornell, and been the proud teacher to several novelists, but never published any works of merit himself. He had come to terms with that early in his career, and realized his talents lay in helping others learn their craft. Pete was African American, but that only served as a physical feature to his logic. This person or that person had a certain complexion, light skinned, dark mahogany, café ole, or pale as snow only worked as a point of reference. His father had been adopted by a Jewish couple living in New York City who passed their last name down to him, so race held more humor for him than substance.

"So here you are, Pete," he said to himself, "a dying black man with a Jewish name, falling apart on a creaky adjustable bed, speaking some of my last words to an empty room, with Death leaning into the doorframe now and again. The docs keep saying I might hallucinate as the end comes, maybe that's all this Death nonsense has been, just a really long hallucination? Hey, you there! Hallucination! I know you're there white boy! You may as well come in and have a seat. Keep these failing old bones a little company in my last hours. I see your shadow, just outside the door, and that is decidedly not a nurse, so come on in and 'pop a squat' as we used to say, or can't Death speak?"

"I speak just fine, Pete, but choose to hold my tongue. Unlike some folks," said the shadow from the doorway in a drawling country cadence.

"Well son the time has passed for being taciturn. I'm sure as shit not getting any younger. You've been stalking my old ass for years now, and I want to know why. Hell at this point a hallucination is better company than no company at all."

"I ain't a hallucination, Pete," the voice said, and the shadow outside the door turned to fill the empty space with the same man Pete had seen before. This time there were no hard to glimpse details, he stood there solid and clearly defined, wearing the same weathered clothes. His gray eyes held the confidence of an older man though he appeared to be no more than forty. Pete shook his head and said, "That's what you'd say even if you were one though. Go on and give me an explanation anyway, you're my hallucination, so you should at least have a good story right, so why?"

The man walked into the room saying, "Why, Pete? That's a complicated question, but I suppose it's time for me to give you a few answers, but be warned they're only going to lead to more questions. Since I already know who you are let me start by introducin' myself. My name was Jasper Reynolds, but now-a-days everybody just calls me Grey."

"I won't say it's nice to meet you, Grey, because something tells me I should reserve that judgment for after you have spoken your piece."

"Fair enough, Pete, fair enough. I've been following you around for some time now, because I believe that I may be ready to move on, and I think you could serve as my replacement," Grey said. Then Grey eased himself into a lounging chair next to Pete's bed and placed his worn boots up on the multipurpose tray table that was only partially tucked under the bed. His boots did not so much as disturb or move a single pea left on Pete's barely touched dinner tray that had yet to be collected. Making note of that Pete said, "If you aren't a hallucination, then why didn't anything move around?"

"Because I didn't want anything to move, Pete. If I don't want to interact with the physical world, then I don't have to," Grey said moving his boot back and forth across the tray by way of elaboration.

"So then… you are Death! Aren't you?"

"I'm not Death, Pete, and I'm right sorry if you've been thinkin' all this time that I was. I'm an agent for the Balance, a warrior with a dirty job that somebody has to do. In a nut shell what I do is keep the whole of existence from being ripped apart into chaos."

"Wow, Grey! Where does a man sign up for that? That sounds like a dream job for an afterlife! Can't I just sit on a cloud and play with a harp, or maybe take a long nap? You need to work on your sales pitch a bit man if you want to be a recruiter."

"Well, Pete," Grey said, "your other options are to move on to the Source or you could stay here on this physical plane becoming more of what you already are."

"What the hell does that mean?" Pete asked as a nurse walked in the room to do her patient assessment. When she leaned over to take Pete's pulse he said, "Hello miss, have you met my friend Death?" He placed a swollen hand to the side of his mouth and whispered, "He says he isn't a hallucination or Death, but, come on, a cowboy in the Finger Lakes?"

The nurse did not acknowledge that Pete had said anything. "She can't hear you, Pete," Grey said. "You're too far gone already and she can't see me unless I want her to." He removed his feet from the tray, leaned forward placing his elbows on his knees, and clasped his hands together under his stubble covered chin. "And if I'm not mistaken, Pete, by the look on her face and by the sound of your labored breathing, I think you're about to join me completely instead of driftin' in and out as you have been. Don't worry a lick. Soon you'll feel better than you have in your entire life. Believe me, there ain't nothing to be scared of."

Pete's death unfolded like so many before his and so many yet to come. The medical staff rushed about trying to prolong a life that would have ended a long time ago if nature had been allowed to run its course. Orders were barked out, machines were fired up, and every lifesaving technique was attempted, but the inevitable end result could no longer be put off. Pete died.

There was little in the way of transition for Pete, one minute he was lying in bed as his body drowned in its own fluid, and the next he was standing beside Grey watching the medical staff's futile efforts to keep him alive. He was dressed in comfortable street clothes instead of his rumpled hospital gown. Plucking at his khaki colored pants he asked, "Grey, is that it? I mean there's my body. I'm looking at me laying in that bed over there. God damn! I look like shit! Wait, I didn't mean that God, sorry. " Pete looked up at the drop ceiling as if expecting to be struck by some form of divine retribution. Scanning the room his eyes glanced over at the mirror in his hospital suite, and stopped. Then as he ran a non-swollen, non-bruised hand over his smooth youthful features he said, "Holy Shit! I look thirty again! Hot damn! Sorry, but this is… Well damn! How the hell did I get out of that hospital johnny? You were right, I feel fantastic! Like I could run a marathon and still have energy left over to go at it all night with the entire Swedish bikini team! God damn this is awesome! Shit, Grey is there a God? Is he going to kick my ass down to hell for that?"

Grey smiled, and placing a hand on Pete's shoulder he steered him toward the open doorway. He said, "Pete, my friend. That is a conversation I think we need to have in a place a bit more comfortable. I don't know about you, but I was never a big fan of hospital food. There's an all-night diner a few blocks from here that serves great cheeseburgers. What say we head there? I find nothing suits profound discussions of the universe like greasy food."

Chapter 2

Choices. It always seems like life is full of choices doesn't it? Choose this and that happens, choose that and this happens, cause and effect, ripples in a pond, and all those colloquialisms. My life was so full of options I guess it shouldn't have surprised me to find that death was full of choices too. No matter how unpalatable the results of those choices may be it doesn't mean that a man ain't got a choice. There are always choices, but some folks may see things differently I suppose.

Stay or leave. Good or evil. "The choice is yours," Harmony had said to me, but what did that really mean? I had never thought of myself as a saintly person mind you, but I certainly was no monster either. I'd made some bad choices in life sure, but I'd made some good ones too. So if I stayed here what kind of force would I become? I wouldn't go about harming people, and I didn't plan on helpin' old ladies cross the street either. We're always faced with the unknown, that don't mean we have to like it though.

There was a stirring at the core of my being like an invisible hand wrenchin' and yankin' on my insides, pulling me back toward the Source. To move on I guess, but quite frankly the idea of something pulling me out of my control, out of myself, well I think you may understand when I say that scared the shit out me! I couldn't imagine no longer being master of my own fate. I've heard folk now-a-days call a person like me a "control freak." I think it was easier when we just said stubborn. I didn't want to lose who I was just yet. I liked being me fine and dandy, why risk changing that?

Standing in that dark alley with Harmony all those years ago I said, "No ma'am, I sure don't feel like going anywhere, I'm doing just fine right here. What did you have in mind?"

She smiled at me, and man alive I would have done just about anything to keep that smile directed at me. "Then come with me now Jasper. I have much to show you," she said and reached a hand out to me.

What would you have done? Stand around in the dark, or take the hand of a beautiful woman when she offered it? Me, I touched that pretty girl's delicate out stretched hand and that, my friends, that is when I moved toward the light. It wasn't the light of movin' on, but the light of Harmony, of the Balance. She engulfed me in light, soothing dim light, with a warm core blendin' to darkness at the edges. I felt peace and agitation all at once. I wanted to stay in the light and throw myself at the darkness all at the same time. This was over in the flash of a thought. The relation of space and time are the purview of smarter men than me, but things *changed, either they did or how I perceived them did. Time flew by so fast that I wasn't even sure it had happened, but it also lasted an eternity. I still keep to a calendar now, because there ain't no going back in time, only forward. How fast or slow that time moves depends not only on point of view, but on state of matter or life or afterlife. Hell even I know what I mean and it confuses me.*

My next conscious thought, after a second or an epoch, was an awareness of laying on my back in a warm meadow filled with bird song, the sharp green tang of broken grass ticklin' my nose, the sun warming my brow, and the pretty freckled face of Harmony looking down on me...........

***

The tires of a passing car sprayed up a fine mist onto the dimly lit sidewalk where Grey and Pete strolled. Most of the buildings they passed as they walked by were dark and locked up for the night, but well maintained, not the derelict urban sprawl that can be readily found around so many hospitals. Pete was buzzing with energy, and basking in the use of a fully functioning body after years of being infirm. He slowed down to examine a newspaper dispenser then had to run to catch up to Grey. Panting he asked, "Wait, Grey, why am I breathing heavy? If I'm dead I shouldn't even need to breathe right? And for that matter why are we walking? Couldn't we just teleport to wherever we're going? You know just think about it and nod our heads 'I Dream of Jeannie' style?"

Grey slowed his pace down to match Pete's and looked him over once before saying, "It don't work that way Pete, but for starters you're only winded because of mental conditioning. You spent the last seventy five years of your life learning how the human body responds to certain conditions. Once we learn to walk, runnin' is never too far behind, and after decades of being winded after quick movements, due to your body's demand for oxygen, your mind, the energy that you are now, still automatically believes you should be winded. That is the same reason your physical appearance looks like you did for the prime of your life, because the mind is conditioned to it. Give it some time and you will adjust. Learn to shape your form however you desire, move at speeds beyond what a mortal body is capable of, leap tall buildings in a single bound, and all that."

A grin worthy of the *Cheshire Cat* split Pete's face, "You didn't say teleportation was out, so will I be able to Barbara Eden myself from place to place?"

Grey stopped walking and turned to face Pete. The damp sidewalk gave off a

18

pungent mildew aroma that permeated the air between them. He cleared his throat and said, "Look, Pete, you are an intelligent man. That is one of the reasons I was drawn to you. Your natural inquisitive state is why you are so bright, so I fully expected a ton of questions. That said, could you try to keep the questions to things that you feel might be important to your decision of what choice you want to make? And not 'Can we fly, or teleport, or walk unseen into a women's locker room?' ….And damn it, I can see you want to ask those questions by the look on your face right now, so to make it easier on myself. Yes, in theory to the first. No, to the second, I don't know why, because quantum mechanics were not something we were taught in my time. And yes to the third, but don't try it until you have better control over yourself, or you'll turn into an urban legend. 'The Black Ghost of Ladies' Fitness,' and don't smile because that wouldn't be as cool as it sounds!...Okay, maybe it would be, but let's keep walking. I'm starvin'."

The lights from the diner shone down brightly on the dark streets and sidewalks, lending an aura of life to an otherwise dead cityscape. People were crowded at the counter, mostly college kids out and about late at night needing a place to burn off some of their exuberance. They inevitably turned up in one of the town's few twenty-four hour businesses. The booths and tables were mostly empty, and the few that were occupied held couples, heads bent together in private conversations. Pink and blue neon lights proclaimed "Don's Eats" from the roof, except the middle "S" was burned out so it read "Don Eats." The gaudy illumination and décor banished any comparison to Hopper's "Nighthawks." This was a place to drink coffee, eat pie, and make monumental life decisions.

Pete and Grey slipped into a booth in the back of the diner where if they turned in their seats they could see the whole establishment spread out before them, a set stage of night-life in a large city. The smells of heavy grease and stale coffee had soaked into the benches, tables, and chairs over the decades since Don's first opened. A perpetual haze hung about the place, even when there was nothing being prepared, as if the diner itself was a sentient being who wanted to smoke, despite the laws that now forbid patrons from doing so. Pete heard a radio playing in the kitchen, loud enough for him to make out John Fogerty's raspy voice shouting over the ambient chatter of the college kids at the counter.

A young waitress looking worn and tired, but still functional made her way over to them and asked, "What can I get you guys?"

She did not put much enthusiasm into her voice. It was a question she had asked a thousand times, and would most likely ask it again a thousand more. She had the look of a woman who subsided on caffeine as much as food for nourishment. Lines had formed at the corners of her eyes from sleep deprivation not aging. The wrinkles around her eyes bunched up more, climbing around to incorporate her forehead when she looked up from her pad and pencil to make eye contact with Grey.

He answered, "I would be mighty grateful my dear if you could bring me a well done cheeseburger, French fries, and a large vanilla Coke if that's possible." Grey reached out a hand and placed it on the girl's forearm as he answered her question. Pete saw a soothing orange pulse of light leave Grey's fingertips and shoot up the waitress's arm to the rest of her body. When it reached her face it seemed to take years of cynicism out of her eyes, the wrinkles vanished, and the weight was pulled off the tired set of her shoulders.

She kept her smiling face on Grey as she said, "Well aren't you just the sweetest thing? Honey, I'll get you whatever you want, as long as you keep grinning at me like that. What about your friend? What can I get him?" She asked without looking in Pete's direction.

"He'll have the same, darlin'. Only make his a chocolate shake please."

She beamed another smile in Grey's direction after she wrote down their order, and turned to leave for the kitchen. When the sound of her heels told them she was out of ear shot Pete looked at Grey and asked in a loud whisper not whisper, "What the hell was that?"

"That, Pete, was politely ordering our dinner. I took the liberty of indulgin' your sweet tooth for you," Grey said blandly, as he looked out over the crowd.

"Bullshit! Not the food. I'm talking about that orange *E.T.* light thing you did with your fingers! What was that? And for that matter how can she see us when the nurses couldn't? And if we're dead why the hell are we eating?"

"Fine, the light was just a little of what I do in my role for the Balance. That young girl is in her late twenties, and her life has been very hard. She is a good person, but the day to day hassles of livin' keep wearing her down. She was pushing her body further than she should, and had aged herself out of balance to her actual years. I gave her a bit of that energy and life back. It wasn't much, but sometimes the little things can make a big difference. Most likely she'll wear herself back out, but that is her choice now. She sees us because I want her to see us. Did you notice that she only looked at me, but not at you? She could sense there was a second person, but not specifically you and or what you looked like. Without digging too deep into the science of it, I slowed our vibration to a level she could see. When you died you were movin' at a higher speed. That is why you felt so light and young.

22

Take a moment and examine how you feel now."

Pete shut his eyes, shifted in his seat a bit, and then shrugged his shoulders. "Heavier, I guess; more solid and cumbersome. Kind of like a gawky teenager again really."

"Exactly right my friend. When we want to interact with life on this level we have to make a sort of physical shell. It ain't a body like we had, but more like a representation of what we were to interact in their lives," Grey said and motioned at the other diners. "We can cause changes at the elementary levels of energy in our true forms. We can place ideas or words in people's minds, harness energy to affect other beings like ourselves, but we cannot touch physical objects or people unless we form this shell for lack of a better term. We can eat in this shell form, because…well damn it every job needs a fringe benefit or nobody would do it right? What better modern benefit could there be other than eatin' all the food you want, and not worryin' about the health ramifications?"

A slight smile crept up at the corners of Pete's mouth when he said, "Well, I wouldn't turn down a little personal attention from a grateful young waitress either or is that outside of your fringe benefits?"

"Sex, when driven by love and not lust, is the ultimate expression of balance. Two

23

of the same, giving up all thought of self to create one, but that ain't often the case is it? Neither you, nor I had children in our physical lives, Pete. If you join us that will be something you'll regret, and I speak from experience there. As far as just having sex, sure, in your shell you could, but I think without your hormones urging you on it would just be one more piece of mental conditioning that you find passes in time."

The waitress set their orders down right after Grey had stopped speaking, and the two of them fell silent. "You two don't need to clam up on account of me. Here's your burgers," she said, then smiling at Grey over her shoulder called, "Enjoy!"

The comfortable quiet of eating good food in pleasant company descended over the table. The ambient noises of the diner drifted over them, clinking silverware, ice rattling in glasses, murmured conversations, the static hum of the radio coming from the kitchen, that farting sound from squeeze ketchup bottles and the occasional laugh at the counter.

"Go ahead and ask me again, Pete." Grey said from around a mouthful of cheeseburger. He pulled a napkin from the dispenser sitting at the condiment laden end of the table. The shoddy paper tore in his hand leaving a little tab sticking out of the upper corner like a white flag of surrender. Grey mumbled, "Damn things never work."

Pete scrunched up his features before saying, "Alright. Is there a God?"

Grey took a sip from his straw before he answered, "I don't know man. Sorry, but I well and truly don't. You feel that tug at the core of your being right now? It's that subtle shift trying to pull you somewhere," Grey asked, and Pete nodded his head in response. "Well, that is what I meant by 'moving on' that pulling is the Source. That's what we call it at least, the Source. As far as we can tell from here it is the Source of all life, all energy. It beckons us to itself when we die and when a new life is formed that is where it comes from. Some folk say the Source is God, because it created everything, and I wouldn't disagree with that logic, but to call it God with the human connotations of religion behind it, with rules of 'thou shall and thou shall not.' That just puts too much of a human face on it for my tastes. It ain't human, with all those inherent personality flaws. The Source is unknowable, until we let go and move on to it that is."

"Okay that makes sense, I guess," Pete said, "but what about my other options? I could stay here and become something else right? More of what I was you said, what did you mean by that?"

"The terms I'll use are only human labels like 'God' they don't really hold the meaning you may think of, given how people can misconstrue things and warp ideas to better suit their own agendas, but you'll come to realize what they are given time and experience. But for lack of a better description Pete, you as a good person could stay here in this realm and slowly evolve into some degree of 'angel,' or a person who was mostly evil would evolve into a 'demon or devil.' Interacting with others of your kind, because like attracts like, and doing more of what you did in life be it giving and helping or taking and hurtin' others. And sticking around means they didn't want to let go of this world just yet, so both sides are always messing with livin' people."

"Or I could join you right? Flirt with pretty young waitresses. Maybe eat greasy food, *E.T.* glow finger touch people, and what else? What would I really do, because that can't be the extent of it?" Pete asked, and started to scoop the last of his milkshake out of the glass with a long metal spoon.

"No, you're right. This ain't it by a long shot. Let's talk simple science, for example an atom is a complete and balanced structure," Grey picked up the red, yellow, and white condiment squeeze bottles. He squirted a large dollop of mayonnaise onto the center of his empty plate. Then he added a few tiny yellow dots of mustard around the edges of the mayo glob. "That atom stays complete through a proper balance of protons, neutrons, and electrons. Protons carry a positive charge and electrons a negative one, but the whole thing would break apart if the neutrons didn't hold it all together. The universe keeps to certain patterns, you follow?" He punctuated this by squeezing a hefty blob of ketchup into the middle of the mayonnaise.

Pete pointed at Grey's sauce laden plate, "You're telling me you're the ketchup."

"Yes, in an overly simplified example. Myself, and the others I work with, would be the neutrons on this level of existence. What I do is more complicated than that, so call this the preview. A small taste of what it means to work for the Balance," Grey said and spun the plate lightly causing the condiments to blend. He gestured to the colored globs that had run together into a chaotic mass. "If somebody doesn't keep the Balance this is what would happen to everything."

"Alright, you want me? I'm curious I'll admit, but as much as I like a good burger, and it would be cool to be a neutron, I loved the *Pointer Sisters,* too. But Grey you're going to need to pull off some really good *ILM* quality effects in your 'preview' to get my vote. Not just crude table art."

"In all honesty, Pete, there is another reason we came to this particular diner. If you'll turn, and look over your shoulder you'll see a scruffy looking fellow who came in after us nursing a cup of coffee sittin' at a table near the register," Grey said pointing with his index finger.

Pete turned and looked to where Grey had directed him, "Yeah okay I'm with you so far, now what?"

"Do you see that dark spot off to his right, around his shoulder? It's probably a bit out of focus. Concentrate on it for a moment and it should resolve itself into an image of what it is. Your senses right now are in their infancy again; you'll have to learn how to see all over again, until you make your choice that is."

Pete strained his vision, squinting like a baseball player into a blinding glare, and said, "No...no it just looks like a dark cloud of...wait! Damn! What the fuck is that thing? It looks like the result of a spider monkey humping a wiener dog! Damn, it's ugly! And why is it pulling on that guy's ears?"

"Yep, that's Phil alright," Grey said with a laugh. "Would you believe that monkey wiener dog used to be an accountant for the Teamsters? Funny things happen to a person when they stay behind, Pete. Without the constant reminder of a body for your mental conditioning to hold onto, well...you start to look more like what you really were on the inside when you were a mortal person. That has a beautiful kind of justice to it if you ask me, and to answer your question, Phil is tugging on that guy's ears because he is trying to convince him to pull that gun he has in his front pocket out and rob the diner."

Grey raised his soft drink up to his lips and had a long pull from the straw. He placed the glass back on the table before easing out of the booth. Then he turned after clearing the confined space and planted both hands on the worn tabletop. He then leaned over to tell Pete in a confident voice, "And now, I'm going to show you some of that *ILM* magic you wanted."

Grey did not run, rush, or sprint over to Phil the monkey wiener dog demon. He walked causally over toward the other booth by the register as if he were strolling over to pay his bill, or to ask the scruffy looking man if he could borrow his salt shaker. When Grey was a few paces from him the man looked up and so did Phil. Each of them widened their eyes to comic proportions as Grey approached the table. The man twisted in his seat with the panic of a cornered animal when Grey leaned over and said, "Son, it ain't worth it. I'll pay for your coffee if you stand up and walk right out that door without looking back. You don't want to do this. Times are tough everywhere and these good people don't deserve to have it taken out on them."

Grey turned his back to the man and started to walk back to the booth he was sharing with Pete. The man jolted up so fast from his table that he knocked his ceramic mug to the floor where it shattered and spilled its stale coffee remnants all over the worn linoleum. He stopped at the door when Phil started bucking and pulling for all he was worth on the man whose hand had slipped back into his coat pocket, fingering the gun it concealed.

Pete watched as Grey slowly walked toward him. There was no emotion on Grey's face, no strain, only the relaxed calm of a man going about his day. The scruffy man pulled his hand out of his coat pocket enough that Pete could see the matte black finish of a small firearm. Grey closed his eyes for a short moment and when he reopened them his storm cloud colored irises and pupils were gone. His eyes were now glowing with a blue light. The same color of light that was pulsing from Grey's right hand in a softball sized sphere. There was no gradual progression that Pete could see. Grey went from a tired looking middle-aged laborer to a glowing statue of power instantly.

Grey spun and launched the sphere of light right at the man's head like a quick draw cowboy right out of a television western. Pete was not sure if the man saw the light or not, but Phil surely did because he screamed and squealed trying to get out of the path of Grey's ball of light. Either Grey's aim was very good or Phil was very slow, but the blue sphere met the demon straight on. The light engulfed the demon in a bubble. It trapped the demon in a cage much like a hamster in a roll around ball. Phil thrashed about as the bubble started to contract on him, tighter and tighter until he could no longer move his limbs. A bright blue egg with a rotten black yolk hung in midair, and then in an explosion of light and shadow Phil the demon was gone.

The diners went on about their meals and conversations. No one paid much attention as the scruffy man left the diner shaking his head, and muttering to himself. The waitress sighed behind the counter when she saw the mess of the coffee cup, and the unpaid check. Grey smiled and winked at her as he pulled a five dollar bill from the faded back pocket of his jeans, and placed it over the man's check.

When Grey (no longer glowing with an aura of power) had meandered back to their booth and slid into his seat looking across at Pete, he asked, "So are you in?"

Chapter 3

I was never much for philosophy and science when I lived in my physical form. I came from a time and place where the deepest thoughts that the common folk had were that a man made his way by the strength of his arms, the sweat from his brow, and by the sharpness of his wits. Thinking about what life meant was for armchair generals and soft footed intellectuals. I don't mean to imply that our way was better, no sir not by a long shot. We had murder in the streets, larceny runnin' rampant like a plague, and everyone seemed to be out for themselves. I guess things haven't really changed all that much, huh? Same shit, different century, how about that for philosophy?

You could see why I was confused when Harmony took my energy into herself. Even saying it that way makes me remember why I didn't care too much for schoolin'. I always learned things the hard way. What knowledge I have now I gained through experience and out of necessity for survival. So you understand why I was confused and asked Harmony, "Where are we?"

She said, "We are here. Here being outside of the world, yet in it. All of this that you perceive." She swept her arms out around herself, and spun like a child doing it for the pleasure of being dizzy. When she stopped she continued talking, "This Jasper is me. I am energy, life, and death. I am everywhere and nowhere. When you are here you are a part of me, for you are inside of me, and I am inside of you. Our energies are commingling to create something greater than we were alone. When I return you to the world there will still be some of me within you, and some of you will stay here. We will be able to commune at anytime, because of this energy that we now share."

Harmony giggled. Lord almighty the girl had a wonderful giggle. I think my confusion was clear on my face, because she stood up and started to twirl again giggling to herself as she moved. "Come with me Jasper. I will show you what I mean."……

***

"Am I in? Good lord man, do you really have to ask? George Lucas, eat your heart out! That was awesome!" Pete shouted. He looked around at all the other patrons going about the business of eating without giving the impression that anything unusual had happened. "But why isn't anybody else reacting?"

Grey leaned back in the booth, turning his body sideways, and placed his back to the window. He crossed his legs so his boots were sticking out into the aisle before he said, "Because they didn't see anything, Pete. Sure they saw me standing there, but Phil, and the energy I manipulated to destroy him, were there at a level beyond what the human eye can see. Think of it like ultraviolet light, infrared or anything else you can't see while alive. There are a few exceptions, of course, when some energy 'spills over' into the physical world. Hell, spill overs are the reason behind many of those instances of what you may have heard people talk about with ghosts or magic."

"You mean like cold spots, EVP, poltergeists, and things like that?"

"Yep, and tons of others including them UFO's your generation is so obsessed with."

"Aw, man, seriously, you mean there aren't any aliens?"

Grey chuckled and shook his head, "Sorry Pete, that ain't my area, but I can tell you that I've never met one. Look, if you're in I think it's time you met the boss. Come with me. She's waiting, and she'll be able to help you understand things a bit more." Grey stood up from the booth with Pete following on his heels. Grey handed the waitress a fifty dollar bill as they passed her cleaning up the ceramic coffee cup shards. He leaned down toward her saying, "Keep the change darlin'. You have yourself a good night now."

They walked on past her as she struggled to squeak out a, "Thanks." Grey and Pete made their way past the register to the scuffed and chipped diner door. Grey leaned forward to open the door for Pete. The exit no longer showed a vista of urban nightlife, but instead a warm sunlit meadow, complete with wildflowers, birds chirping, insects humming, and white cabbage butterflies dancing about in the tall grass. Pete stopped just shy of crossing the threshold, eyeing the new surroundings. He placed his hands on either side of the door and leaned his neck and shoulders out of the building. Grey laughed to himself as Pete looked left, then slowly turned his head to the right, then quickly back to the left again. "Um, Grey? Did I miss something? I thought you said no teleportation. You did say no teleportation right? Because last I checked this door opened up onto a west side street, not…what is this 'Little House on the Prairie'?"

"We didn't teleport, Pete," Grey confirmed. Stepping around Pete, he swept his arm out the door in an encompassing gesture. "This is Harmony, our boss you'd say. That is if you still want to join me? She is everywhere at all times, she is the Balance. So for us to join her we simply change the way we are. Use the idea of us vibrating at a higher level if that works for you, a little string theory for the college professor, eh? It's safe my friend, just walk on out."

"I thought you said science wasn't your thing," Pete said as he tentatively placed his right foot out the door onto the lush green grass, then jerked it back quickly. Nothing seemed untoward or dangerous to him so he tried it again with his left foot, slightly out the door, touched the ground, and then drew it back again. Grey rolled his eyes then stepped behind Pete and shoved him out the door. Pete stumbled, tripping with arms aflutter out the door, and landed on his hands and knees. He glared over his shoulder at Grey and said, "That was not cool. That's all I'm saying. Just not cool."

The door closed, disappearing completely behind Grey as he stepped down after Pete to offer him a hand up. Pete took the outstretched hand reluctantly but dusted himself off once he was back on his feet. The contrast between cool autumn night when he had entered the diner to leaving into a warm spring afternoon was disconcerting and a bit disorienting, but in a pleasant way to Pete's thinking. He did not mind the cold damp autumns as much in his youth, but as his body aged the cold seemed to seep into his joints. The warm meadow was a pleasant change. *Hmmm*, Pete thought to himself. *That must be more of that mental conditioning. I don't even have bones left to ache.*

Pete looked over to Grey who had his face turned up to the sun with a look of a man enjoying it for the first time after a long cold northern winter. Glancing around Pete realized his description of "Little House on the Prairie" was not too far from the truth. Turning in place he saw rolling hills all the way out to the horizon and what looked like a working farm and log cabin just over the next rise.

"Grey! Hey Grey!" a booming basso voice shouted out, breaking into Pete's thoughts. He looked in the direction the voice had come from to find a giant Viking looking man running up to them. There was a big grin spread across his bearded face. The grin traveled all the way up to his shining blue eyes. Beads and ribbons hung from braids in his wild auburn hair and beard. He was waving both arms in great flourishes trampling tall grasses and wildflowers indiscriminately. His bulk scattered swarms of moths and butterflies in his wake as he approached them. When he was close enough to no longer shout he said, "Hey Grey! Is this the newbie?"

"Hello Zeus," Grey said smiling, "and yeah this is Pete. Pete, meet Zeus." Grey motioned back and forth between the two men. Zeus stuck out a massive bear claw of a hand at Pete, "Glad to meet you Pete! It's always good to have another comrade in arms."

Pete brought his own hand forth only to watch it disappear inside the large man's paw. Blue and lavender light pulsed from Zeus' hand up Pete's arm. Pete fell to his knees jerking his hand back as if it had been burned and exclaimed, "Jesus! What was that?"

"You'll have to excuse Pete, Zeus," Grey said reaching down to pull Pete back up to his feet. "He hasn't had much of a taste for things yet. He only just saw me use some energy to destroy Phil a few moments ago, and he hasn't been touched by anyone other than me yet either. I've been holdin' back on that for the moment."

Zeus looked crestfallen for a moment, then smiled brightly again saying, "Sorry Pete. I meant no offense. You see it's been a long time since we had a new recruit, and I just got a little overzealous like a big old hound dog jumping around yapping at the chance to meet a new friend. I didn't mean to surprise you, but trust me you'll get used to new experiences. A little shared energy is going to be the least of your troubles real soon. It seems like every day I come across some weird new wonder out there." He chuckled ruefully and turned his attention to Grey. "You finally took out Phil huh? Well, that tiny turd has had it coming for a while now, hasn't he?" Zeus nudged Grey in the ribs as he said the last part, sending the smaller man stumbling a few steps back.

Zeus' boisterous demeanor was infectious. He reminded Pete of Dickens' "Ghost of Christmas Present." He looked the big man up and down taking in his denim and worn black leather attire and thought, *well if the Ghost of Christmas present decided to lead a motorcycle gang that is.* All three men were smiling broadly at each other when Pete said, "No problem Zeus. It's cool. You just surprised me a bit. It felt like the world's biggest joy buzzer, but with light. Just not what I was expecting I guess."

The big man nodded his head, and slapped Pete on the back a couple of times sending blue sparks into to the air with each thump. He said, "Well Pete, brace yourself because you're about to get the surprise of your life. The boss is all set for you two. She told me to send you fellows in on my way out, so go on in."

"Thanks Zeus," Grey said, waving over his shoulder as he turned and started to walk in the direction of the log cabin.

"Good to see you again Grey, and nice to meet you Pete," Zeus said, nodding to each man in turn as he started to move off in the opposite direction of Grey.

"Yeah, it was good to meet you too," Pete said. Then he thought of a question and shouted at Zeus' retreating back, "Hey is your name really Zeus? I mean, I know Grey used to be Jasper, so I'm just curious if Zeus was your birth name, or if it was a nickname. You know, because you're all breaded, broad, and badass."

"It's more than a nickname, Pete," Zeus said as he started back toward them. "It's more like a description of who we are. You'll find that all of us have different opinions on this, but you seem like the inquisitive sort. I bet you watched Grey toast Phil and then asked why that little bugger looked the way he did right?"

Pete nodded his head. Zeus had drawn up close to Pete and Grey and slipped his arm around Pete's shoulder in a friendly "just between us boys" gesture. "Well then I hope Grey explained a bit about our true forms, about how what we looked like in life isn't exactly who we were. I did not look like this for starters, no sir, but over time as you drop that sense of what you thought you were, you will start to realize what you really are. Confusing as all hell at first, but then as you drop some of that mental conditioning, you will see how the rest of us perceive each other and you will change accordingly. Nobody looks like they did in their physical life. Well…except for that stubborn son of a bitch next to you. Grey looks just the same as he did when I met him ages ago, and Harmony says that's how he looked when he was alive. Stubborn and contrary to the core, but I guess that's why he's her favorite. He is what he was. No masks. No hiding."

Pete turned to look over at Grey, but he had turned his back on the two of them while Zeus was talking. His hands were tucked into the back pockets of his jeans acting as a brace for his slightly arched back. Again he had his head tilted toward the sky as if soaking in the sun was the most important thing he could be doing. He rolled his neck around a bit, changed the direction he was facing, but he never opened his eyes or gave any indication that he had heard what Zeus had said.

Pete looked back at Zeus and asked, "So what was your birth name Zeus? Who were you before?"

Placing a meaty palm across where his heart had been when he had a physical body Zeus said, "My name was Francis Bancroft Ogelsbee."

Pete chuckled and said, "Really, wow man no wonder you go by Zeus now."

Zeus' open and friendly face grew clouded with anger. His brows pushed so far down his forehead that his eyes became tiny little slits under a heavy awning of furry eyebrows. He let go of Pete's shoulder and turned so that they were facing each other. Pete's nose came to Zeus' sternum, and that barrel chest rumbled with deliberate pauses and emphasis making each word a sentence, he said, "What. Is. So. Funny?"

The color of Pete's face turned ashen when he stammered out, "Um… well you know…. you're such a big guy now, big …big and strong, you could tear me into little pieces for sure, so it just struck me sort of funny that your name was Francis…the rest was good though…Sorry."

Zeus' expression did not shift one centimeter. It stayed solidly angry as if his displeasure had cast his features in bronze or stone. "My mother named me Francis." He all but growled at Pete. Orange sparks of light were dancing in Zeus' slowly disappearing irises adding to the surreal aspect of his statue like mien.

Pete looked around nervously from side to side and uttered, "Oh okay…Um well …I'm sure she was a very nice lady." He was lifting his hands up in a placatory gesture and glanced over in Grey's direction saying, "Um …Grey a little help here please."

That was when Zeus' face split into an enormous grin with a huge bellow of a laugh rolling out from his chest. "I'm just fucking with you kid. Oh too easy. Ha! It's just too easy." Zeus slapped Pete on the shoulder as he turned away wiping a tear from his eye before it could soak into his beard. "This one is going to be fun Grey." He said as he walked away still chuckling to himself.

"What just happened?" Pete asked standing stock still and watched the retreating giant as he cleared the closest rise. Zeus' laughs echoed back to them across the hillside.

"That was just Zeus being Zeus, Pete. You'll get used to it," Grey said. He had walked up behind Pete while his gaze was elsewhere, and laughed a bit shaking his head.

Pete stirred, and raising his eyebrows he said, "I'll take your word for it. So, when do I get my 'nickname not a nickname'?"

"I haven't a clue, Pete. It will happen when it happens. You can't just say 'I want a new name.' Pete served you well enough for seventy-five years didn't it? I think it will serve you just fine for a bit longer," Grey said turning his back by way of attempting to close the subject.

Pete was not to be deterred. He continued, "You don't understand Grey. Jasper isn't a common name, but at least it isn't a slang synonym for penis. If your name had been Jimmy, Peter, Dick, or Willy you'd understand. Trust me. Now, how about 'X' huh? My middle name is Malcolm, and I have a commanding African presence. That would be a good one right?"

Grey sighed, and said, "Not going to happen Pete…sorry."

"How about 'Slim'?"

"Nope."

"Oh come on! Maybe just stick a 'Big' in front of Pete?"

"Sure!"

"Really?"

"Nope."

"You're killing me, Grey. You're absolutely killing me."

"Harmony wants to meet you Pete, so come on," Grey said as he started walking in the direction of the small farm Pete had seen earlier. Following a few steps behind Grey, Pete was muttering unintelligibly under his breath. They followed the swath of destruction Zeus had mown through the meadow scattering miniature flocks of butterflies with each step. After a few strides, Pete stopped griping and started watching the approaching homestead.

They walked in silence until they reached the sun-bleached wood of the porch. Then Grey turned to Pete with one foot on the first step and a hand on the worn railing, "Pete, I don't know what will happen to you, or how

Harmony will speak to you. She appears different to each of us, and up to this point I have been your guide for want of a better term, and you have perceived things as I do. I think of the world as it was when my body died. That is why you think we are on a farm in some sun-dappled meadow because that is how I felt the afterlife or heaven should be like. I always feel a sense of completeness when I'm with Harmony. It's like coming home. I can't go in there with you this time. This is your final step, and you have to take it alone."

Grey offered Pete his hand, and he took it. This time Grey allowed himself to open up with energy flowing out from him. When Pete felt the sparks of life jump from Grey to him, and back again, he did not flinch away from it as he had with Zeus. They held the grip longer than most men would feel comfortable holding the hand of another man, but it held a current of finality that Pete could not discount. "Is she really going to change things that much for me Grey? You're making me feel like this may be a farewell."

Grey nodded his head, and scratched his chin in contemplation with his free hand. After a moment he said, "Perhaps, or perhaps nothing will change at all. We'll see what we see. Good luck Pete."

Pete nodded, and they broke the grip. Grey walked down to a rocking chair set on the porch and slid into place. He closed his eyes and settled in with the weariness of an old man slipping into a hot bath. Pete watched him, then swallowed his resolve and walked up to the front door. He reached for the knob, but paused when a symbol burned into the wood caught his eye. He traced the tip of his thumb over the dark scorch marks recognizing it from a class he had taught one semester titled "Symbolism in Modern Literature." The course had been an abysmal failure, but many of the common symbols had stuck with him. This was a crude Libra, or set of balanced scales. The academic in Pete started to kick in as he wondered if this Harmony was the origin for different mythological beings, and if so which ones? Before Pete could pin down specific characters out of legend the door opened on its own, and a soft sultry female voice that seemed to come from everywhere said, "Peter, please come in." "Okay, that wasn't too creepy I guess," Pete said when he started moving into the room. From the cabin's exterior he had expected to walk into a cozy well lived-in room, paneled in woods and decorated toward other frontier motifs. What he stumbled into was "Willy Wonka's Chocolate Factory" complete with a milk chocolate waterfall. A gorgeous young black woman sat leaning against a tree made from chocolate-covered pretzels. Dressed in a red silk evening gown, she smiled seductively at Pete and said, "Hello Peter."

She reached out and patted a tuft of spun candy grass at her side asking, "Will you come over and sit next to me? There is no sense in me shouting over the waterfall."

"Yes ma'am. Uh, are you Harmony?" Pete stayed standing and made no move to go nearer to her. He glanced around at the candied expanse, but his eyes kept being drawn back to the woman by the tree.

"That is one of my names, Peter, but I have many. Why have you come here, Peter?" she asked and crossed her arms over her stomach just under her breasts, pushing them slightly out of her already revealing attire.

"Uh…Grey," Pete said in an attempt to articulate. She stood up from her repose, and allowed Pete to glimpse her full figure as he continued. "You know Grey, right?" He motioned over his shoulder at the now closed door. She smiled and nodded. "Well he brought me here, and then this giant scary Viking guy said you were expecting us, so um… wait don't you know why I'm here already?"

"Yes, Peter, I know," Harmony said reaching up to pluck a caramel apple from the tree. "But I want to hear you tell me yourself, so I know you understand what it is you are doing."

"Oh, well you see, I'm here…hmm…well..." Pete stopped to take a minute to think. "Look ma'am, I know you probably want some intricate philosophical reasoning for why I'm here, but honestly, I'm here because I want to learn how to shoot balls of blue light at ugly spider monkey wiener dog demons!" Pete said, then flinched a little before he added, "Do I still get the job?"

Melodious laughter seemed to fill the cavernous room. It came from everywhere, behind trees, around rocks, and out of flowers. Pete's mind told him the laughter should have been coming from the woman standing under the tree because she was laughing to be sure, but the sound was all around him.

"Oh yes, Peter, yes, you still get the job," she said with traces of the laughter in her tone. "I can see why Grey wanted you to join us. I would also have accepted that you wanted to live some of the adventures you had only read about in your physical life because you were born into a time and place that your talents were not appreciated in. You were out of balance in your life whether you knew it or not. Much like many of my other soldiers you want to expand your mind, learn all you can, and to be a help to humanity and life before you move on."

"Well, yeah, that too," Pete said as he reached up to scratch the back of his neck in a self-conscious gesture. "Yeah, when you say it like that. It makes my answer seem kind of stupid."

"No, Peter," she said. "You want what you want. As long as your heart is true I do not ask for more. If you are ready Peter, then please come over here and take my hand."

Pete walked over to Harmony and did as she asked. The second they made contact everything vanished for Pete. The chocolate factory vanished. Harmony vanished. Pete vanished, and for an eternity or only a moment there was nothing but light, pulsing, comforting and all-encompassing. He drifted in that light, and very reluctantly stirred when he sensed someone calling his name.

When Pete came back to himself he was again in the chocolate factory, but there was no sign of Harmony. "Wow, what the hell was that?"

"That was us connecting, Peter." Harmony's voice spoke from within Pete's head. "Now that we have shared our energies I can be with you at all times to help advise you, guide you, and instruct you. To tell you what I need from you to help me keep the Balance. All you have to do to reach me is concentrate on the place in your mind where you feel me now. We are bonded, my warrior, and now would you please go ask Grey if he would come in and join us, because I have a mission for the two of you."

Chapter 4

Human nature seems to divide people into two different camps. The first being those who want to stand out from the crowd shining saying, "Look at me! I am something special!" They think the world should pay attention to them for some reason or other. You see this mind set in politicians, celebrities of all types: singers, actors, professional athletes, and the like. The second group is made up of those who want to blend in with the crowd, escapin' notice at all costs. The humorous part to me is that most times the few who do get their chance to stand out are not the ones that really are special, and the ones that want to just go about their lives innocuously? Well friend, fate always seems to have different plans doesn't she?

I think whatever it is that makes a man or woman stand out from the crowd becomes tarnished when that same crowd tells them that they are special. You hear folk use the French term "je ne sais quoi." I suppose that's as good a description as any. That "I don't know what" seems to disappear by degrees when that person starts to think of themselves as special. The more they believe the legends, stories, and myths about themselves then the less extraordinary they become. The myths that go along with greatness or fame never represent what the person really was or is. I speak from experience here. I've met more "legends" than I can count. They're never more than people with faults just like you and me. They put their pants on one leg at a time...well except for Wild Bill Hickok, that crazy son of a bitch liked to wear skirts. He called 'em kilts, but they were skirts believe you me. You take my meaning though; a legend is only that, a legend or story, not a real person.

When I lived I always thought of myself as a member of the blendin' in sect. I wanted to go about my days in peace and quiet. Maybe work a hard day's labor then grab a beer come sundown, taking each day as it came, without worrying if other folks liked me or not. Please take no offence from this, but I say fuck what other people think about me. Who needs that kind of stress? Life gives a man enough problems without going and creating more for himself by playing "high school popularity contests" like that. If you blend in then the world doesn't expect much out of you. That may sound cowardly or lazy to you, but remember that not every man sets out in this world to be a hero. The smart fellow leaves those dreams behind with his other childhood toys.

I knew next to none of that the first time I stood in Harmony's prairie home. I stood there staring at her dancing like some sort of goober. Butterflies hovered around her in swirls and eddies flying in syncopation with her motions. I knew nothing of art back then either, but now I'd say she put me in mind of an Andrew Wyeth painting come to life.

"Come to me Jasper!" she called. "Come dance with me! I have been waiting for someone like you to come along for an eternity." Harmony twirled in the meadow, her simple cotton dress slowly changing colors to match whatever cluster of wildflowers she was closest to. "You are special Jasper. You will be the first one to stand apart. You will be the one who can help me to do the things that must be done. You will be my finest warrior, my first knight. You will make the changes the others have not been able to."

Yes sir, fate does have a twisted and sadistic sense of humor doesn't she.........

***

Grey was sitting in the same rocking chair basking in the sun when Pete walked out of Harmony's cabin. Only from Pete's perspective the chair was now made out of licorice and the porch was made of peanut brittle. Grey had his boots propped up on the brittle railing. His scuffed rawhide toes pointed out to the former prairie meadow that had been replaced with rolling hills of confection sugar spun to look like trees and shrubs. Pete glanced over his shoulder to see that the log cabin had transformed into a gingerbread house.

"That's different." Pete said to himself. He did not think that Grey was aware of him, so he tentatively leaned toward the frosting that lined the nearest windowsill. His tongue had barely touched the surface when Harmony's voice came from inside his mind. "Of course it is Peter."

Pete jumped back clutching a fist to his chest like a toddler caught with his hand in a cookie jar, yelling, "Damn it woman! Don't do that! You nearly gave me a heart...never mind."

Her voice spoke again in a silken apology, "I am sorry Peter, but you will become accustomed to it. What I meant was you did not expect to see things the same way that Grey does after we connected. Did you?"

Still holding his hand to his chest Pete said, "No, I guess not, so things are different only for me then right? Grey still thinks he's rocking away the afternoon on the Ponderosa, but to me he could be a new character for Candy Land, the caramel cowboy."

"Yes, I suppose that would be one way of saying it. All of my paladins perceive me differently. Grey was a simple man. I do not mean that in a derisive way, far from it. He was and is true to his nature. He loved the land

53

he came from. For Grey the grass was green enough right where he was. That is where he draws his power from, his solidity. Peter, you on the other hand were a man of imagination, a man of dreams, curiosity, and what ifs? That is where your power comes from, and why Grey was to drawn to you, because your energies complement each other. You perceive me here as your first fantasy, what made such an impression on your early mind. You were raised in a family that was not overly religious. When you first read Roald Dahl's fable it impressed on you an image of what you felt heaven should be like, and whether consciously or not you retained that image your whole life. That is why you see me like this."

Grey slowly cracked open his eyes. Looking in Pete's direction he said, "You alright there Pete? You look a little shakier than I thought you'd be." Pete nodded an affirmative and said, "Harmony wanted me to tell you to come in now, because she has a job for us."

"Yeah, I know," Grey said standing up from the chair and walking over to the open doorway. He stopped, placing his hand against to what appeared to Pete as a hard candied door jamb. "She sent you out here, so you'd have a better feel for how things have changed. It will make what she has to tell us easier for you to comprehend if you can accept how you perceive things, and not dwell on the changes. How'd she look to you anyway?"

Pete craned his neck about as if trying to see where Harmony could be hiding. "Um…she can hear us right?"

Grey laughed and slapped Pete on the shoulder before saying, "Pete, buddy I don't mean to make you paranoid, but she knows what you're going to say, even before you say it."

"Oh, so if I said she was smoking hot, she knew I was going to say that?" Harmony's lilting giggle came from everywhere around them. Pete's chin drooped a bit as he said, "I'll take that as a big yes."

"I expected no less my friend," Grey said. "She is, well technically she isn't really a she. She isn't anything, but when she interacts with those of us who are or were mortals she typically picks the gender that you were most attracted to. It helps keep us beggin' for her attention, and because of the intimate nature of the bond she creates, the human psyche tends to react better when bonded with their emotional opposite. Creating a balance, even and especially within us. Of course like everything else there's always an exception to the rule, so I was just curious."

Harmony's voice purred out of the open doorway, "Boys I appreciate Pete's need to learn, but I do have a very pressing issue that needs Grey's particular touch, so please come in, and I will explain further."

Grey motioned to Pete in an "after you" gesture, and they walked through the cabin door, each into their own version of Harmony's room. Pete back into Wonka's iconic chocolate factory, and Grey into a comfortably lived in log cabin complete with handmade furniture and quilts. Harmony sat in the same spot Pete had first seen her under the tree, but to Grey she was reclined in a rocking chair identical to the one he had just vacated. She stood and moved toward them, gliding more than walking with the ethereal grace of a ballerina.

Once she reached them she slipped her hand into Grey's, sending sparks of light pulsing up his arm in such a large quantity that many fell off him to the floor where they blinked like dying fireflies before racing over to Harmony's feet and scaling her leg, completing the circuit. She looked Grey directly in the eyes before she spoke, and the gesture was so intimate that it made Pete feel voyeuristic just standing there. Harmony's voice broke the tableau. "Grey, it's Raven. She needs your help, and you know how little she listens to me. The town that I sent her to is being corrupted by a demonic influence. The children are lashing out violently in excess of what any young mind should. The corruption seems to be widespread to the surrounding area, but thankfully contained to just this single town at the moment. I need you to go there and help Raven find the source of this unbalance, and not only keep it from spreading further, but destroy it if you can. Take Pete with you. Teach him what he will need to know in his role as one of the Balance."

Then she turned to face Pete with a smirk and an arched eyebrow. She said, "You know what to do Grey, show him how to shoot balls of blue light at ugly spider monkey wiener dog demons."

Grey gave Pete a questioning look but responded to Harmony by saying, "Of course, darlin'. I'll show him everything he'll need. Pete, are you ready?"

Pete had been staring intently at Harmony and not really paying much attention to the conversation. He was not sure if she appeared so physically appealing to him because as Grey had said, he would seek her attention, or if it was leftover mental conditioning. Whichever the case Pete had been unable to draw his focus much further than Harmony's chest, so when Grey had spoken his name it had made him realize he had been asked a question. He shook himself in what he hoped would be the ethereal form of a cold shower and said, "Sorry, Grey, what did you say?"

"I asked if you were ready to leave to go help Raven." Grey said with a lopsided grin pulling at the corner of his mouth.

"No, I'm not," Pete said shaking his head for emphasis. "I'm sure this comes as a surprise, but I have some questions. Who is Raven? Where are we going? And why do the two of you look like Romeo and Juliet made out of sparklers? And honestly man, why can't I stop staring at her boobs?" He said pointing at Harmony's cleavage.

Harmony smiled and responded to the questions instead of Grey. "First Peter, you boys can leave and head toward the horizon. I will direct you to where I need you from there, because time is running short on this. I can answer your questions as you travel, and as I told you earlier all you have to do to commune with me is concentrate on the part of yourself you feel pulsing with my energy, and I will be there. So please follow Grey."

Grey had already left the cabin and was stepping off the porch when Pete started moving to catch up. "I know this will take time for you to understand Peter. It was an adjustment for all of them. To answer your questions in order: Raven is another soldier like Grey. Grey actually brought her to me, when she had passed away in Malign's last war. That would be World War II to you Peter. Raven was a young woman who was swept up in Der Fuhrer's march toward madness. She has worked for me ever since, and I am sending you and Grey to her as backup in a small town in Illinois. As to why Grey and I share so much energy, that is the nature of our relationship. He and I have a partnership that I have not allowed any other."

She stopped speaking, and Pete had started to wonder if she was not going to address his last question. Then she spoke again in a whisper. "It could be one of two reasons for your final question Peter. The first reason being that you are newly born into this form of life, and like any infant you are drawn to breasts for sustenance."

"Oh, thanks. That isn't too psychoanalytical or anything," Pete said, quickening his pace a bit to close the gap between himself and Grey.

"The other reason Peter," Harmony purred. "It could be that I have a great rack."

Pete tripped a bit and laughed out loud. "Yes ma'am, I suppose it could be that too."

When he had stopped chuckling Harmony continued in a serious tone of voice. "Grey will help you where he can, but if you have a question that our taciturn friend does not give you a satisfactory answer to then please ask me. Luck be with you boys."

Pete felt Harmony's presence lessen within him. It did not disappear completely but seemed more like leaving the light on in a closet then shutting the door. The rest of the room is dark but for the slivers of light peeking out of the cracks, still there only muted. It gave him a sense of privacy that he was not aware he was missing until she gave it back to him.

When their short trek to the horizon, and the doorway of blue light waiting there to take them to their destination, was almost complete Grey turned to Pete. With the same half smile he wore earlier he asked, "Is that the reason you gave her when she asked why you were there?"

"What?" Pete asked unsure of what Grey was talking about.

Grey answered, nodding his head in the direction of the homestead now several hills behind them, "When Harmony asked you why you had come to see her, did you really say 'To shoot balls of blue light at spider monkey wiener dog demons'? You did, didn't you?"

Judging by the sheepish look on Pete's face Grey shook his head and blew out a deep breath. "Wow, the woman asks you a deep philosophical question to measure your spirit, your determination, and you respond like a thirteen year old boy. Classy, Pete, real classy."

A look of umbrage clouded Pete's face as he said, "Oh fine Niche. What was your response?"

"She never asked me that, Pete. As far as I know I'm the only one she's never asked. I don't know why, and don't bother asking her, because she won't tell you either. She and I will contradict each other at times, and I apologize in advance for that, but she'll keep her secrets just like I do. It'll be up to you to decide who to believe or how hard to press for answers. Hell, every time someone does ask her why she and I don't always agree all she says is, 'Because he's Grey'."

Chapter 5

Change is a powerful thing. Whether it's for better or worse, either you embrace it or it rolls right on over you like the tide. No man can stop it, and the stubborn are crushed under its weight. You can't deny that the old adage of change being the only constant holds a strong dose of truth. Sometimes the change is outside of your control, sometimes you get to initiate the change yourself, and sometimes…well sometimes you are the change.

Dancin' with that pretty little brunette named Harmony in a field of wildflowers I felt change stirring the wind around us. It was in me, in her, and in everything I could see, hear, and feel. If it weren't for the clarity in which my surroundings presented themselves I would have sworn I was dreaming, but I had never in my recollection had such a vivid dream before. I could feel her body pressed against my side, soft and firm in different places. It had to be real, or as real as real could be for a dead man.

Yeah, that's right I was dead, and with that thought I pulled away from Harmony. I didn't want to, but I could feel myself getting caught up in the moment and I needed some answers. Believe you me, but that was the hardest embrace I had ever broken. Being dead and confused can make a man do things he wouldn't normally do. So instead of holdin' that comfortable weight tight to me I pushed a space between us.

For a split second I was sure I saw hurt in her eyes. It didn't look like she knew what the emotion was. Maybe change could come for everybody, even a being like Harmony. I asked her, "Ma'am, what do you mean by special?"

The hurt in her eyes was gone. It was replaced with a pearly white smile, and instead of answering me she leaned forward, stood on her tiptoes, and kissed me. No, calling that a kiss would be a huge understatement. She touched me for the first time, with what she was, not just how she said we had connected before, but this time with her whole being. We experienced every emotion the human mind can endure, and some that I didn't know existed at all in the matter of those few seconds of contact.

This time she was the one to break the embrace first. She leaned back still looking me in the eyes and said, "Jasper you are special, because you are the first who is strong enough to help me dispassionately in my work. You can handle the power I will give you, and wield it judiciously; not be swayed by your emotions. You will do what needs to be done to maintain the Balance of life. The Balance is inherently contrary and precarious. One *moment hate is called for, and the next…love. You are special Jasper, because you are the first. The first whose eyes I can meet, and see more than their color. See past the gray, and see who you are, the first Jasper, the first who I love."……..*

***

Leaving the light behind, Pete and Grey walked out of their respective versions of Harmony into a cool dry autumn night. The star strewn sky was clear of any cloud or jet contrail, and unpolluted by either moon or the ambient light of a large city. It was early enough that condensation had yet to form on the grass, so their shoes left no marks on the scraggly weed choked turf of the neighborhood park that Harmony had directed them to. The maintenance workers had already tucked the picnic tables together in that leapfrog stacking style they use in an attempt to keep all of the tables protected under the overhang of a shelter to minimize weathering. The baseball diamonds were starting to sprout grass on the baselines with the spring and summer seasons so far away, the soccer fields looked derelict, even the playground had that worn down appearance of too many children playing too rough over too many years.

The park was surrounded on all sides by narrow one way streets with mostly single story ranch homes creating a hedge of buildings. That made it difficult for Pete to judge how large or small the community really was. A few porch lights were on adding minute glowing pools, but most of the houses were completely dark. What street lights that were not burned out flickered sporadically, threatening to give out completely at any moment, providing minimal illumination.

The only clear sounds Pete could distinguish were a few late season crickets singing their last, and katydids screeching like band saws. Turning to Grey he said, "Seems like a quiet town to me, Grey. Where do we find this Raven?"

"Hush!" Grey snapped. He had his head cocked slightly like a dog who hears a siren miles away before any of the people around it. Without anything better to do, Pete shrugged cocking his head in imitation, and strained his hearing in hopes of picking up whatever it was that had grabbed Grey's attention. At first he heard nothing but the insects, but then a slight drone started echoing around between the houses. It sounded like an engine of some kind being pressed harder than the designers had intended. As the drone grew louder and closer Pete could hear voices shouting out in whoops and hollers. The voices stopped suddenly, and then there was a resounding crash followed by even louder whoops and hollers.

Bright headlights swept over the park as an automobile rounded the corner. The vehicle was swerving drunkenly heading the wrong way on a one way street. When Pete focused he could make out a rundown Ford pickup truck almost overflowing with bodies in both the cab and the bed. A few of the people in the truck bed were swinging aluminum baseball bats at the passing mailboxes. "Well that explains the loud crash," Pete said, as one of the vandals connected. He looked over to where Grey had been standing, and saw nothing. "Shit! Grey, damn it where are you?"

"Psst over here," Grey's voice whispered from a small copse of trees and shrubs that still held onto most of their foliage providing him a decent amount of cover. "Pete, get over here now. I don't want them to know we're here yet."

Pete started to head over to Grey, but before he had gone a few steps a spotlight swung around from the truck blinding him. "See! Ha! I told you I seen something moving Tommy! Didn't I say that," yelled a squawky bird like voice from the truck. The rusty Ford had rounded another corner of the park, and was now headed directly for Pete. "Hey! What the fuck you doing in our park dude?" one of the passengers demanded.

"Yeah motherfucker, you ain't supposed to be out after dark around here!" another voice agreed. Pete could still only make out the vague shapes of people and not the distinct faces of individuals.

"It can be bad for your health," said yet another, followed by a round of whoops and hollers. The truck had now stopped, having driven up onto the soccer field but was unable to get any closer to Pete without running over the playground equipment. The driver of the truck, a teenager closing in on his twenties Pete could now make out, at least had enough sense not to try taking his truck over the merry-go-round and swing set that stood between them. Behind the spotlight there was another teenage boy who was scrawnier looking than the others. His spiky blond hair was shaved into a Mohawk, giving his head a rooster like appearance as he bobbed back and forth from his perch.

There were shadows moving about the bed of the truck, pitch black swirls and voids jostling among the other passengers. The patches of darkness looked much like the demon Phil from the diner before Pete had concentrated enough to get a better look, only much, much larger. With all the movement and the bright halogen light he was having trouble making out definitive shapes.

The boys holding the baseball bats jumped out of the truck bed when the driver turned the engine off. The others were right on their heels but for the scrawny boy with the Mohawk who still held his place leaning out over the cab roof to get a better view. When they were within a few yards Pete was able to make out the dark shapes clearly. They were lithe and lanky. To Pete's eye the demons, and he was sure now that was what they were, looked like stretched out panthers standing on their hind legs. Their thin narrow eyes glowed in a deep russet color. There was a demon for each of the five boys approaching him, with one extra prancing around at the edges. *Apparently Mohawk the Rooster boy's demon did not want to miss out on the action*, Pete thought, while he attempted to keep a calm facade.

Pete had the presence of mind to focus on that closet door Harmony had closed earlier. He gave it a mental knock, but nothing happened. "Shit!" Pete said to himself. He knocked on the door harder, with the same results. "Shit! Shit! Shit!" Then directing his attention to the group of boys and demons in front of him, who had stopped just out of reach, he said, "Good evening boys. Isn't it a lovely night? So this is your park huh? Maybe you should put up a sign or spray-paint some gang lingo to discourage trespassers."

In his mind Pete was no longer knocking on Harmony's door, but pounding on it and occasionally screaming, "Damn it woman! Open the damn door!"

"I haven't seen you before man," The truck driver said, "and I know everybody from town, so you ain't from here."

"Yeah Tommy's right, we don't know you dude!" chimed in another boy. "So who are you?"

Pete watched as a panther demon slunk up behind the boy, Tommy, according to his friends. The lithe shadow wrapped its paws around his torso like a lover embracing him from behind. It slid a paw up and along the side of his face, adding just the slightest amount of pressure to tilt his ear to its mouth. After a short unintelligible whisper Tommy shivered in pleasure, grinning he asked, "More importantly, is anybody going to miss you?"

The other boys all wailed like a pack of hyenas, as if Tommy's comment were the height of wit. Pete had spent the bulk of his adult life teaching men about this age. He could tell the other boys were nothing without their alpha, Tommy. He told these boys how to think, how to act, and what to do. *Okay*, Pete thought to himself, *they say you stem fear with knowledge. I figured this kid out after five seconds. Then why am I still scared shitless?*

Tommy was not that much larger than the other boys physically. Even in his purple and gold varsity jacket his shoulder width was no more imposing than your average high school senior. Pete noted by the year that

Tommy had only graduated the spring before. *That is, of course, assuming he was smart enough to graduate*, he thought to himself. Pete was jerked out of his one sided mental conversation when the boys and demons made a quick motion as if to pounce. He flinched, waiting for the first blow to land when the unmistakable sound of a shotgun shell being chambered came from behind Tommy's shoulder. Both boys and demons froze as Grey's voice said in a soft cadence, "Maybe you should ask yourself the same question, boy. Is anybody going to miss you? If I pulled this here trigger right now, would anybody give two shits? I'm a gambling man myself, how about you?"

The six demons started hissing and snarling when Grey suddenly appeared among them. They scampered to the edges of the group of young men, keeping their red eyes trained on every move and flinch of muscle Grey made. The tension of the moment thrummed like a downed power line until Tommy started chuckling. Pete thought it sounded forced, as if Tommy did not want to lose face in front of his crew, but there was a definite undercurrent of fear in his laugh. It reminded Pete of a man whistling as he walked through a graveyard, hollow, and tinny. It came through in his speech when he said, "I don't know who you are either mister, but you sure have balls!"

A demon, it could have been the same one, Pete could not tell them apart, slid up behind him again while its fellows continued to hiss. The demon seemed to lend Tommy the confidence he was lacking on his own, because his voice came out more forcefully when he said, "Since you haven't pulled that trigger yet I'm betting you don't want to. See I'm a betting man too, Hoss, so me and my friends are just going to walk back to my truck now, alright?" The rest of them were all eyeing Grey carefully, both demon and human, wary and perhaps looking for an opening, to flee or attack Pete was unsure.

Grey walked backward for a few steps giving him enough room to edge around to Pete's side. The shotgun never wavered from its line with the boy's head. When he was face to face with Tommy and shoulder to shoulder with Pete he said, "I think that sounds like a good idea son. In fact you may want to drop your friends off at their homes. Let their mommies tuck them in and go catch a little shut eye yourself."

Tommy just grinned at them. The panther unwound itself before he started walking backward. None of them turned their backs on Grey and Pete until they were far enough away that the spotlight no longer distinctly illuminated them as individuals. Then the engine revved loudly, throwing up big chunks of sod as it peeled off through the soccer field back to the street. It was not until the truck was completely gone and could no longer be heard that Pete turned to Grey, and said, "What the hell took you so long? And why didn't you just blue light fry those kitty cat demons? And where the hell was Harmony? 'I'll be with you at all times' my ass! I was concentrating on that spot as hard as a damn psychic friend man! Dionne Warwick would have been proud of my ass!"

Grey rolled his neck and tossed the shotgun at a near garbage can, but it dissipated before ever reaching the rim. "Calm down Pete. She agreed with me that we shouldn't tip our hand just yet that we're here, so she pulled her presence in tightly to keep them from noticing her. I didn't destroy them Pete, because at that moment they were not upsetting the Balance. They were only doing what their kind has done forever, and that is causing trouble. The boys didn't have guns, so they probably wouldn't have killed you anyway. I ain't allowed to harm angel, demon, or mortal just on the grounds of what they might do. Only when they have crossed the point of no return can I use lethal force."

Pete looked confused, and said, "Oh…so how do you know when to light up?"

"Trust me Pete you'll know, with experience you'll learn. That's why you're here with me now ain't it, to learn?"

A rusty grating sound of metal on metal came from the swing set. Both men were strung so tightly from the previous encounter that their heads snapped up at the sound without hesitation. A little girl of about eight or nine years old wearing a pink sweater and bib overalls was sitting in the middle swing slowly pumping her legs back and forth. There was a Raggedy Anne doll propped in her lap; she cradled it like she would a younger sister. Her far set brown eyes stared at them with open contempt, but she did not say a word. Her auburn hair was plaited into long pigtails trailing down the sides of her head. The plaits swung in opposite of her momentum: she moved forward and the pigtails swayed back, she swung backward and the plaits moved forward.

"What the fuck?" Pete exclaimed. "It has to be after midnight Grey. What is a little girl doing out here so late man? And where did she come from because she sure as shit wasn't there a second ago."

"That is no little girl, Pete," Grey said. "I'm afraid your little scare was for nothing. Our cover was blown anyway."

The little girl giggled, and started to sing. She had a lilting voice that would have been at home in any choir.

"Little gray cowboy came to play.

Little gray cowboy shouldn't stay.

Little gray cowboy will have to pay.

So, little gray cowboy run away."

When she finished, she hugged the doll close and looked down at her, laughing like they were sharing a private joke. The girl stroked the doll's check lovingly. Pete could see that she had tiny yellow dots painted on her fingernails. He focused harder, as he had earlier to see the panther demons, and realized the dots were happy faces. She cooed gently to the doll like a mother to her infant. After a few moments the cooing, laughing, and giggling subsided. The girl brought her head back up to face Grey, ignoring Pete completely, but this time a third eye burned out in their direction from her fair skinned forehead. The eye was a deep burgundy color, staring unblinking and pupil-less at them. Pete flinched, taking a casual backward step, so he was slightly behind Grey, placing Grey between him and the demon girl.

She had stopped swinging on the rusty set. The crickets had ceased their chirruping. The katydids had fallen still. There was no breeze stirring the dry leaves, so the night was completely silent.

When she opened her mouth to speak a bestial voice rumbled forth. It was a noise that had no business coming out of the mouth of a human, let alone a little girl. It growled, "Run away, Grey, run away."

Chapter 6

Fear is a tricky thing ain't it? The academics will say it leads to two choices: fight or flight. That after countless millennia, when faced with real fear it comes down to an instinct to either flight to preserve your life, or fight for your own or someone else's life. I always laugh when someone says that. Fight or flight? We as a species with all those accumulated years of "instinct" seem to ignore our instinct of pride. You might be of a religious bent and consider pride a sin, but it ain't, I'm sorry. Disagree with me if you like but pride is an instinct. Because how else could you explain why those same academics kindly omitted the most common response I see, and that is to freeze. Nobody likes to admit to it, but we've all done it a time or two when the shit really hits the fan. Fight, flight, or freeze my friend...that's just how it is.

Freezin' in the face of fear doesn't make you a weak person. No sir, it just makes you a person. The mind can only process so much terror before it shuts down. That stopping point is different for everyone, and subject to external factors or the whims of fate. A child may thrive under the pressure of a math test, but freeze in place when a dodge ball comes flyin' at his or her face. We all have different strengths and different weaknesses.

My weakness was intimacy. I'll own up to it and ignore my prideful instinct. In life I had been with plenty of women, but I hadn't cared one way or another for them emotionally. They were just a body that my body craved. It never went past physical need for me. Did that make me a bad person? I never lied to get them to sleep with me. I never told them I loved them or that we were going to be anything more than a pair of strangers holding on to each other to push back the night. We both always had needs, some stronger than others, but we always met those same needs.

So again, did that make me a bad person? I don't see it that way. My mother died when I was young, and I never knew my father. The bonds that other people make and learn from were not there as examples for me. Analyze that however you want to if it makes you feel superior. But folks, I met Freud, knew him quite well as a matter of fact. That little man had more demons poking at him (literally and figuratively) than you could count, still does come to think of it, so I don't put much stock in head shrinkin'.

Yes sir, I froze a time or two in both my lives. Case in point being when Harmony told me she loved me. Well I'm not proud of it, but I froze. Just like a damn deer in front of a semi-truck's headlights. I stood there blinking at her stupidly, but it didn't seem to bother her any because she just giggled and said, "It's okay Jasper. Why that scares you is one of the many reasons I love you."………

***

Pete turned to Grey and with worry evident in his eyes said, "Look, Grey, I know you're supposed to be this super badass, and I guess that makes me a badass in training. Historically speaking it is not common for the badasses to run away. Literary heroes always stand their ground, with all that 'you shall not pass!' shit. That looks good on paper, and even better on a movie screen. But right now I think it would be a real good idea to listen to the scary three eyed girl with the dolly, and get the hell out of here!"

Grey lifted his chin in the direction of the swing set, "It's alright Pete. It's gone already." Without any explanation or elaboration he walked away from Pete, heading over to the picnic shelter where he yanked a table out from under the stack. Grey eyed a level patch of grass a few yards away, and with a slight flick of his wrist, as if he were shooing away a fly, he threw the heavy wooden table across the distance. It landed in a creaking heap but stayed upright and stable. Grey strolled over. *No shit*, Pete thought, *he's actually moseying.* Then Grey climbed up to sit on the table top, his scuffed boots resting on the bench seat, his back to Pete, and he stared out into the night.

Pete started to head toward Grey, but Harmony's presence flooded back into him like a tidal wave before he had taken two steps. "Peter, I am so sorry to have done that to you. It is very early in our relationship and I want you to be able to trust me. Trust me now when I say that it would not be a good idea to go sit with Grey at the moment."

Pete spoke in a whisper, "Oh now I should trust you?"

"You do not have to whisper Peter. In fact you do not need to speak at all. Remember, you can just think and I will respond."

Pete's eyes grew wide, and he threw his arms out to his sides before shouting, "Oh sure! I was thinking 'help me, help me' at the top of my mental lungs earlier, but it didn't work then did it?"

"I know holding back from you like that when you were terrified is not the way to engender that trust. Again I am sorry."

"Hey, hey now I wouldn't say I was terrified," Pete disagreed shaking his head in negation.

"Peter, remember, I know what you are thinking and feeling. That is the core of our bond, how we share, and how I can help you. There is nothing wrong with being afraid."

"Well damn it woman! There were six giant upright panther things egging those testosterone pumped white boys on. Any self-respecting brother would have been scared shitless!" Pete said. "In towns like this where the opening of deer hunting season is considered a holiday, I was damn lucky every single one of them wasn't carrying a shot gun."

"I am sorry Peter, but Grey was right. The element of surprise has been the key to many victories throughout history. When all attributes are equal, surprise can make all the difference. If it is any consolation I would have brought you back to me before they could have destroyed you."

"Destroyed me! What do you mean destroyed me? I'm already dead, aren't I? Are you telling me I can die twice?" Pete asked, still continuing to speak aloud.

"Grey should have told you this before," Harmony said. "He has a tendency to omit things that he feels are distracting or philosophical. He would say…," then her voice changed within Pete's mind to an exact mimic of Grey's, "I don't put much stock in far off and fancy thoughts." Then in her own voice again she said, "Peter all things are made of energy. Energy can never be created or destroyed."

Pete rolled his eyes and said, "Oh now we're talking Einstein. Sure, sure why not? He work for you too lady?"

"As a matter of fact, Grey offered him a place with us, but he went right back to the Source. He said, 'The only place he belonged was with the unknown.' The theory is sound no matter who gets credit for expounding it. Truthfully it was our cowboy friend sitting over there, though he claims not to care about such things, who gave Albert the seeds for his theory. Only he phrased it a bit more colloquially."

"I'll bet he did," Pete groused, "so I still need to be scared of death huh? Great, you'd think a guy could let a few of the old stresses go after he flatlines."

"No Peter, not death," Harmony corrected, her voice had lost any sense of joviality. "Annihilation. You would cease to be you, and would become a part of whoever took your energy. Or even worse you could be torn apart into individual particles, completely scattered and dispersed."

"Oh thanks, that sounds so much better than dying. The fine print nobody talks about until it's too late, huh? I should have known that between that blue light ball thing and your magic boobs that those were meant to distract me from the scary shit!" Pete threw his arms up in the air in exasperation.

"Peter, as you are now, energy inhabiting a place in the physical world, you can be taken by another entity like you. It can be demon or angel. They would incorporate your energy into them, granting them more power. That is how Malign has become so powerful over the millennia. Among those who stay behind that is all that is really important; good or evil does not matter. Those are convenient labels people use. Power is what life is made of. Power is why we exist. Power is everything to them, and soon it will be to you too." Harmony's voice trailed off wistfully.

"Oh yeah that's me all over, a power crazy retired literary professor."

She laughed softy, and said, "Perhaps you will be the first not to, Peter. I have been wrong from time to time. One can only hope."

"Thanks for the vote of confidence lady. Since I have you chatting, you mentioned this Malign before. Who is she?"

"Malign is the strongest existing entity for evil. She is an embodiment of chaos. Most of the major conflicts of the world have been of her design. She will claim to be the Devil, though it was she who corrupted the angel Lucifer and allowed him to take the blame, but honestly she is as close to that creature as any I have known. To a greater or lesser degree most of the human mythology about the devil is based on her interactions with mankind."

"Great, this keeps getting better and better. A power hunger crazy she devil. Let me guess, she's a white girl too isn't she? I don't care about a person's race, but my momma always told me to stay away from the white girls, because you never knew which ones were crazy until it was too late," Pete said and started walking again to where Grey was sitting by the picnic shelter. "Well, Harmony, while we're on the topic of crazy white people, what's got Grey's boxers bunching? Or is he always moody like this?"

"That is Grey's story to tell Peter, so I have to let him decide if and when he wants to tell you. Although since we know how forthcoming he is I do feel you are owed a warning. Grey and that demon you just met have a past. Grey is too strong to let it affect his judgment, but he is also too stubborn or 'moody' for me not to warn you about it. Keep your eyes open Peter and learn from Grey's example. Perhaps teach him how to be a tad less moody, if you can." With that said the Harmony door inside Pete's mind seemed to close, but this time she left it cracked open a bit.

Pete started to talk to himself. He knew both Harmony and Grey could hear him, but his emotions were running high, and the effects of so much change so quickly were troubling his freshly deceased mind. "Annihilation, sure great…'help me keep the balance, Pete'…sure why not…oh look at the shiny ball of light, Pete, pretty huh…oh, Pete, did you notice my rack? Aren't they spectacular?" He stopped muttering and shouted to Grey as he approached the picnic table, "Nice night, huh Grey?"

"Yep," was the only response he was awarded.

"Growing up in New York City we didn't have night skies like this. Nope, we were lucky to see the North Star. Did you have clear skies where you grew up?"

"Yep."

"Oh screw this small talk beating around the bush bullshit! Yeah that tiny three eyed demon girl was creepy man, but you are way too sulky for somebody whose eyes can glow too! What is going on?"

"Harmony wouldn't tell you, would she?"

"No."

Grey laughed and shook his head. He turned his body a bit and lay back on the table letting his knees and feet hang off the end. He tucked both arms behind his head as he looked up at the star strewn sky that Pete had commented on but did not say anything further.

"Fine, don't tell your replacement everything he needs to know!" Pete yelled exasperated. "Why would I need to know anything, right? What would be important, hmm? Like…oh, I don't know…demons you may have pissed off before and oh, just a little piece of philosophical fluff here Pete, but demons can kill you permanently and take all your energy. Fine! Just great! Keep your own counsel for now Grey, but if you need to tell me anything…you know, anything life alerting and important! I'll be right over here!" Pete motioned to the playground as he said this. He did not realize he was motioning at the playground until he turned around to stomp off, but that was not going to hinder him. He walked in a very wide arc around the swing set keeping his eyes on it at all times in case the little girl reappeared. Not wanting to turn his back to the swings he headed toward one of the playground's spring riders, because it was facing in the right direction for his demonic vigil.

"Just over here Grey, if you need me!" Pete yelled. Then he started quietly muttering again, "Sitting on the bright pink seahorse. Yeah that's me the apprentice badass demon slayer. All the white she devils will run in fear when they see me come riding to save the day on a pink seahorse, 'Hi Ho Pinkie, away!'" Pete sat down on the rider, but was instantly thrown off balance since he had not sat on a spring rider since he was a boy. He fell from the side of his mount into the recycled tire mulch of the playground. Spitting a small piece of rubber from his lips he said, "Oh yeah, Pete, real badass."

Chapter 7

Expectations can cause us so much heartache through all of our life, be it in a physical flesh and blood body or a creature of energy. The ironic part is that we can't function properly without them. We are conditioned from the very beginning to believe that if we do one thing we can expect a certain number of possible responses. You hear this referred to as "cause and effect" right? More terms from the academics, thank you boys and girls. I just call it life. Your parents had sex, and about nine months later there you were, new life; cause and effect. Energy swirling about in the void collapsed in on itself, bang, or "Big Bang" I guess, galaxies and stars were born, with the planets eventually followed suit to provide life. Cause and effect.

Yeah that's how things always start right? With the pretty and the positive shining out like a newborn baby laughing; if things started out shitty nobody would ever do something more than once in this universe, would they? Well, there will always be some damn fool willing to, I suppose.

Harmony showed me what the world was like from her point of view. How she could feel, no...see maybe? No, still not right. There just ain't the right verb in any language to describe what it is that she does or how she does it. Think of tossin' all five of your senses into a blender, and hittin' puree, then experiencing them all at once and you may come close, but you'd still never fully understand her perspective. My mind translated her world into images I could comprehend. I saw a roaring fire lit under a block of ice. The steady drip made the flames sizzle, but it kept burnin'. "Never too much of one or the other, Jasper," said Harmony, her voice coming from everywhere at once. "If the fire melts the ice, all is lost, or if the ice puts the fire out…"

I interrupted, "All is lost," finishing for her.

"Exactly so," she said. "But look closer." She directed my vision to a single drop of water about to fall from the block of ice. I could see the face of a young boy being egged on by friends to jump from a barn loft into a pile of hay. There were other black shapes capering about the children, demons I would soon learn. The boys did not seem to notice them. One of the shadowy shapes had moved a rusty pitchfork under the straw, tines pointed up right where the boy would land. "Hey kid!" I yelled at the water drop, "Don't do it! Hey stop!"

"It is up to me, Jasper," Harmony said. "I have to weigh and measure each life, to see if the actions of the self or others will upset the Balance, or if it will be just one more

drop." As she said the last the boy leapt from his perch, and the droplet of water fell. I turned my head. I did not want to see the end result, but I still heard the sizzle of water touching flame. Harmony spoke to me softly, "This is now your job too, Jasper my love. I need you."

One man's beginning, and another man's ending. Cause and effect.

Dealing in the Balance of things like I do, it makes the ugly harsh truths harder to ignore. I learned that lesson when I heard a small drop of water sizzle. Hell, if I ignored the uglier side of things none of us would be here right now, trust me on that one. When the result of things matches your expectations you get that positive sense of accomplishment. It happens like that from time to time. I hadn't expected my job to give me such heartache, but it did.

So when those expectations don't match up with what does happen, and life knocks you on your ass, what do you do? Do you fall to the ground, bitchin' and moaning about what's not fair? Or do you get up, plant your feet under you again, and say, "Shit happens." Because that's the even less academic way of saying "cause and effect" ain't it? Shit happens……..

***

Pete sat in the mulch with his knees drawn up to his chest and his arms locked around them. The crickets had started their song back up, and he closed his eyes, tilted his head back against the spring rider he had fallen off of, and listened to them. The crunch of boots on the mulch interrupted the chirruping. He opened his eyes to slits making sure that it was Grey approaching and not some new demon. Upon confirmation of his identity Pete closed his eyes again and said, "What do you want, Grey?"

Grey stood in front of Pete with his hands in his pockets. He did not shift, sway, or fidget like most people do when faced with an uncomfortable moment. He stood there silently, lean and solid like a statue made from flesh instead of stone or clay. Then he leaned forward reaching his hand out to Pete. "Take my hand, Pete."

Pete's eyes came open only half way before he asked derisively, "Why? You going to joy buzzer sparkle away my agitation, or maybe orange light *E.T.* me into a good mood?"

"No Pete," Grey said. Taking a deep breath and blowing out a sigh he continued, "This is a crossroads for you. You made a choice before, sure, but you are still faced with the same choice, and as far as I know you always will be. If you want out all you have to do is sit there feelin' sorry for yourself, and sooner or later that pulling sensation is going to get strong enough that you will just move on. Adios, see you 'round, bye-bye, nice knowing you Pete. Or you give up and run back to the Source, screw waiting around for it to happen, right? Just run. Or you get up, dust yourself off, and give the universe the middle finger. Take another swing at it. Those are your choices. They're the same now as before. All I'm offering you is my hand, and someone to stand at your back for a time. I know from experience that a little help goes a long way Pete. I never pegged you for the type to roll over for anything, but the choice is still yours."

Pete opened his eyes completely this time and said, "Give the universe the middle finger huh?"

"It's what gets me through," Grey said with a single nod of his head and a lopsided grin. Pete reached up and took Grey's proffered hand. The crackling blue light that Pete had experienced before with Zeus started up this time with Grey, but this time Pete felt a real sense of camaraderie and connection. *Maybe this is one of those changes Grey was talking about when I connected with Harmony*, Pete thought. The blue light shifted to a deep indigo and raced up Pete's arm to his shoulder, neck, and head.

When the sparks and glimmers had climbed high enough to obscure Pete's vision he started catching images in the light. They were not a definitive sequence of events, but more like flashes of a movie played on fast forward: Grey lying face down on a dust covered road, a tall dark haired man with a third eye (just like that little girl demon) in the center of his forehead was standing over him; Grey back on his feet, arms thrown back, a scream of rage on his face and blue light flowing from both his hands at a pack of demons all with that third eye in their foreheads; Grey and Harmony in a close lovers' embrace; Grey and Harmony yelling at each other and gesticulating harshly, then Grey's face filling the indigo light completely, his eyes no longer brimming with light at all, but instead he had the empty sockets of a corpse with black inky darkness deeper than any well. A scream of rage washed out from his mouth, so loud and forcefully that Pete staggered back breaking the embrace. "Jesus Christ!" Pete yelled.

"What Pete? What did you see?" Grey asked leaning down to crouch over Pete as he fell back down to the mulch.

"You, man. I saw you," Pete said panting, trying to catch a breath that he no longer needed. "I saw you and demons with three eyes. You with Harmony, the two of you arguing and hugging. I just saw you man."

"That happens sometimes Pete. When the connection between two of us is strong enough we're shown glimpses of what the other is, was, or could be. In those instances you can't trust what you see to be true Pete. Your mind just filtered the energy we shared and turned it into images you could comprehend," Grey said. He reached out to steady Pete, and when his hand touched Pete's shoulder this time there were no sparks. Grey held himself back so that it was only one man helping another to stand.

Once his feet were under him Pete staggered over to the merry-go-round and collapsed onto his back with a groan. Grey walked over with him and sat down. He rested the insides of his biceps on the handrails, letting his hands and finger dangle. "I should have told you more than I did Pete. For what it's worth I'm sorry, but I had watched you for so long, looking for a replacement. I was worried if you didn't decide to join me I would have wasted all that time. I'm tired Pete, tired and worn out. I've been at this longer than any of the others. Something about what we do just wears a person down. Maybe it's because unlike the others that stay we don't keep any energy for ourselves. We just channel it through Harmony or utilize what we can pull from around us and inside us; maybe steal a bit from the Source, but we never keep it."

Pete grunted inarticulately in response. Whether in affirmation, conciliation, or pain

Grey could not tell, so he continued, "The demon with the third eye is known as Legion. That little girl and her doll are just a pair of demons it has subverted to its cause."

"For we are many?" Pete's voice wearily drifted up from the middle of the mostly primer gray merry-go-round, but with more syllables than grunts. Grey took that for a good sign.

"Yeah, that's the one. Only don't give it all that much credit. It had one good line that that Mark fellow recorded and it landed in the Bible. Nice and creepy. 'For we are many,' yeah right. Trust me it has never been more than a dozen demons at once, but that doesn't inspire enough fear if it said, 'For we are about a dozen.' Legion is kind of a one hit wonder in that regard. Demons feed on negativity, and fear is a nice appetizer for that. That third eye thing is showing Legion's control over that particular demon or human. Legion uses up other demons as tools and vessels, and goes through them faster than a heroin addict goes through needles. It preys on fear and loves to influence the young, because youth is so easily scared, especially those in late adolescence; you were a teacher, you know that."

"Yep, just enough knowledge to think they know everything and not enough experience to realize when they're being manipulated. Sounds like the perfect fodder for a demon," Pete agreed rolling onto his side to look at Grey.

"Legion is responsible for a lot of the rebellious youth behavior seen in early history. I should have realized with all this cultural turmoil children have shown in the past few decades that it was still hanging around. That Kent State fiasco and those Columbine kids come to mind. Not to mention any of a number of others that never hit the mainstream media. That son of a bitch is even responsible for my death, but something tells me you figured that out already."

"I thought you said not to trust what I saw?" Pete asked and sat up. He leaned against the handlebar closest to Grey and scuffed his shoes in the cracked dirt moat that encircled every merry-go-round in every playground, the result of thousands of Nikes, Reeboks, and Converse plowing up the soil in play.

"So I did Pete, so I did," Grey agreed. "But if you keep using my own words against me I may as well stop talking, right? We can play the 'but you said' game all night if you want. Dawn comes quickly enough. If you want to hear about my history with Legion before we go huntin' that slippery pecker head down, then I need to keep on rollin' without interruptions. This ain't something I enjoy reliving. Maybe we could talk about your heart failure instead? That could be fun right?"

"Point taken, Grey. My lips are sealed; please continue," Pete said, waving his arm in a grand sweeping 'The floor's all yours' gesture.

Grey looked up at the stars for a moment. He breathed in the night air, and felt all the sensations of life tingle around him. He did not need the breath. Without lungs in need of respiration the motion was only for the comfort it provided and not integral to life. After all these years Grey found that in moments of discomfort or stress he always went back to the motions of life. All those small physical tics like breathing, swallowing, opening and closing his eyes, or running a hand through his hair. None of that was really there outside of the shell body he had created, but the repetitive actions soothed his psyche when he was upset, and dredging up his past always caused him angst.

"I'll take certain liberties with my story Pete, because in my time watchin' you I learned that you were a pop culture fanatic. Movies, books, and television were all escapes from the drudgery that daily life had turned into from my time to yours.

"Legion instigated New Mexico's Lincoln County Cattle War. Of course I didn't know that until after I died, and Harmony showed me what really happened. I had worked on and off for John Tunstall for a few years. Drivin' cattle mostly, but occasionally some handy work too, fence repair and the like. He was a good man, honest in a time and place where honesty did a man more harm than good.

"When I heard about his death I was sad to be sure, but that was the way of the world back then. It didn't surprise me none. John refused to play the game the rest of the good old boys did out in cattle country, and he paid the price with his life. I didn't go saddling up with Dick Brewer and Billy Bonney's Regulators. That just wasn't my way, and before you ask, Billy was more 'Scut Farkus' than Emilio Estevez, trust me.

"While those boys were out raising holy hell, claiming the law was on their side and gunnin' down all those responsible for John's death, I was trying to scrape by as I had my whole life as a farm hand. Picking up odd jobs here and there by day, and blowin' off steam in the local tavern come night. It wasn't a bad life, simple work and simple pleasures.

"One particular night I was playing cards, and enjoying a few drinks when a couple guys from the Murphy and Dolan side of the cattle war came in. They were already drunk, and looking for trouble. The war had escalated from warranted law into vigilantism on Bonney's part. I had heard Brewer was dead by then too, another dead boy in a rich man's war. One of those Murphy boys recognized me as having worked for John

Tunstall. It didn't matter none to them that I had also worked for their boss on occasion as well. They were angry, and looking for something to lash out at.

"I was the perfect target. I didn't have any close friends there, so no one stopped them from draggin' me out back. I still to this day believe they only intended to rough me up a bit, but that was not what Legion had in mind. No sir, it had those boys worked up into a lather. They would have believed anything he whispered in their ears. When I tried to cover my ribs Legion shouted 'He's going for a gun,' and that was enough for them. Flashes of fire in a dark alley, and the next thing I know Harmony is chatting me up.

"My story with Harmony is our own and none of your business, thank you very much. She showed me how things were and are. I learned it was Legion who was responsible for my death and many more, and against Harmony's advice I went gunnin' after it. The game between Legion and me was long bouts of back and forth so many times I've lost count. It won a bit then I would win a bit. I had thought up until earlier tonight that Zeus and I had finally gotten the better of Legion years ago in Tunguska, but apparently I was wrong.

"Not this time. I am going to show you how to fight, Pete, and with your help once we meet up with Raven I will end this. I'm going to destroy Legion once and for all, and you are going to help me."

Chapter 8

Life is about power. Who has it, who wants it, and to what lengths are they willing to go to get it. Humanity flatters themselves when they say only people crave power. Sure people can be the subtlest animal in their efforts to acquire power, I'll give you all credit on that, but all life is about shiftin' and balancing power.

The tiniest atoms end up struggling over electrons to attain balance. Power. Black holes devour energy like giant interstellar vacuums. Power. The struggle happens outside your front door, it carries over into your home, hell it even happens inside of your body. Right at this very moment viruses and bacteria are both fightin' inside you for power.

You show me a man who says, "I don't want power, I just want to share," and I'll show you a liar, and sadly a self-deluding liar at that. We may believe that someone's actions are selfless, but in my experience that is never the case. There are always ulterior motives. The minister guides his flock because he has a calling. He helps bring salvation to those willing to listen, why? Because he's either a good man who wants to go to heaven, ulterior motive. Or maybe he likes the feeling he gets when he preaches, or helps others. Self-gratification, ulterior motive... I can go on and on, but I don't want to disparage nobody. I just want to illustrate my point.

Harmony had told me she loved me, and so help me I believed her. Love is just another way to gain power. In my opinion what you do with that power dictates whether you are a good or bad person. It would be wonderful if you could share yourself with someone completely. I know that is what Harmony wanted from me. I was just so damned afraid that she saw something in me that wasn't there. It's a terrifying sensation when someone gives you their love.

"I have watched so many drops fall, Jasper," she whispered. "I had to. If I had attempted to save but one, I would had lost them all. I am sorry; it is a burden, a burden I needed to share, one that none of your predecessors seemed to understand. I learned how to feel through them. That is how I know what I feel for you is real, by judging what was lacking in my relationship with them- love."

She had all but said I had no choice in the matter. That she would know what I was thinking or feeling at all times with that bond we shared. I even think she believed that, and probably still does, but no matter how close two people are there is always a secret corner tucked away somewhere that is solely the domain of one.

What lurks in that domain? Something wonderful, something powerful, or something terrible? Quite possibly all of the above, yet there lies our connection to the Source. Only there is where we are whole, complete, and ourselves. Power……

***

Pete stared at Grey from across the rusty handrail. They made eye contact in silence for several long seconds before Grey spoke, "I mean it, Pete. I plan to finish what was started a long time ago, and I don't think I can do it without your help. Will you help me?"

"No more secrets?" Pete asked in return. "No more half-truths, Grey? If I'm going to have your back in this I can't be left in the dark. I wanted an adventure my whole life, and I've had more in the last…shit man! I don't even know how long I've been dead. I guess it really doesn't matter, but since my death it's been one new experience after another. Sure it's been one hell of ride, but I want out of the dark. I want some light! That's my price if I'm going to help you. I will stand with you, but I want the complete truth, and everything I need to know before it's an afterthought of, 'Oh gee, maybe I should have told old Pete that before the demons ate him'."

"Alright, the whole truth, at least as far as I know it, agreed?" Grey asked.

"Fair enough," Pete said, then casually ran his hand down the rail, and kicked his foot a step to start the merry-go-round moving. In a nonchalant tone of voice he continued, "Sooo is it time for the *ILM* crash course, because I was thinking now might be a good time for me to learn that ball of light trick, and maybe the glowing eye thingy too. I don't know if that does anything, but it looks fucking cool."

Grey chuckled ruefully, "Yeah, I reckon this would be a good time for that. I'm sure Harmony has been in touch with Raven and is sending her our way. No sense wastin' this opportunity."

Harmony moved forward in both of their minds and said, "Yes, Grey, Raven is on her way to you right now, and Septemsab'aa is with her. He has been aiding her where he can, but he fears to overstep his bounds. It will be an excellent opportunity for him to meet Peter, and teach him where the boundaries lie." Then she faded into the background once again, giving them the impression that she was busy elsewhere.

"Who is Sep-tem-sab'aa?" Pete asked.

"I'll give you the short Cliffs Notes version, Pete," Grey said. "Septemsab'aa is Malign's opposite. She's the super evil bitch where he's the really good guy. There has to be a balance to her power. We work with him often because his nature as an angel is to help, so he lends a hand where he can. But he is limited in what aid he can provide."

"Okay got it," Pete said nodding his head. "Malign evil white she devil, dude with the long foreign name good guy."

"We call him Sep for short, Pete. It's just easier. Follow me," Grey said as he jumped off the slowly rotating merry-go-round, and headed toward the weed choked baseball diamond. Motioning for Pete to follow, Grey started to explain while he walked, "Channeling light or positive energy is easy. All you have to do is focus on that place in yourself where you feel the Source pulling on you. It may not seem like it, but that is a two way door, just like Harmony's where you can pull power from. In a pinch Harmony can feed you some of her power as well, and if you get really good at it you can pull some from the world around you. But taking energy from the Source will be the quickest and most potent reservoir, because it is all but inexhaustible."

"Ha!" Pete laughed out loud, and stopped walking. He turned to Grey and said, "I think you just told me to 'Use the Source'."

Without a hint of derision or sarcasm in his voice Grey said to Pete, "And where do you think the idea for what you are referencing came from? The Source of life is just that, the

Source. It always has been and always will be. It was there long before its rhyming cinematic counterpart."

"Has anybody ever told you that you just suck all the fun out of things, Grey?" Pete asked in exasperation.

"Yeah, Zeus does all the time," Grey said and steered Pete over toward the beaten down hump that was once the pitcher's mound. It was now just a small lump of dirt with barely a rise of elevation. He lifted his right hand out from his side, and faster than thought a blue ball of light crackled and fizzed in his palm. He held it out to Pete and said, "Take it."

Pete tentatively reached out and took the ball in his hand. It started falling apart almost at once, turning into an amorphous jellyfish like blob that moved up Pete's forearm. "Whoa! Hold on there. Grey, what's it doing?"

"You're losing control of it, Pete. It's searching for a way to blend with you. To become a part of you, energy wants to bond, and be stable. Just hold the image of the ball in your mind. Focus on what you want it to do, and not what you see or feel it doing," Grey instructed stepping a few paces away from Pete.

Pete closed his eyes, and his face slowly melted into a flat visage of concentration. Little by little the light amoeba inched back down his arm, past his wrist, and settled into the palm of his outstretched hand. "Ha! Check that out! I did it, not bad for a first try huh? You know I think I could be a natural at this, sort of a prodigy maybe? You know 'Prodigy' would be a cool name for…"

Pete stopped mid-sentence, shrieking as the light ball shot from his hand like a comet, spinning around him once before it buried itself into his chest, and knocked him flat out on the ground. He laid there on his back looking up at the stars until Grey's face came into view looking down on him. With one eye brow raised all Grey said was, "Nope," and walked back out of Pete's line of sight.

Tiny wisps of smoke rose from Pete's hair and chest as he sat up and said, "I know you aren't laughing over there, Grey."

"Me? I would never," Grey said holding a hand to his chest in a mock offended manner. "You ready to try again, Prodigy?"

"Asshole," Pete muttered under his breath, but walked back to the pitcher's mound. This time Grey was waiting with a slightly larger ball of light. It was about the size of a grapefruit and pulsed with a verdant green hue. Grey rolled it around his hand flipping it from palm to back, back to palm over and over like a stage magician. Then he started tossing it back and forth from right hand to left. The green light split in midair into several smaller balls which Grey deftly started to juggle in a three ball cascade. A sly grin crept onto his face, and the three balls divided again into six, yet Grey continued to juggle without pause.

"Asshole," Pete said again. "Alright, Grey, I get your point. You can stop showing off now."

"Sure thing, Pete. Here, catch," Grey said and he tossed his hand toward Pete. All six balls coalesced back into a single sphere and sailed toward Pete, covering the short distance between them in an eye blink.

"Shit!" Pete exclaimed. He ducked down and stuck his right hand up in the air like any first year little league player hoping to catch the ball by luck more than skill. The result was the same whether it was luck or not. The green ball rotated and spun on its axis in Pete's outstretched palm. He squinted with one eye up at his hand, not moving out of his crouch. Then Pete closed his eye, and blinked them both open. The dubious look on his face confessing more than any admission that he did not believe what he was seeing. A huge smile broke through as Pete stood up saying, "Alright! Now that's what I'm talking about!"

Grey flinched and said, "You didn't just say that, did you?"

"Give me a break," Pete said still smiling. He held his hand out carefully as if holding something he was worried about dropping and breaking. "That's something every black man should get to say at least once in his life, and you'd be surprised how few opportunities come up in a college literature classroom."

"Okay, cliché out of your system?" Grey asked, and after Pete nodded he continued, "Then go ahead and see if you can manipulate it a bit. Move it around, or toss it back and forth a couple of times. Examine where the control comes from inside of you. Once you find that place, that calm, remember it, and you'll always have power to call." Grey started walking away from Pete still standing on the pitcher's mound, and headed toward home plate. When he was there he turned around, and squatted down into a catcher's stance. Where previously the balls of light would form there now appeared a globe of darkness that swirled violently. The void twisted and turned in Grey's hands until a small center concavity appeared in the dark mass like a miniature black hole.

"Now, Pete, when you're ready throw it back to me, but keep it controlled and focused in your mind after you release it, or it's going to come right back at you like before," Grey said adjusting his stance a bit. Without hesitation Pete cocked his arm back, and let fly. The green ball of light soared through the night like a small meteorite right into the void Grey held ready for it. There was a bright flash as the opposing energies met. Then the light was slowly swallowed up by the dark globe. "Very good. Concentrate on that place again and see if you can produce one on your own this time."

Pete shut his eyes in focus and in hopes of blocking out any external distractions. He could sense the power from Harmony just waiting for him to call it, but he had been using that place in himself enough to communicate with her that he felt confident in his ability to use it already. He wanted to touch "The Source" as Grey called it, Power with a capital "P". Pete focused on the place that was tugging on him, cajoling him to let go, and grabbed that energy. At first his mental grip was yanked back like a metaphysical game of tug-a-war. Grey's voice intruded on Pete's focus, echoing in a raspy shout, seeming to travel over a great distance, "Pete! Pete, let go! You're trying to pull in the whole damn Source, man!"

Pete dropped his mental hold on the Source and tumbled to his hands and knees panting. He grasped at the cracked dirt and dry weeds that his fingers were tangling in. When he had enough control again he opened his eyes. Pete could see lines of energy pulsing out from his fingers, connecting them to a spider web of power coursing out from him to the ends of his vision. Between each line of light there was an area with a dark gaping maw tugging at the energy. In a winded whisper Pete said, "Beautiful…"

"Yeah, Pete, it is." Grey said as he leaned over to help Pete back to his feet. "But no man can handle it all, trust me. Now, try it again, but grab just a bit. I like to think of it as fishin'. Toss your line in, get a bite, and pull back just a bit. Don't go gunning for the white whale on your first try."

When Pete was back in control of himself, and his feet were stable under him once more he noticed that the lines and voids were gone. The world was back to how he had always perceived it. Grey had gone back to home plate. Once more Pete closed his eyes in concentration. It was easier this time for him to find the Source tugging at his core. He reached out to it, feeling the Source pulse and wash through him, life and death together. Separating a piece from the whole was tricky work. Pete casually fished his grip in that ocean of power and pulled on a small section. A chunk of energy, burning like an ember, gave way and crashed into him lending a thrumming aura of power. He mentally pushed that aura of power down and out from his core to his hand where small crackles and jolts of red light started jumping from his fingertips.

"Grey? Why is it red?" Pete asked, concern evident in his voice.

"It's just how you perceive it, Pete. Color as you think of it really doesn't matter in energy. The sun appears yellow to the human eye, but that doesn't mean shit to the sun. Red could be how you are feeling, warm perhaps? Don't pay it any mind. You're doing well. See if you can manipulate it into a shape you can wield. A sphere is just the most natural form for controlled energy, but not the only structure," Grey explained. Then he manipulated his black void catcher's mitt into a long spear, and with a deft swirl of his hands it flattened out into a large shield. Another flick of motion and Grey was back to holding his small void again.

Sparks and glimmers cascaded off the golf ball sized sphere in Pete's right hand. He brought his left hand up to cover his right like his was trapping a firefly. He cracked his top hand a bit to see what had been contained, and a small round ember of light flickered solidly in his hand. There were no longer embers bouncing off the round flame in his hand. It was completely under his control. Pete smiled again, and said, "Hey, Grey, check it out! Too bad I quit smoking. This could be really cool at parties!"

Pete moved his left hand back down to his side, and the little red ball in his right hand flickered a bit. He focused on it again, and this time the light grew brighter then larger to the size of a grapefruit. The sphere grew steadily larger to resemble a volleyball. Realizing the energy was starting to get away from him Pete tried to shrink the globe, yet it still increased to a beach ball in circumference. Pete yelled, "Shit! Shit shit shit…wait, wait."

The light dimmed and shrank back to a manageable size again when Pete asked, "Are you ready for it, Grey?" He tossed his red meteor across the field before Grey responded with a nod. The red ball collapsed and disappeared into Grey's void just like the green one had previously done.

They kept repeating this sequence over and over until the first glimpses of dawn lightened the eastern horizon. The color of Pete's light changed, running the spectrum, as the hours wore on. The power flowed faster and stronger as Pete became more confident with his ability. Pete launched auras of force out to home plate just as fast as Grey could devour them. The dawn had crept in completely as Pete yawned. He paused after doing so and asked, "Wait, why am I feeling tired? We don't need to sleep, do we?"

"No, we don't," Grey answered. "But when we operate on this level in a physical shell we are more subject to our mental conditioning. You feel tired because your body would have been worn out by now. You could rest if you needed to or let yourself ascend back to a higher level of vibration. Those options would help, but time would still pass while you did that. And time is pressing.

Demons with their natural affinity for darkness are less active during daylight giving us an advantage in runnin' them to ground. Your two best options are either let Harmony lend you some of her strength or go get something to eat. Food doesn't really provide us nourishment, but it does give you a bit of down time to relax. Maybe recharge your batteries, so to speak. That is what I plan on doing myself, because our ride is here."

Grey nodded his head toward the narrow parking lot lining the side of the park nearest to them. Pete turned as he heard the distinctive sound of car doors slamming. From the distance separating them he could make out a white minivan back lit by the rising sun, and a pair of figures moving in his direction.

Chapter 9

Men and women, two sides of the same coin, in relationships must maintain a state of balance. I don't mean to imply that men and women are opposites, like good and evil. People always want to view existence in black and white, right? It's a protective tendency that has them do so. I don't blame them none for it mind you, but it tends to bleed over into everything they view, like the differences in gender.

You could say that a woman is more predisposed to making decisions based on emotions, or that a man always thinks with his pecker. You'd be right, and you'd be wrong. Those are generalities, y'all live by those, some call them stereotypes, and others call them suppositions. All it boils down to is that if repeatedly more than half the time a generality holds true, then that generality is considered an established fact. Does it mean that the other forty nine percent of the time when things or people do not fit that generality are then considered false? No, but we don't talk much about that do we? The academics that so rightly love me don't want you to pay attention to the percentage that did not fit into their experiment, or world view if we're talkin' regular folk and their prejudices.

So there will be folks who don't like others based on gender, color, or religion. They don't think of them as being a person first. No they are just their generality, all women are the same, right? "Pay no attention to the man behind the curtain," as the saying goes. There is a kernel of truth in most lies, and most of our established truths are sugar coated lies. You have to look at something from every angle before you can say you have seen it if you don't want to make a generality.

All too often people let those generalities affect how they relate to one another. They base how they interpret their emotions on those same suppositions. They think because something gives them pleasure that they love it, or if it causes them pain, they hate it.

My eyes, or what passed for them now, told me Harmony was a woman. My mind was rational enough to realize she could not possess a gender, or mayhap she was both. It was confusing, but when she showed me the world through her point of view I could feel part of her that she was keeping walled away. I don't think she knew, or to this day knows, that I felt it. An alien perspective that was showing me things in a way I could understand. I could feel desire to be like me, a person, but it was confused. I felt like a peeping Tom, so I left it alone and did not seek to further understand it, or her, or him.

I guess when you try to understand someone else, you should always make sure that you have fully examined the old maxim of "Know Thyself" before you go placing labels and generalities on another…….

***

Pete watched the pair as they approached. One was a tall slender woman with ink black hair dressed in tight leather pants matching her hair color, and a pale blue tee-shirt that complemented her eyes. She swayed toward them with a feminine grace that brought to Pete's mind the panther demons from the night before. She was all fluid motion blending one step into the next, grace.

So mesmerizing was the woman that Pete had forgotten about the other figure until they were almost standing before him. The man stood a head shorter than his companion, and where she was long limbed and supple, he was stocky. He was not corpulent or obese, but sturdy, giving the impression of a boulder resting in an ocean's surf. He had immaculately coiffed salt and pepper hair, but the coloring was patchy, not an even blending. Dressed in a cream and khaki business suit complementing his complexion, he had the skin tone of someone from a Middle Eastern country. *He's swarthy*, Pete thought. *You always read about people who are described as "swarthy," but you never get to use it yourself. He looks like a modern, hip pirate.* As if the man had read Pete's thoughts he smiled, turning his head slightly so Pete could see a small gold hoop earring in his left earlobe.

"Grey!" The woman shouted, bringing Pete's attention back to her as she ran the last few yards to throw herself into Grey's arms. Whereas before with Harmony sparks of color shot off of them in the places their bodies met, this time Pete did not get that embarrassing feeling of voyeurism. It was more like watching a father and daughter who did not spend as much time together as either would like.

Grey twirled the woman around once, put her down, and then ran his open palm down the side of her face. It left a quickly vanishing trace of blue on her cheek as he said, "Raven, it's been too long darlin'. You look as beautiful as ever."

Raven smiled at Grey then turned to face Pete. Her bright happy expression vanished, black eyebrows beetling down to glare at him. She looked Pete up and down a few times. Then with her husky voice dripping contempt she said, "So this is the guy who is going to be your replacement? He doesn't look like much. Do you really think he's up to it?"

Pete rocked his head back like Raven had slapped him. "Nice to meet you too," he said. Then with his best lopsided grin he drawled, "Hey, lady, I may not look like much, but I got it where it counts!"

"Cute," Raven said. Jabbing a finger at his chest she continued, "Listen up *Solo*, Grey is irreplaceable. He has taken on more demons and kept the universe from falling apart more times than any of us can count! You could follow him for millennia and never even come close to what he can do!" Raven advanced a few aggressive steps toward Pete as she spoke. Pete put his hands up in a placatory gesture and retreated backward a couple paces as she came closer.

"Whoa, lady, chill out!" Pete said.

"Chill out! You want me to chill out?" she asked in an accusatory tone of voice. "Legion is poised to tip the Balance over and spread chaos and destruction. Our greatest soldier's new apprentice is cracking *Star Wars* jokes, and I'm supposed to 'Chill Out'?" Raven threw her hands up in exasperation and turned her back to Pete.

Pete let his hands fall back to his sides, blew out a long sigh, and shook his head. Under his breath he muttered, "Crazy ass white women."

"That's it!" Raven yelled. She spun around with a Smith and Wesson 500 Magnum pointed directly at Pete's nose. Only a few yards separated the two of them, so there was no doubt in Pete's mind that if she pulled the trigger he would take a shot right between his eyes. A cluster of dark bangs had fallen in across Ravens cheek. She blew out a breath to move them and with a cynical laugh she said, "I'll just save Legion the trouble and do it myself."

Pete had no time to register her words when she pulled the trigger sending a bright lavender bullet shaped charge directly at him. Even when it was over, Pete was not sure if it had been through talent, survival instinct, intercession of fate's hand, or pure and simple beginner's luck. He had thrown out his right hand creating a small red shield directly in front of his palm that deflected the bullet. It ricocheted off at an odd angle toward the picnic shelter where it struck a garbage can toppling the bin over. The raccoon that had been rummaging through the trash went streaking away, screeching at them as it fled.

Raven cocked a well sculpted eyebrow at Pete. She flicked her wrist and the handgun vanished from her grip. She gave him another visual once over nodding her head. "Not bad for a single night's training Grey. Maybe there is hope for him yet."

Pete still held his shield out and ready. He continued to hold it in place even when Raven walked away from him. He was still holding it firmly in front of his hand when she had reached Grey, who was standing at home plate with a sardonic smile on his face. Pete shook his head and finally let the energy he held dissipate. Then looking up at the sky he said, "You were right, momma. Damn, were you ever right!"

Chapter 10

I often wonder why people make the assumptions that they do. Is it a result of their conditioning like their expectations, or is it something else that leads them to assume certain ideas? There is no good without evil; one necessitates the existence of the other. Good and evil all come from the same source, the Source, and I guess that is as close to an argument for God as you can get.

Is the Source God? You could use that title sure, but that word means something different to every single sentient being to ever hear it. I can't give you an answer to a question beyond your ken, but I can say that both good and evil must always exist in a state of balance, so your God is the nicest man I ever did meet. He's also an asshole too. He has to be to let children die, wars destroy, and hate sweep across nations.

Yet people still assume that good always triumphs over evil. Those angels with flaming swords will conquer the vengeful demon hoards. Never giving thought to the fact that any aggressive action is evil, whether in defense or not. If an angel is to stay good all it can do to evil is turn the other cheek or at most stand defensively in front of the object of a demon's interest, and be absorbed. I've known a few who learned to manipulate positive energy to trap a demon, allowing them or those the angel was protecting to escape without an aggressive altercation.

Positive charges can turn to negative, and most angels are inherently good and will not jeopardize their energy being converted to evil ends. It takes a real, pardon me if this sounds like an oxymoron, but a real badass angel to penny up and try to trap a demon.

Then where are the archangels you may be thinking of, Christian mythologies' hit men?

Pleased to meet you.

Harmony's warriors have been mistaken for the archangels, wizards and sorcerers for that matter too, because we so often go up against the demons and the darkness. Evil by its nature will try to destroy and consume everything, so when the mortal world happens to catch a glimpse of us fightin' those that would do them harm they think, "Hey that must be an angel." We don't care mind you; it's just their assumption. We all assume from time to time.

After I had been working with Harmony for a while she told me about Legion. What it had done, and where. That demonic butterfly flapped its wings and poof, there I was dead in an alley outside a shitty saloon that served watered down whisky. I asked her why she didn't intervene, stop me from dying. I knew by now that she could have. She said, "It was just your time, Jasper; I could not."

But friend, if you've been paying attention you know she was the one to make that decision right? So like me maybe you ask yourself, "Did she let him die because she wanted him to help her? Was it his time, or was what that little brunette thought of as love clouding her judgment?" I still ask myself those same questions in that secret place that we all have, remember?

Maybe you'd assume I went off halfcocked looking for revenge despite the fact that Harmony asked of me not to. Maybe you'd be right, but maybe Harmony can make assumptions too. Maybe she assumed I'd do what she wanted, or maybe if she knew me well enough to say she loved me then she assumed I'd do what I wanted in either case. Maybe I went gunnin' for Legion as a way to transfer my anger over those unknowable answers, to too many questions. Life always seems to have a lot of maybes, don't it?

None of that mattered to me. There was a war on. There's always a war on, but it don't always spill over into the physical world. (When it does, that's when you should take notice friends because if everyday folk notice the energy we toss about, then it's time to duck and cover.) It was my turn to go on the offensive. I had power, knowledge, and direction. At least I assumed I did…….

***

Grey folded his arms across his chest, looking between Pete and Raven with his eyebrows raised he said, "I suppose an introduction would be rather silly at this point, but, Pete, this is Raven, and, Raven, this is Pete. Now I need to have a nice chat with Sep, and I would really appreciate it if you two children would play nice while the grown-ups talk business, okay?"

"Oh, shut up, Grey," Raven said redirecting her glare from Pete to him. "I needed to test his mettle. If he's going to go up against Legion with us I had to see if he would freeze like a newbie, or if he had enough balls to stand his ground." Then she cast her eyes down from Grey's face, looking less confident and more like a shy school girl when she continued, "I'm sorry I didn't warn you it was Legion. I suspected it was based on the stories you've told me, but I wasn't sure until Sep confirmed it…sorry."

"Your guilt is unfounded, Raven," Septemsab'aa said, speaking for the first time. His voice was slightly accented in a dialect Pete could not identify, and until he had spoken up Pete had again forgotten about him. He could not decide if this was because Raven the human firework stole the spotlight or if it was something that the man did on purpose. *A blending in with the background maybe*, Pete thought. *I'll have to ask Grey about that. Some kind of camouflage or something.*

Sep continued, "There is no way you could have known it was the Gadarene demon. Even Harmony believed it to be destroyed last time it challenged Grey. Only a fool would be upset with you child, and Grey may be many things, but never a fool. Am I right, my friend?" He asked, turning his face toward Grey. He smiled, displaying a set of teeth so white they almost glowed out from his tan features, and winked in Grey's direction.

"When aren't you, Sep?" Grey said with a sigh. "It's good to see you as well old friend. Thank you for watchin' over her. She and Harmony have been at odds lately, more than normal, and whether they'll admit it or not, their relationship isn't what it should be. I thank you for your help."

Grey walked over to Sep to shake hands. Pete had finally come to expect the flash and flair of shared energies, but this time nothing happened, only a handshake between two men. Pete made a mental note to ask Harmony or Grey about it later. He was accumulating quite the number of unasked queries, but for now he did not want to miss out on the exchanges and introductions. Raven had already made him feel inadequate, and he was determined not to let her see him slip up in

124

any way. Grey gestured to him and called, "Pete, come over here and meet Sep."

Pete went over and grasped Sep's hand. He pumped it up and down twice then let go with the same results as Grey. There were no sparks or zaps manifesting in the gesture. He thought, *maybe we can't share energy with an angel*. Sep interrupted his churning thoughts when he said, "It is a pleasure to meet you Peter. I hope Raven did not scare you over much. She can be a bit zealous at times. One cannot help but admire her enthusiasm."

"Aw it's no big deal," Pete said shrugging his shoulders in a nonchalant manner. "You know how it is. Crazy ass white women pull giant energy firing hand cannons on me all the time. I just have that kind of way with 'em you know?"

Sep laughed, then turning his beaming smile up a notch he said, "I imagine you do Peter, but do not let her intimidate you. Yes, Grey is handing you quite a large pair of shoes to fill, but I trust he will not let you try them on until he knows you are ready."

Raven had come over to stand behind them. She was not saying anything, refusing to chime in on the conversation, whether out of frustration or simple pique, Pete could not tell. He kept watching her as she glanced at each of them, a different set of emotions flashing in her eyes depending on who she was regarding.

125

Grey noticed her from the corner of his eye and smiled. She smiled back, but wrapped her arms over her breasts tightly as if to ward off a chill. Grey smacked Pete on the shoulder to get his attention and winked at Sep before he walked over to Raven, the unspoken male equivalent of 'You two stay and talk. I'm going to speak with her in private.'

When Grey reached Raven he did not stop walking or utter a sound. She fell into step with him knowing what he wanted without needing to hear it. They walked in silence for a while just enjoying each other's company and the warm early morning sun. Grey was the first to break the quiet, "What's bothering you, darlin'?"

"This, just all of this," she said motioning her hands in a large sweeping gesture to encompass the other men. "Grey, I'm not good with change, you know that. I don't like the thought of you moving on. It's not just you leaving me here, but everybody else needs you too."

"We've been over this Raven," Grey said with a sigh.

"Yeah I know," she whispered growing silent for a minute. When she continued it was in a more forceful voice, "And guess what. We're going over it again because maybe this time will be different. Maybe this time I'll be able to change your mind, and if not this time? Then we'll go over it again and again until I do. You don't…Are you laughing at me?" she demanded.

"No ma'am," Grey said doing his best to stifle the chuckle that had crept up on him despite his best efforts.

"I didn't think so," Raven said waspishly. They stopped walking and stood in silence facing each other, both with a thousand things on their minds to say, and a million reasons not to say them. Raven sighed, shook her head, and said, "Fine Grey, I'll let it go for now because I know you, and I know you're about ready to change the subject in your oh so subtle male fashion, and ask if there's a place to eat around here? There is, and quite honestly I'm glad it's only fast food, because I know that's your last choice in any town, so there." She emphasized her speech by crossing her arms and tapping her foot impatiently.

Grey just smiled at her. Leaning in he kissed her on the forehead, and said, "Thanks darlin'."

***

Pete and Sep had been watching them from a distance. Not in an attempt to eavesdrop, but out of that lack of conversational material that sometimes crops up when two people are introduced, then moments later left alone by their mutual acquaintance. When they saw Grey lean in and kiss Raven's forehead Pete asked, "So what's their story?"

"Just like everyone else's, Peter, long and in-depth, only slightly longer and slightly more in-depth than most I suppose," Sep answered in an offhanded manner. Turning his attention fully to Pete he continued, "He pulled her out of the ashes of Auschwitz when she was a young woman, and brought her to Harmony when he saw her strength. They have been understandably close ever since. He was her spiritual Florence Nightingale, well if Florence had kicked some serious metaphysical ass that is, but I believe the metaphor is still sound." His focus had drifted from Pete at some point in his explanation, and he was nodding his head as if in agreement with someone Pete could not see.

"Okay," Pete said slowly, "and why don't Raven and Harmony get along so well?"

Sep turned his attention and smile back to Pete saying, "Have you ever known a mother and daughter who did? Harmony is wonderful in what she does, do not take my meaning wrong, but how she chooses to interact with each of you is a personal relationship. I do not know why she chose to view Raven as a daughter, but she can be

128

single-minded at times, and closed off in what she will and will not share with me. I believe all her interactions with mankind have changed her over the millennia. She is far older than I, and to my knowledge I am the eldest to have stayed here among the human race. Her counsel has always been her own."

"Sooo you're the 'Really Good Guy' huh?" Pete asked changing the subject.

"I see our friend Grey is still using his Cliffs Notes version of things," Sep said laughing out loud this time. Pete decided he liked Sep, based on his laugh alone. It brought to mind the old black and white swashbuckling movies he used to watch as a child. When Sep had downgraded his laugh to a rueful chuckle he said, "I suppose I should take comfort in his stability. Yes, in a simplified equation I would be the 'Really Good Guy.' I notice our friends are coming back, and knowing Grey as I do I can only assume we are going to go somewhere he can get a hamburger. Yes indeed, stability."

Chapter 11

We take comfort and solace where we can. Nobody can go on toiling through the pains of life forever. I hear it called "me time" or a "sanity break" by modern folk. Some people find it in physical contact with others, a simple touch or embrace. Others find peace in the baser actions of life; eating, procreating, and defecating. Maybe that's why children find dick, fart, burp, and poop jokes so funny. It's something they can all relate to, so they laugh at life's great equalizers. Make no mistake, friend, that is the greatest source of comfort and solace, laughter.

I always found it best to combine the more socially expectable choices though. Connections are best made when you sit down to a meal with pleasant company. Breaking bread and sharin' fellowship are common symbols throughout human mythology for a good reason. Just like those children giggling at a fart, we can identify with those concepts. Jesus had his "last supper" among his closest friends, families put aside differences every holiday to eat together, and men and women dance about their courtships over meals.

Common threads connect every life and will continue to connect them as long as the Balance holds. I have sat in on many a war council, and in all honesty those moments are the clearest in my long memory. When the underlying theme is that this could be your last meal, you enjoy it more. Everything sticks out in a hyperrealism as your subconscious whispers, "Enjoy that bite partner, because it could be your last."

Zeus went with me in 1908 when Legion and I fought what I thought was our last battle. Zeus followed me wherever I went back then, and I have never known a man to enjoy a meal more than that Sasquatch. He and I camped out on the open tundra the eve before battle and slow roasted an entire pig over our campfire. I tell you I can still taste it, more than a hundred years later. Hell, for that matter I can still hear him laughing telling jokes over that fire while we dined. Yes sir, food and fellowship; not much more a man can ask for…….

***

Pete sighed with relief when the fast food restaurant came into sight. He had never been so happy to see those gaudy yellow lights, the giant plate-glass windows, and smell the cheap grease mixing with the car emissions from the drive-thru line. The four of them had ridden in an awkward silence since they had climbed into the minivan back at the park. It had only been a few miles drive from one end of town to the other, but with many one-way streets, stop signs and lights the trip lasted the better part of twenty minutes. Pete kept thinking, *Time may not have the same meaning when you're dead, but lord it can still drag on by.* Looking around, Pete noticed there were more cars in attendance at this early hour than he would have anticipated for such a small town. He sighed and unbuckled his seatbelt before Raven had finished settling the minivan into a spot far out from the entrance.

Sep said, "You know, that was hardly necessary," smiling as he pointed to the now retracted seatbelt. Pete glanced up at the rearview mirror hesitantly meeting Raven's unreadable sunglass covered gaze. "Yeah, well, let's just say I have some trust issues, alright?" he muttered under his breath he muttered, "I'd say for a good reason too."

Pete slid the rear door open and stepped out. Raven still watching him from behind her shades waited until he took his first step out of the van and let her foot slightly off the break. She had yet to shift to park and Pete stumbled as the van lurched forward a foot. He glared back over his shoulder at her. She smiled sweetly in response. Grey ignored them both and Sep said, "Children, come now. That is no way to act. Please, if you are going to be so immature wait until I have left your company."

Sep stepped out of the van placing a hand on Pete's shoulder in passing and walked toward the entrance. The others followed him. Since he was the first to reach the door he held it open for his companions with a smile and a bow directing them to go ahead of him. Cold recycled air heavy with the aromas of grease, meat, and industrial cleaners smacked them in the face when they passed through the second set of doors which Grey held open. The young woman behind the counter looked surly and tired when they approached. Glaring at Pete as he walked up to her she asked, "Can I hep'yew?"

"Um yeah," Pete said, looking at the illuminated menu and its variety of choices and sizes for what he thought of as essentially the same food. "I'll have the number one value meal with a chocolate milkshake please."

Rolling her eyes and chomping her gum the girl said, "It's before eleven mister, you hav'ta order off'a the breakfast menu!" snapping at Pete as if he were slow, stupid, or both.

"Oh, sorry," Pete stammered. "I'll just have a coffee and some hash browns I guess." The girl entered his order glaring at him with the same disdain most people reserve for the things they have to scrape off the bottom of their shoes. She gave him his total, and Pete was surprised to find he had a wad of cash in his back pocket when he reached for it just like

Grey had in the other diner a life time ago. *Huh, another fringe benefit?* Pete thought in question to himself.

"What'll you have?" the girl asked Grey without looking up from her register.

Grey reached out and placed his hand on the girl's arm. Small sparks of violet light radiated from his fingertips up to the girl's shoulder. Her head snapped up to attention, smile shining as she chomped her gum. Grey gave her a lopsided grin and drawled, "I know it's an inconvenience, but I could really go for a cheeseburger and fries darlin', if it ain't too much trouble please."

"No problem at all," the girl said. She keyed in his order and asked, "Would you like anything to drink?"

Pete did not listen long enough to hear Grey's choice of beverage. He was busy grumbling to himself, "Oh that's just wrong." Another worker, this one a pimply faced youth right out of a sitcom fast food restaurant, complete with pubescent voice crack said, "Here's your order sir" to Pete, and slid a spartan tray in his direction.

Pete picked up his tray, walked into the dining area, and slid into an open booth. He had cracked the plastic lid off his coffee when Sep sat down on the bench across from him. "Not hungry Sep?" Pete asked while he stirred several packets of sugar into his coffee.

134

"No, not for this food anyway, and I use that term quite loosely here," Sep said with derision dripping from his voice. "I am not what you would call a fan of the modern American fare, too many chemicals. All of those preservatives sour my stomach. When I choose to eat I want it to be real food from the earth, not grown in a lab, thank you." He picked up Pete's hash brown patty, looked at it, shook it a bit causing it to wobble gelatinously, and then let it drop back onto Pete's tray with a plopping sound.

Pete shrugged, tore a piece off the patty, dipped it in some ketchup, and tossed it into his mouth. After wiping his finger on a napkin he continued to empty sugar packets into his coffee until Grey and Raven joined them. Pete noticed that they both had cheeseburgers and French fries on their trays when they sat down, and he shook his head in annoyance. "You know you're going to have to teach me that one too before you re..." Pete said but tapered off when Raven shot him an icy stare, "Before we go out to breakfast again," he finished smiling at Raven, but her expression remained the same.

Grey was not looking at either of them though. He was staring intently out the window past Raven as she shot the paper covering tube from her straw across the table at Pete. Ignoring her Pete followed Grey's line of sight in time to see a familiar worn down Ford pickup truck pull into an open parking space. It appeared Tommy and his friends had not taken Grey's advice because they were all dressed in the same clothes as the night before, but having taught college age boys for forty years Pete could not discount the possibility that they had all just been too lazy to change clothes too. The only noticeable difference was the absence of their demon companions.

Tommy stopped when he saw Grey through the window. The fear that the panther demon had helped him smother jumped back into his eyes. His friends were not paying attention and they bumped into him, piling up comically at his back. Pete was not sure if it was the absence of the demons spurring them on, the light of day with witnesses about, or the fact that Grey's eyes had gone completely gray, glowing without a trace of pupil or iris as he stared the boys down. Whichever the case was, Tommy turned around scattering his groupies like a swarm of flies. They regrouped in his wake and were close on his heels as he hightailed it back to his vehicle.

"Friends of yours?" Sep asked quizzically, raising a silver eyebrow.

Raven laughed and started eating her cheeseburger. Grey turned to Sep, color returning to his eyes, and said, "We met last night when they tried to push Pete around a bit. They had some of Legion's panthers goading them on."

"Yes, that makes sense," Sep said. "Their leader, the one who took the most interest in you Grey, his name is Thomas McDougal. His family is the local big name, and Tommy there has been riding on that his whole life just as his father did before him, and so on for quite a few generations. Young Tommy graduated high school last spring and has been hanging around with his group of sycophants ever since. Even his family's money could not keep him in the local community college. He is of the dimwitted sort who is only bright when it comes to being mean."

"I've dealt with his type more than a time or two Sep," Grey said with a hint of annoyance creeping into his typical drawl.

"Of course you have, Ramadi. I did not mean to imply that you have not. I only wanted to paint a picture for you and Peter of what the day life around here is like," Sep said in a placatory tone of voice.

"Fair enough Sep," Grey said. "I didn't mean to sound testy. I'm just more tired lately than normal, and my patience isn't what it was."

The table grew quiet but for the ambient sounds of the other diner's chatter coupled with the eating and drinking noises from those at the booth who were partaking. Pete emptied more sugar packets into his coffee and Raven started in on her French fries. Grey left his tray untouched as he stared out the window. Pete glanced over at Grey between sips, watching the man sit there statue-like was unnerving, so Pete poked him on the shoulder and asked, "Dude you okay?"

Grey nodded his head and passed his untouched food over to Pete. "I'm not hungry, Pete. You go ahead and take it. I'm going for a walk outside. Clear my head a bit. Something about this ain't sitting right with me. Maybe a stroll will help me work it out. I can always grab another burger when I get back."

Grey slid out from the booth and walked toward the door. All three of his compatriots watched him go: Raven with worry, Pete with curiosity, and Sep with sadness. After the doors had shut on Grey's back, Sep touched Raven on the arm to grab her attention. He looked her in the eyes and said, "Behave." Then he was gone. No fading or flashing of light, just one moment there, and the next an empty seat.

Raven turned and stared at Pete while she ate her French fries. Her blue eyes never left him as she ate. Her hands moved in a practiced rhythm: pick up, dip in ketchup, and move to mouth. She never once looked down to double check where items were on the table. It was more unnerving to Pete than Grey's far off stare. He started to slide out from the booth saying, "Uh, I have to use the bathroom."

"No you don't," Raven said. "You won't ever have to use the bathroom again if you don't want to in your current state."

"Fine then, I want to, because you scare the shit out of me, alright woman?" Pete asked.

Raven smiled and said, "I'll take that as a compliment. Sit back down and eat your food, and I'll dial the mega-bitch act down a bit, sound fair?" taking a bite of fry and dropping her gaze from his for the first time in minutes.

Pete nodded but still kept a wary eye on her as he started in on his meal.

***

Grey walked a few blocks and sat down on the worn concrete steps that led up to the local public library. He sat for a few moments slowly breathing in and out, watching as the town started its day. He rolled his neck around, doing it just to enjoy the repetitive physical action, rubbing a hand on the nape loosening up nonexistent muscles. When he stretched his legs out onto the sidewalk he crossed them, announcing to the empty step at his side, "You may as well show yourself Sep: I know you're there."

Sep appeared next to Grey sitting in the same position he had been in the restaurant. His hands were folded primly in his lap, and his eyebrows were raised in a silent query. Grey sighed and ignoring the unspoken question said, "Please don't let Pete see you do that Sep, or he'll start in on teleportation again."

"Oh…well allow me to apologize in advance, because I left the table in the same fashion," Sep said lifting a hand for a gold light to come perch upon. He stroked it with his index finger a few times then it moved off, circling Grey once before scaling a nearby maple tree and disappearing. A few moments later the light reappeared, carrying a newspaper that it deposited in Sep's lap before flying off in the opposite direction. He unfolded the paper and placed his right ankle up onto his left knee. As he perused the entertainment section he said, "Peter is a good man Grey. A fine protégé. He will be quite the warrior given enough time and encouragement."

"Yep, but that ain't what's on my mind, so stop fishing," Grey ordered. "And tell Harmony to quit worrying. I know she'll deny it, but I can feel it coming off her in waves. Plus, I probably shouldn't tell you this, but the bond she and I share has grown so strong lately that I can hear some of what goes on when I'm not with her. Conversations between the two of you for instance, or conversations she has with

140

other soldiers. I know she worries. Hell, I've given her more than enough right to over the years, but time is just catching up with me. Nothing wears on a man like findin' out what he thought was a finished job turns out not to be done."

"Ah," Sep said neither agreeing nor disagreeing with Grey. He simply sat next to him with compassion in his eyes. He had seen this type of malaise before on other men in Grey's position, but Sep had grown closer to Grey than any of the others. It pained him to see his friend in such turmoil. There was something about Grey that all of his predecessors did not have: an ease of camaraderie, a sly wit, and a quiet strength sure, but there was an indefinable quality that Sep with his millennia of life could not define.

"Why're you still here Sep? You've stayed longer than is your norm. It can't be to buffer Raven, because you just left poor Pete alone with her to check up on me. You aren't going to sacrifice yourself taking out Legion are you? None of your folk are ready to step up and fill that void if you did…so why?"

Sep placed his hand on Grey's shoulder and said, "Because my friend, Harmony is not the only one who worries. Ramadi there are times where I do not feel you comprehend how much influence you have, not only among your people, but on both sides of the fence as well."

"Oh I'm fully aware of that Sep," Grey said in a sarcastic tone. "It's one of the main reasons why I feel so weathered lately. But feeling tired is a man's own business. Everybody assumes if he goes off to think a spell that he's sulking. It ain't sulking, it's thinking. I got one more battle to fight, one I thought was over a century ago, one more imbalance to redress, 'Once more unto the breach dear friends' right? My problems are nothing new. Despite what you and Harmony have led yourselves and deluded others into believing, I'm a man, and I'm tired. I've earned a break. You may not be ready to move on after all this time, but try walkin' in my shoes for a bit old friend, and you may change your mind."

"Jasper Reynolds, always the consummate philosopher," Sep replied. "You must always be as you are and do as you feel. You are a living example of free will. You do not need a baby sitter or therapist. I did not mean for my staying to imply that you did." Sep looked to the street as the traffic increased. Motorists were out running errands or starting their work day increasing the ambient noise. "I did stay because I thought you could use a friend."

Grey smirked, chuffed a small laugh, and said, "Yeah, Sep, that I can always use."

The two friends sat in silence for a while watching the morning progress toward noon. Demons were retreating further and further into the shadows, taking shelter where it could be found. Some were forced to seek sanctuary in the earth, sinking down beneath rock and soil as the sun crept to its zenith. Grey pointed to a demon whose eyes were visibly peeking out from under a rock and said, "I always wondered if that was why folks believe hell is underground."

The angels were venturing forth with the day's light, rejoicing in the warm of life as the demons fled. Sep considered his response before commenting, "I forget what it was like to know as little as they do. To be scared yet always more afraid of acknowledging that fear and looking weak. A terrible state is the mortal coil. Your rationale is as sound as always my friend. One holy man or woman witnessed a demon rising or taking refuge at some point. They record their observations, and the next thing you know human mythologies start to place Hades in the earth."

"It never ceases to impress me," Sep said changing the subject. He motioned to the other angels as they moved about the town, "There are times when I think the power of dawn may be why I continue to stay."

"I could see that," Grey responded laconically with a nod.

"No, that feels too close to a lie for my tastes," Sep amended. "I think it's my fear that still keeps me here."

"I could see that too," Grey repeated.

"I envy your courage Ramadi," Sep said looking over at Grey, folding up the newspaper and placing it on the step next to him. "I stayed here so long ago, not out of compassion, but out of fear of the unknown. I was terrified of that feeling of the Source pulling me toward it. All my good deeds came about out of fear."

"And you feel that cheapens them somehow?" Grey asked.

"No, good is good," Sep said. "I only wished I had been nobler in it like you, my friend. I believe fear is why I stay. Perhaps it is no longer fear of the Source, but fear of what would happen if I left. Would my leaving cause a power vacuum? Fear made me stay, and it still does. Only the fear changed, and I am still here." Sep smiled widely, stood up, and touched Grey on the shoulder asking, "Why is it, Grey, that whenever I try to help counsel you, I am the one who ends up making therapeutic progress?"

"That's just life Sep," Grey said. "We do what we can with what we have."

"Yes indeed Grey, yes indeed. Harmony will not like me saying this, but it seems you are always right my friend. Perhaps I should have learned that by now. I will leave you to your business. Please give my regards to Pete and Raven. They both need you now more than I do. I will be watching from a distance and sending my hope with you."

Sep vanished from where he stood. Grey sat and watched the world go by for a few moments more before standing up and walking back toward the restaurant.

***

"So, Raven, why the gun?" Pete asked.

"Because I enjoy the phallic symbolism," Raven said in a deadpan voice without batting an eye.

Pete choked a bit on his coffee and said, "Well that explains why it was so big I guess."

"It's simple psychology Pete," Raven said as a handgun appeared in her right palm. To illustrate her point she waved the Magnum around in flourishes while she spoke, causing Pete to flinch or duck his head when she flicked her wrist in his direction. "I like the manifestation of something powerful that I can direct my strength with. It gives me focus and containment. Balls of light like Grey prefers are too sloppy and imprecise for my personality."

Pete stared at her wide eyed, jerking his head in the direction of the other diners, and made loud throat clearing sounds. After nearly a minute of this she stopped her explanation and snapped, "What?"

"What?" Pete asked, "You're waving a damn hand cannon in the middle of a fast food restaurant. Somebody is going to call the cops!"

"Relax, Pete," she said. "I'm not letting them see the gun. It's only there as a demonstration for you. You really have a lot to learn yet. Where was I?...Oh yeah, besides, demons don't exactly have a long shelf life with a few notable exceptions like Legion. Most of them remember how their human lives were preoccupied with violence. Handguns are a pervasive symbol of aggression all over the world. What says 'Violence' more than a ridiculously large handgun? Hmm? Simple psychology."

"Do you think we could be friends if I admitted you were more of a man than I am? That you make me feel inadequate?" Pete asked.

"Oh sweetie," Raven said and patted Pete on the hand. "I already knew that, but that's big of you to admit it."

"You know they used to call me 'Big Pete' back in high school?"

"No. They didn't," Grey's voice said from behind Pete. "I do know what they used to call you in Mrs. Cribbage's eighth grade math class though. Do you think Raven would like to know what it was, Pete?"

"Not cool, Grey! And I wasn't even talking to you," Pete said.

Raven was laughing when she noticed that Sep was not with Grey, "Where's Sep?"

"He decided it was time to step back," Grey answered. "He didn't want to risk tipping things in one direction or the other by being here when things go down, but he wanted me to say 'goodbye' for him."

Raven nodded in understanding and Grey continued, "Are you two ready? We have things to do before night fall. Sep said that Legion has been influencing all the youth of this town, but it has been concentratin' its efforts on that Tommy kid. We need to track him and his friends down. Let them lead us to Legion. That way we can finish that damn thing off this time. It leaves pieces of itself rooted in places like a cancer."

The girl from the register walked up behind Grey and tapped him on the shoulder. He turned around to face her asking, "Yes, darlin'?"

She handed him a takeout bag that was sagging with food. She said, "I thought you might want a couple of burgers to go, on the house."

"Thank you, darlin'," Grey said taking the bag from her. She smiled as if he had just professed his undying love for her and skipped back to the counter. *Skipped*, Pete thought, *the girl actually skipped. Unbelievable.* He shook his head.

Chapter 12

When we have a physical body, we are conditioned to rely solely on our five senses. If an experience can't be quantified through them then most of us shrug it off as unimportant or nonexistent. Does that make us more animal than man? I've seen men who behaved worse than animals and some animals who had more dignity than some men. Relying on your five senses only (pardon the phrasing) makes sense. It's what you have, so go with it, but never forget the mind as well. Some Asian cultures call the mind the "sixth sense." I can stand behind that. Without the cognitive control and interpretation of the mind the other five senses wouldn't mean shit.

If you're scientific or analytical by nature you may see that there is more out there than we can perceive. How vast and extensive the universe is. It's easy for most of us to lose track of what infinite really means. The scope and scale of it go beyond our ken. In outer space, beyond what we can see, there are great forges producin' stars and galaxies; there's some power for you. Inner space, again beyond what our unaided sight can perceive, tiny spheres of energy revolvin' around each other coalescing into molecules. Split one of those spheres or mash a couple together in just the right way, and there's even more power. Amazing how often things come back to power from this side of life. I told you power is everything.

Always keep in mind that we can see none of this. It happens on a scale that our puny five senses cannot come close to noticing, but does that mean it ain't there? The wisest man is the one who admits he don't know a damn thing.

I'm not sure what it says about me that when Harmony showed me the world through her eyes, what a demon was and the things it was capable of doing, likewise with angels, that I just accepted things at face value. No arguments, no questions, only point me in the direction you need me and fire. Does that make me a loaded gun, a trained dog? No, I'm my own man, but I realize the world is a whole hell of a lot bigger than me, and sometimes it's best to take the word of those who can perceive more than you……

***

"We need to let go and move out of the physical world if we're going to follow those boys around," Grey said from around a mouthful of hamburger. "I don't want to provoke them into doing anything more stupid than they would otherwise do, and they'll be easier to track from there than riding around in that truck."

"It's a minivan Grey," Raven corrected.

"You know I only see those vehicles in two classes' darlin': cars and trucks. The rest of those names you like to use don't mean shit," Grey said and grabbed a fry off of Pete's tray. "You aren't all that attached to your mini-truck are you Raven? I was planning on leaving it here."

Raven gave him a sarcastic over the top smile that was not really a smile, but otherwise said nothing.

"Higher vibration, right Grey?" Pete asked. "You know, not teleportation, because that's impossible and all, so Sep was just vibrating really hard earlier when he vanished from that seat." He finished by pointing to the open seat next to Raven.

"Raven darlin', would you mind giving Pete here that same smile, because I don't think I can do it right," Grey said and walked away from the booth without waiting to see if she did or not. He casually pushed through the first set of doors into the breezeway that keeps the climate trapped inside. He vanished before he reached the second set.

"Still looks like teleporting to me," Pete groused as he followed Raven out of the booth in Grey's wake.

***

The world looked different to Pete this time when he shifted into his pure energy form. He was not sure if it was because this was the first time he had experienced it in daylight. Maybe it was that he was becoming accustomed to the ebb and flow of energy around him or just growing into his power more. Most likely it was a bit of each.

The dark spots that Pete had had to concentrate so hard on previously, to see the shapes within, popped out in relief against the bright sunlight. There were long limbs and grasping talons groping out from the shadows looking like they were trying to drag the dark in for cover. New shapes, previously hidden by the night, danced about in front of Pete. Large soft amorphous blobs floated around, butterfly and moth shapes hovered and glided, and bipedal forms vaguely resembling the human structure moved about glowing with an inner light. "Wow," Pete said.

"Is this your first time seeing it in the daylight?" Raven asked him.

"Yeah," was the most Pete could articulate past his sensory overload. If asked to describe it visually Pete would have been at a loss, because it went beyond what the human eye could process. Even a sensory blending of touch with vision or sound with taste would have fallen significantly short of accuracy. Mouth hanging agape Pete asked, "Is it always like this?"

"Yes, but after a time you grow used to it," Raven said. "Still…you can see why so many choose to stay behind. Some places are livelier with them than others. I'd say you're seeing so many here as a counterbalance to Legion's influence."

"Yeah…" Pete said trailing off in thought. When he spoke again there was a suspicious edge to his voice. "Convenient thing I died at night, huh Grey? If I saw all these fairy lights I may have been less likely to join the afterlife armed forces."

Grey shrugged his shoulders and smirked, "Some might say that's an argument for fate or mayhap it's destiny Pete."

Pete watched mesmerized as a woman pushing a stroller stopped and leaned over to see what her baby was laughing at. She scattered the flock of soft pastel lights that were the cause of her child's amusement. "Who's a silly baby?" she cooed pulling her head back and started to walk once again.

After she had retreated the lights zipped around her, regrouping over the child once more. The entire group of lights, mother, and child were moving down the sidewalk in Pete's direction. When mother and child drew close enough Pete could see definition within the lights: colorful, bright, and simple faces peered out from the light, characters that would have made Jim Henson proud. They flowed past him in a swirl of color.

One small lavender globe swirled off from the herd. It hovered in front of Pete for a moment, and then buzzed several circuits around his head. In a high-pitched whisper of a male voice he said, "I overheard you earlier. You have the aura of a rookie about you so I will say this once, and only once. Don't call us fairies! It's demeaning." The light flew off in a shot, shedding sparks in its wake, to catch up with the other swirls around the retreating stroller.

Pete looked over at Raven with his face scrunched up in an unspoken question. She shrugged her shoulders saying, "Everybody's different Pete. That little guy might have been a seven foot tall professional wrestler in life, and his self-image won't let him to think of himself as a glowing cartoon character. Who knows, people are people. They can still be in denial after death."

Pete shifted his focus about the downtown and Main Street where most of the buildings were vacant but in a better state of repair than many Midwestern small towns. The glowing eyes of demons could be seen lurking in the shadowed recesses of closed businesses, while angels danced about in the open shops. Across the street he saw a rundown old man sitting on a rundown old park bench holding a rundown old hat in his age palsied hands. Next to the man sat the most distinct form Pete had seen yet, a woman in her comfortable middle years dressed several decades out of fashion. She pulsed with a faint golden aura and sat looking at the old man with a concerned smile. Raven looked where Pete's attention was focused and said, "She passed on not very long ago, a few days, maybe as much as a week. A lot of couples do that. The one who dies first waits around for the other before moving on. At least it looks like she doesn't have all that long to wait."

Grey cleared his throat and said, "Pete I hate to rush you. I remember what it was like the first time too, but we need to get movin'. I tagged that boy Tommy earlier when we saw him outside that burger joint so I know where he is, but we need to watch where he goes and see what he does."

"Tagged?" Pete asked.

"Yeah, I kept my physical shell in place, but reached out into this level as well and slapped a bit of myself on him so we could hone in on it later," Grey said. Then his eyes started to drift to murky gray orbs again as he continued, "What? You think I was giving him the evil eye earlier just for shits and giggles? I didn't do it last night because I didn't want to tip our hand, remember? But that don't matter now. Sadly though mine wasn't the only mark on that boy. Legion has all but taken him over."

"Cool, spiritual multitasking and game tagging…you'll have to show me how to do those," Pete said.

"Good luck," Raven said. "He's the only one who can do it."

"Oh," Pete muttered, his bubble of enthusiasm visibly burst. Grey was already moving away from them, not waiting around to answer any more questions. His back was already rounding a corner, so Raven and Pete had to push themselves to catch up. Moving at an accelerated speed was one of the skills that Pete seemed to take to quickly. Without having to concentrate on holding his physical shell together, movement and action were all mere thought. There was no longer any pesky meat needing chemical prodding or stimulation to move in the direction he wanted. He flowed and moved with a speed that made Olympian sprinters look like geriatric tortoises.

Catching up to Tommy and his entourage proved a quick trip. They were hanging out around the side alley of what the street sign claimed to be 'McDougal Plumbing' drinking beer, smoking both tobacco and marijuana, whistling and catcalling at any woman who went by and doing their best to imitate every hoodlum they had ever seen on television or in movies. In the shadows around the boys Pete could see the shapes of the panther demons swirling and scampering. The demons were doing their best to stay away from the light encroaching on their dark domain.

"Can those panther demons see us Grey?" Pete asked, but before Grey could answer the demons hissed and backed away into the farthest corner of the alley with the darkest shadows. It looked to Pete as if one or two of them had sunk into the stained concrete and were sticking only their heads and shoulders above ground. The demons made piteous mewling sounds as if they were in pain, and a third eye opened up on each of their foreheads. The demon in the middle writhed, trying to move as far away as it could. Then it howled in pain, body seizing and arching as if there was an electrical current running through it.

It suddenly stopped all movement and noise. Gathering its limbs together it hesitantly approached the edge of the alley like a beaten dog afraid to take food from the hand that had done the beating. Its jaws snapped open and instead of a feline hissing noise escaping past its razor-sharp fangs, the baritone snarl that the little girl demon had previously spoken to them in poured out. Legion's spleen filled voice said, "These boys are mine Grey! Their sins are many and unrepentant. Go back to your little Balance whore, and stay out of my business or this time I will devour you too."

Grey stepped up and placed the tips of his boots into the shadow of the alley, so half of him was in the sunlight and the other half intruded into the shadows. He squatted down on his haunches, resting his elbows on his knees, and clasped his hands together. Grey leaned forward so his eyes were a hand span away from the demons and said, "We're both students of history, you and me." He moved his index finger back and forth indicating Legion's eye, and himself. Laughing ruefully he added, "Hell, we are history."

The demon only responded by snarling a bit in its throat neither agreeing nor disagreeing. Grey continued, "Yeah, it's always good to learn from your mistakes and the mistakes of others. That's what history teaches us right?" Grey paused, but when no response was forthcoming he nodded his head agreeing with his own statement. "Take Jesus; I never met him personally, but I hear tell you did. We have a lot of mutual friends, Jesus and me, and they all agree he was a pretty nice guy. He cut you a little too much slack in my opinion though, exorcising you out of that man back in Gadarenes. Yep that was pretty nice of him, but me? I ain't a nice guy."

Black shadows started swirling in Grey's left hand as he stood up, and blue light started coalescing in the other. He stood there for a second with hands out at his sides. One palm glowed with a blue fire, the other palm disappearing into a void. At twice the speed of a cobra strike he grabbed the demon around the scruff with the hand shrouded in shadow. The demon screamed, and for the first time to Pete it sounded human as it wailed, "Nooooo, please."

Grey ignored its pleading as he dragged it out from the cover of darkness into the light where it screamed and thrashed about. Pete and Raven both stepped back to give him room as the demon thrashed in his grip. Grey switched his hold so the panther was facing him, his fingers tightened around the monster's throat while he held it at arm's length. Then he pulled the demon in close to him so they were face to face. The demon's voice had degenerated into inarticulate hissing. Grey looked at the creature for a moment with cold emotionless eyes, and then picked up his speech where he had left off. "Yes sir, Jesus was a real nice guy, but me? I ain't a nice guy. Me? I'm going to fucking kill you."

The demon shrieked louder as the shadows from Grey's hand swallowed it in a pulsing void. Grey brought his other hand around in a boxer's right hook punch. The shining light met the black void encasing the demon, and both disappeared in a violent explosion.

When Pete's vision had cleared he could see Grey brushing his hands together like a man dusting off a hard day's labor. He retreated to the other side of the street sitting down on the curb where he could still see Tommy and his gang. He leaned back into a nearby lamppost, laced his hands behind his head, and appeared to go to sleep.

Pete turned to Raven, looked straight into her eyes and said, "Okay fine, you were absolutely right. I will never, ever, ever be that cool."

Chapter 13

Emotions are hard things to quantify. Anger, hate, and fear can be indistinguishable from each other at times. Just like love, happiness, and compassion. What is the controllin' factor behind such states of mind? Is it all just chemicals? I say that's doubtful, but then again I have a leg up so to speak. I've been sans body for some time, meaning no chemical compounds or hormones to muddy the waters of thought for me, yet I can still get righteously pissed off. Just ask anybody who was there in '62 when Chernobog tried prodding Kennedy and Khrushchev into starting World War III. Y'all heard it called a crisis, but you should have seen it from this side…let's just say me losing my temper is not a pretty sight.

It could be a holdover of conditioning I suppose. I don't remember anything before I was born into my human body, so did I exist before? I don't rightly know. I only bring that up because if our physical form is the first state in which we think as an individual, then it could be an argument for chemical conditioning. This is what we're born with, so we stick with it.

It feels more likely to me that emotions are just the mind's way of dealing with positive and negative energies; just another version of the same story I suppose. Everyone I knew in life was obsessed with greed, positively controlled by it, acquiring as much material wealth as possible. I myself never understood why; it must still be the effects of fear. Fear driving them to have things in case some moment comes and they need that something. They should have had it, but they didn't, so what then? Driven by greed born of fear?

So maybe it's all just conditioned mental states that bring emotions over into this existence too. Maybe that is just who and what we are? Only now fear drives us toward power and energy instead of money and possessions. It'd be nice to think that we grow emotionally, but most times it seems like we always stay a bunch of selfish children hoarding our toys.

Or maybe not………

I once watched a young boy throw himself at his stepfather to stop that drunkard from beating his mother and baby brother to death. Was that emotion guiding his actions? He couldn't have been more than ten years old. He didn't have anything to gain from his sacrifice but to try and have another day with the only two people he loved. Is that still greed do you think? Did he honestly think he would win, that he could hold his mother or baby brother one more time? Was that fear of losing them a chemical reaction, an instinct?

He never did get to hold his mother or brother again. Sure she held him, and his little brother as their bodies cooled against her breast. I asked that little boy's spirit, "Son, I understand why you did that, but you do understand that you had no chance?"

He looked back at his mother as she wept. Without looking at me he said, "She should've left him months ago, but she didn't. I may have had no chance mister, but I also had no choice."

I heard every one of those aforementioned emotions love, hate, anger, compassion, fear, happiness, and more, all in that boy's simple response. Yes sir, hard to quantify………

***

Raven and Pete went over to join Grey across the street in his stakeout of the demons and their human play things. The boys had not seen or heard any of what had transpired, but on some level they must have felt the loss of one of the demons, because they had retreated further into the alley just as the other monsters had. Tommy especially kept looking wearily around like a toddler afraid to be discovered with his arm up to the elbow in a cookie jar.

This was the first time Pete had given any particular notice to the boy and his friends besides their initial discovery. Last night in the dark they were faces and shapes, with only the occasional feature like the one boy's Mohawk to set them apart. At this level of energy in full daylight Pete could make out individual features, but there were veins of purple and black shooting around under their skin, pulsing in a distinctly unhealthy fashion that kept distracting him. Tommy was the most afflicted, thick ropey cords ventured out of his shirt, ran up his neck, and onto his face where they gathered in a pool at the center of his forehead. Pete could barely make out the starting of a third eye there like all the other creatures under Legion's control.

"Gross," Pete muttered, but asked his companions, "so what do we do now?"

"We wait," Grey said. "This is not where Legion is stayin'. It's hidden somewhere, but close to have this much control over its rabble in the daylight. That boy Tommy is close to death. I take it by your comment you can see it bubbling around in him. Legion will need to be close by for his death if it's going to claim him as one of its own. So we wait, and when that happens, we strike."

Raven grinned over at Pete when Grey stopped talking. Another Smith and Wesson 500 Magnum was in her hand, and she was spinning it around in a fashion to make any movie gunfighter envious.

From across in the alley they heard one of the boys say, "Hey Tommy I'm hungry! Let's go down to Giono's and get some pizza!"

"Hells yeah!" another chimed in. "Maybe Julie will be working. I fucking love her tits!" He illustrated his point cupping his closest friend's chest in a lewd suggestive fashion.

Tommy grinned lasciviously, "Yeah, sounds like a plan," he said and started down the back of the alley to where his truck was parked. They all piled in, pounding hands on the roof of the cab, or roughhousing and playing grab ass. Tommy revved the engine before peeling out onto the street just barely avoiding a head on collision with a postal service van when he went left to center. He pressed hard on his horn, stuck his left arm out the window, and flipped the other driver the middle finger.

"You know," Pete said, "you always see kids behave like that on TV or in a movie, and you think nobody acts like that big of a dumbass in real life, but sure enough just wander into pretty much any small American town and you'll have your pick of dumbasses who will do just that."

The panther demons had stayed in the safety of the alley shadows but melted through the wall of the closest building in the direction the truck had gone. Pete could see them racing off to keep pace with the truck through the building's front window, and then after flowing into the opposite wall they were gone. Grey stood up and casually started walking in the same direction, in no rush this time since he knew their destination.

Raven took a few hurried steps to catch up to Grey. Touching him on the shoulder she asked, "Tell me I'm not the only one who feels like this is a set-up?"

"Oh it's a set-up alright," Grey said, "but I plan on using that to our advantage. If you know your enemy is settin' a trap for you then you can anticipate it, and turn it back on him. That's classic warfare tactics darlin'."

Pete was only listening to them with half an ear. His father used to always accuse him of daydreaming as a boy, because he would rather play inside his mind than with a ball any day. He had never outgrown his propensity to woolgather, but he had learned the right time and place for it as an adult. With the new dimensions to the world that his current state had opened his eyes to, Pete was finding it very hard to focus. He was aware that he was moving after Grey and Raven, but he was caught up marveling in the new sights. The day had passed on more than he had realized with the shadows between buildings lengthening out providing ample cover for the creatures who dwelled there to venture forth with much more than a glowing set of eyes or a clawed talon. Their faces leered out from behind dumpsters or peered out from dark corners. There were so many different forms and shapes in certain places that Pete had a bit of trouble distinguishing some from others. When he looked closely he could see that some demons were mixing in and out of each other. *Like a twisted dark side version of an M.C. Escher painting*, Pete thought.

The beings of light that had distracted him earlier were still there interacting gently with the world. The difference this time was that all of them stopped when Grey was near and watched him walk by. That morning they had all gone about their business not paying attention to Grey or his companions, but now their focus was riveted on them. *No*, Pete decided, *not us, on Grey*. All of the creatures were watching Grey warily, be they light or dark. Faces or what passed for them intently focused in Grey's direction, not returning to what they had been doing until he was well past them. A few of the smaller angels and demons flew or ran away when Pete's new mentor drew near.

Pete noticed how far he had lagged behind Raven and Grey in his distraction and started running to catch up to them. He had the mixed emotions of feeling like a toady hurrying to tag along with his chosen bully, but it also felt like the right and righteous path to take. Grey was doing what those angels could not do. Someone had to keep those demons from causing too much damage. *If those goodie two shoes did not want to get their hands dirty then let them stare at Grey*, Pete thought. Grey did what was necessary, what they were incapable of. Pete felt himself getting riled up with these ideas when Grey's voice interrupted his train of thought.

"It's alright Pete," Grey said. "They can't help being what they are. They want the world to be sunshine and rainbows, but they don't realize that without the darkness the light is meaningless. You'll get used to their stares. They don't mean anything by it. They're just afraid. It ain't a bad thing to let fear make you wary."

In his daydreaming state Pete had not realized how quickly he had caught up to Raven and Grey. He was also unaware of how much of what he was thinking and feeling in this state could bleed over to others. *Are my thoughts really my own?* Pete ventured to himself, *or perhaps Grey was just that perceptive?*

"But," Grey added, "it is fun to let those slippery fuckers in the shadows stew a bit in their own fear. You got to take the good with the bad Pete. You pick how to view which is which."

Harmony's door quickly opened wide in Pete's mind before he could respond, and she said, "He deals with his emotions in his own way Peter, even if you disagree with him. Please keep it between us for now. He needs his armor in place for the coming battle. All of his armor." She paused long enough that Pete thought she was done speaking. Then she added, "Grey is very perceptive, never discount that, but only I can sense what you are thinking. If you want your thoughts to be private, please let me know and I will stop listening, in a manner of speaking." As quickly as she had appeared, she also retreated. Noticing the expressions on the others' faces, Pete knew she had only spoken to him. *You're going to have to learn to keep your expression neutral man*, Pete thought when Raven cocked an eyebrow at him.

Grey smiled without saying a word, nodding his head once. He turned back in the direction the rundown Ford had gone and started walking again.

***

The old downtown district they had found themselves in when Grey had confronted Legion progressively changed as they followed Tommy and his crew. The old brick buildings had progressed to old Victorian homes. The older homes had progressed to newer ranches and apartment complexes. The newer homes and apartments had progressed to fringe quick stop convenient plazas most of which were only half occupied by small chain businesses. The windows in the vacant stores all held sun faded for rent or lease signs.

The three of them stood on a sidewalk that looked freshly laid. It ran parallel to the street with a grassy strip acting as a verdant buffer between traffic and any pedestrian who may use it. The sidewalk ended on the other side of the strip plaza where a large field was under construction. A huge placard claiming 'McDougal Commercial Excavating and Construction' sat along the street where a state route provided an exit from the town.

"Christ, Sep wasn't kidding was he?" Pete asked Raven as he pointed to the sign.

"No he wasn't. That boy's family has controlled this little town for a very long time." She shook her head and continued, "The world is full of small towns just like this Pete. With the technology age people are just now realizing how many big fish in small ponds were actually out there, because those fish are now being swallowed whole by a few whales who think the world is their pond."

"Wow lady," Pete said. "If you didn't scare me so much I'd comment on how cynical that sounded. I've seen enough to know you're right, but still…" He trailed off without further elaboration.

"We have balance everywhere Pete," Grey interjected before Raven could spit out the box of nails Pete thought she looked like she was chewing on. "My girl Raven here is our cynic. Zeus is our optimist. Hell you met him; you know what he's like, my friend. Somebody has got to offset that much exuberance."

The synthesized bell chime of the door to Giono's pizza interrupted their discussion. They turned to see a couple dressed in business casual wear storm out of the restaurant. Their agitated voices could be easily heard in the mostly empty plaza as they walked toward the only vehicle in the parking lot other than Tommy's truck. The woman's voice held a high-pitched note of frustration as she said, "That was ridiculous! Who do those boys think they are?"

"I know honey, but in a small town like dis?" the man said. His voice held the long "a" and blended "th"s and "d"s that marked a Chicago accent. He spoke like a man who was used to acting in the role of spousal placater. "What do you expect? We should have just waited until we got back to Chicago to stop for food."

"No shit? You think?" she snapped at him. "But that poor girl…I mean my God haven't they heard of sexual harassment out here?"

"Do you want me to call da police? I mean I will if you think I should, but dat will mean statements and reports. We'll be here all night, and out here you know it will still be real 'paper' work too."

"No, no I want to get home. I guess out here she's probably used to being treated like that."

"Sure, it's probably deir version of flirting."

The rest of their conversation was closed off when they shut the doors to their car. They drove out onto the street without pausing to look for traffic and shot off down the state route passing the construction site billboard.

"Hey, Pete," Raven said, "you want to come on over to my end of the Balance pool? The cynicism end is nice and warm right now after that couple just pissed all over it. Why get out and use the bathroom? Why should they inconvenience themselves at all? They have better things to do. It's like that all over the world, every day."

"Yeah," Pete agreed. Then he turned to Grey saying, "You might want to tell Zeus to be extra optimistic next time you see him, because I think I'm joining Raven's team."

Grey ignored them both, and stared at the large picture window of the pizzeria. He marched off in that direction without saying a word. Pete looked at Raven and asked, "Does he do that all the time, just ignore everybody if he doesn't feel like talking?"

"Mm hmm," she said nodding, "but he gets the job done. You saw it for yourself in that alley. Are you going to argue with that?"

"Good point," Pete conceded. "So, we tag along and follow his lead? Is that the plan?"

"Works for me," Raven said.

They both walked over to where Grey was standing with his arms folded across his chest looking into the window. Pete followed his gaze, and found if he concentrated he could see and hear everything going on in the restaurant: Tommy, his friends, their panther demons now down by one, a young girl maybe the same age as them behind the counter, and another woman a bit older in the kitchen portion of the restaurant. Their dialogue seemed to vibrate out through the window. The girl yelled, "Stop it Tommy!"

"Oh come on Julie," Tommy whined. "The yuppies are gone. It's just me and the boys now, show us those tits. Just like back in the day, huh?" He reached across the counter and grabbed Julie's right breast and laughed.

"Thomas McDougal!" The woman from the kitchen yelled, "You leave that poor girl alone right now, or I'll call the cops!"

"Go ahead, you dried up old cunt," Tommy said with a chorus of hoots and hollers from his groupies. Even the demons seemed to be laughing as he continued, "My Uncle Bobby's on duty tonight. I'm sure he's desperate enough to take a go at you if you're jealous."

This brought on a larger fit of revelry from both demons and boys alike. One of the boys, the fellow with the blonde Mohawk, was laughing so hard he knocked his soft drink all over the boy seated next to him. The soaked boy sat startled for a moment then grabbed his half eaten slice of pizza now soggy with Pepsi and rubbed it into Mohawk's face. A demon had curled itself up and around the boys shoulder whispering in his ear goading him on. While he tried to dry himself off with napkins he snarled, "There, you little bitch! Now you really are a pizza face!"

Raven and Pete stood on either side of Grey when he started to shake his head. He looked over at Raven and said, "I know it's the age of women's liberation and all that, darlin', but I reckon there should always be at least one man workin' in any business that might draw this type of crowd. Boys are less likely to mess around if a man is present to keep them corralled."

174

"Oh I don't know Grey. Maybe it just takes the right type of woman," Raven said with a grin that could have been confused with a sneer in certain lights. She watched the boys and demons through the window, and Pete could see a small twinkle of deepest indigo light flash in her eyes.

"What type of woman would that be?" Grey asked her innocently.

"Pete?" Raven redirected the question at him without turning from her vigil.

"Uh…um…A crazy ass white woman?" Pete said and flinched, but Raven just smiled, and nodded her head. She pushed in the swinging door with more force than was necessary. It swung open banging against the rubberized doorstop, and as the bell chime sounded Pete heard her say, "Damn right."

***

Pete and Grey watched from the outside window as Raven swaggered into the pizzeria. In her physical shell she moved like a woman who had walked right out of the pages of a men's magazine. Tight black leather and soft feminine curves looking almost unreal in the overhead florescent lights, Raven approached the counter without paying attention to Tommy or any of his goons. She gave the impression that she was the only one in the restaurant with the girl behind the counter.

"God I'm starving girl, what's your best pizza?" Raven asked placing her palms flat on the red Formica topped counter. She started to tap her fingers as she leaned forward toward the girl at the register.

"Um… I like our deluxe," Julie suggested.

"Alright, make it a large, and toss in a two liter of Pepsi too," Raven said, still completely ignoring the leers Tommy was sending her way. His toadies had all stopped messing around and were paying undivided attention to Raven's leather clad posterior as she shifted from foot to foot waiting for Julie to ring up her order.

"Will that be for here or to go?" Julie asked as she typed keys on her register. When she looked up at Raven her eyes pleaded for Raven to say, "For here."

"I suppose this seems like a quiet enough place," Raven said looking around. Her gaze swept over all the other occupants without acknowledging their presence. She added, "I do just like to relax when I eat you know? Sort of stress relief and unwinding from the day."

"I know something else that's good for stress relief pretty lady," Tommy sneered. He was leaning with his left elbow on the counter looking back over his shoulder for support from his groupies. They all snickered and muttered barely audible obscene comments to each other. The demons were not chiming into the merriment this time. They stood stock-still, eyes fixed on Raven as she silently swung her arm out in an arch. The boys fell silent too when a handgun appeared out of thin air in her palm.

Tommy heard a clicking sound next to his ear and turned his head back toward Raven. The 'Aren't I a stud' grin died on his face when he saw the barrel of her hand cannon only inches from his face. Raven was still facing forward, looking right at Julie behind the counter, but her left arm was extended out toward Tommy, elbow just shy of being locked as it held up the obscenely large Smith and Wesson.

Julie stared wide eyed at her and jumped a bit when Raven said, "I think I may be more woman than you can handle kiddo. I'm what they refer to as a 'high maintenance' type of girl. Now I saw a bit of what was going on in here before I walked in, and I just don't appreciate that kind of treatment, and I don't think this young lady here does either."

Tommy was sputtering and stammering an unintelligible stream of, "Umm ahhhh."

"In fact," Raven continued, ignoring his vocalization, "I think you owe her an apology, don't you?"

"Sssorry," Tommy managed to articulate.

"Yes, yes you are," Raven agreed. "Now I think it's time you and your friends left. Go on, bye-bye."

Still facing Julie behind the counter, never deigning to look in Tommy's direction Raven waved at him, a quick motion with her right hand like she would have given to a small child, folding her fingers up and down rapidly.

Tommy was a bully at heart, but he was not a stupid bully. A gun was a gun, and he did not have one to match hers, currently, so he nodded to his friends in an unspoken signal to leave. He had moved a pace toward the exit himself, but stopped jerking both of his hands to his temples, and dropped to his knees shrieking. Julie retreated into the kitchen as quickly as she could move knocking Tommy's unattended soda across the counter in her flight. Raven finally turned to Tommy and watched in disgust as he thrashed about. The Pepsi had run down the edges of the counter and was steadily dripping on his head, plastering his hair to the side of his face as he

178

contorted. His friends were screaming at her in a chorus of, "What did you do?"

"You crazy bitch!"

"What the fuck? Tommy? Tommy you alright man?"

"Use your cell! Call the cops man!"

Raven calmly said, "Shut up," turning her left hand, still burdened with the handgun, in their direction. She raised her right hand, in which an exact replica of the gun from her left appeared, and leveled it at Tommy's pain racked face. Tommy's screams tapered off, and for the space of a few breaths he made no sound at all. Then a chuckle started to bubble up from his chest. The laugh was several octaves lower than Tommy's usual tone. When he finally spoke it was no longer Tommy's voice that issued forth, but Legion's animalistic baritone coming from Tommy's mouth. "So, Grey sends his little bird to set these boys straight. It's a pity, little bird, that you met the old cowboy first. We could have had so much fun together, you and I."

"Tttommy? You alright man?" asked the boy with the blonde Mohawk.

"I'm fine Kevin," said Tommy in Legion's voice causing all of the boys to flinch away from him. Ignoring them Legion dug in Tommy's front pocket and tossed Kevin the keys to his truck, "Warm her up for me. We're leaving, but I want to talk to this bitch first."

Kevin and the rest of the boys shuffled out toward the exit without turning their backs on Raven and her gun as it tracked their every movement. As they stumbled through the door it looked as if they were not sure who to be more afraid of: her, or their friend and his new basso voice.

The door chimed when it swung closed, leaving only the five remaining panther demons in the pizza parlor with Legion and Raven. Legion laughed as the panthers slunk around the dining area, under booths, around the counter, and along the walls like human sized spiders. Raven's eyes darted about quickly attempting to keep track of them all. Legion stopped laughing and said, "So little bird, make your move. You will not kill this body will you? Yes it has been rude and sadistic, but it has crossed no lines. This boy, this meat is mine, but not yet. So I say again, make your move." Legion spread Tommy's hands out, palms open in a supplicating gesture.

Raven drew in a deep breath dropping her guns to her sides where they vanished. Legion tilted Tommy's head back and laughed loudly. "Your kind is always so predictable, so impotent. You cannot act until we do. That must anger one who burns like you do little bird. It does, does it not? You wish to fight, but must wait until your master lets you off of your leash."

Legion closed the gap between them so that she could smell the corruption wafting off of Tommy's body. The seams of his varsity jacket were tearing, his teeth were stained nicotine yellow, and it had been days since the boy had changed his clothes, but those were not the sources of the odor. It was Tommy's soul that she could smell. The boy's spirit was rotting his flesh from the inside out.

The panther demons had closed about her in a loose ring, purring with excitement. They were enjoying the tension of the moment, feeding on the negative emotions like maggots on carrion. Legion was so close to her now that she could feel Tommy's body reacting to the excitement brushing up against the front of her thigh. The demon leaned in toward Raven as if he meant to kiss her and said, "You know little bird it is never too late to change your mind. Perhaps you would like to lend me some of your fire?"

Raven placed her hands on both of Tommy's shoulders and leaned in completing the kiss. The panther demons roared with excitement and pleasure. Then Raven drove her right knee into Tommy's groin with enough force to knock him completely backward. He toppled over onto the pizza covered table his friends had recently vacated, scattering disposable plates and drenching his back in more soda pop.

Raven turned her back on the possessed boy as he lay stunned and whimpering. She walked toward the exit but spun on her heal, twin Smith and Wessons appearing instantly to fire into the nearest panther demon as it leapt to block her escape. It wailed in agony as the bullets of cerulean light chewed holes in its shadowy hide. The demon's body collapsed into a black heap and dissolved when it had been riddled with more bullets than it could bear.

Another panther had tried to jump on her from behind as Raven destroyed its compatriot, but she was faster than it judged. She spun again pouring blue light from her guns into the airborne demon's midsection, tearing it completely in two. The bottom half fell to the floor and dissolved. The upper half soared over Raven's head and splattered into the front window where Pete and Grey were still looking in. Pete jumped when it landed against the plate glass, then he watched as it oozed down the surface leaving a trail of black ichor behind.

"Crazy ass white woman," Pete said, but this time in awe, not fear.

Chapter 14

Regret, do you reckon it's an emotion, or a state of mind? Is there a difference between those two? A state of mind ain't always an emotion, but an emotion is always a state of mind, kind of like rectangles and squares. You can regret your actions, the outcome of someone else's actions, the actions of fate, the weather, a needless death, a needful death for that matter too I guess. There are all sorts of things you can regret.

I sure have earned me my fair share over the years. Compared to the other folk in my profession I've been around a good long clip, but when you look to the likes of Sep, Malign, Lucifer, or even Harmony? My century and a half seems paltry indeed.

Harmony once told me the hardest part of doing what it is we do was regret. Regret, because all our actions are integral if the rest of the world is to go on existin', but that don't mean we can't look back and regret what was necessary.

I do love that little freckled brunette despite, or maybe because, of all the other things she may be. Her pain is my pain; that's what love is, ain't it? But imagine the kind of pain she's got to feel over her regret. A being that has been alive so long that she could walk the earth before the rest of us monkeys even thought up the word regret. She has felt it over every negative action that has been necessary for the Balance. She is the Balance, so think on that. What kind of guilt must that be? To know all that negative, death, hate, and violence was there because of you.

Boggles the mind it does. It makes a man like me, with my silly paltry regrets, look the fool in the grand scheme……

***

Kevin's Mohawk stuck up over the bed of the truck shaking as he rapidly breathed in and out. He was ducking down with the other lackeys waiting until the crazy woman walked out of the pizzeria before he ran in to check on Tommy. He and his fellow sycophants had seen nothing of the fight between Raven and the panther demons, but they had seen their friend kiss the woman with the guns. Then they watched her knee him in the balls so hard he fell onto their table. When Raven stalked out the front door the other boys stayed hidden from her, and Kevin scuttled in to help Tommy.

Raven had let go of her physical shell when she was halfway to Grey and Pete who had gone over to a small outdoor eatery section adjacent to Giono's. The men had sat down in

184

the utilitarian black wrought iron patio chairs that served as ambiance to the pizza parlor. Grey had his feet propped up on the table, boots tapping against a bundled up umbrella.

The other boys who had stayed with Tommy's truck were sitting around smoking, and waiting for the two inside the restaurant to come out. One of the boys sitting in the bed of the truck noticed Raven's disappearance and said, "Dude! Where'd she go?"

"I don't know man. I wasn't looking," said another. "I was looking in the window."

"Maybe she went around back?" the first boy suggested.

"Maybe, who gives a shit?" chimed in another. "The crazy bitch is gone, and I bet Tommy's gunna be pissed!"

They could see Tommy was already getting to his feet and shrugging Kevin off when he tried to help him up. He stormed out the door with Kevin right behind him. "Where'd that bitch go?" He asked.

Kevin was the only one to venture a response. "Tommy do you really think you should go chasing after her? Remember the guns?" He molded his hands into tiny imitations of Raven's magnums.

"Yeah, well she ain't the only one who has one," Tommy shouted. "Come on! We're going to my Uncle's house. I got a key, and we'll load up from his collection. Then go hunting for that bitch!"

The boys all crowded into Tommy's truck, some more reluctantly than others. The sun was sitting low enough on the horizon that the three remaining panther demons had risked coming out of the restaurant and piled into the truck bed with the boys. Tommy revved the engine and tore off through the parking lot. The bumper of his beat up Ford nicked a newspaper dispenser launching it into a cartwheel spin. Papers flew everywhere when the dispenser crashed back to the blacktopped lot, breaking open the locking mechanism.

A sports section fetched up around the legs of the chair Grey was sitting in. Taking his boots off the metal table he stooped down and picked the paper up. Sticking his feet back up he unfolded it and started to read. Over the top of the paper he looked to Raven. "Well, darlin' I don't know if you made things better, or worse."

"They had it coming Grey," Raven said. "Besides, the pizza joint is hardly where Legion has set up shop. At worst I cost us another day. At best I flushed them out, and they'll go running to Legion whether they realize it or not."

"That, and it was cool!" Pete chimed in, smiling at both of them.

Grey looked sternly at Pete for a moment, but then he reluctantly nodded and said, "Yeah, and it was cool. But now I have to go in there and see if I can't calm those two ladies down some. Normally I wouldn't care all that much if the local authorities got involved, but I have a feelin' that when the shit does hit the fan around here I'm going to want as few innocent bystanders around as possible."

Grey sighed, folded the paper under his arm, stood up, and left the two of them outside as the autumn day settled toward dusk. Pete craned his neck to watch through the window but did not bother listening in as Grey motioned to the employees with warm light glowing around him. The women gradually went from agitated to serene as Grey spoke to them. The older one even went back into the kitchen and brought him out a slice of pizza. Pete chuffed, hooked a thumb in Grey's direction and said, "He always been like that with the ladies?"

Raven snorted, "Oh yeah, that man could charm his way into a nun's panties. There are times when I'd love to have seen what he was like as a living person."

"The way I hear it he was just like he is now," Pete said.

"That's what I hear too, but to quote Grey himself, 'A man and his legend are never exactly the same person,' so I wonder sometimes." Raven looked sincerely at Pete. "Look I'm sorry for the way I treated you when we first met, Pete. It's just…he means so much to me, and I don't like the idea of him leaving me here alone."

"Forget about it," Pete said. "I've known the man only a short while, and I don't like the idea of losing him either. I only hope…"

A rhythmic ticking noise interrupted Pete and made him leave his hope unstated. He turned his head around to see where the sound was coming from. Raven had already found the source because a frown line creased her forehead. Pete followed her gaze, and saw a familiar girl with long auburn pigtails. This time she and her doll where wearing matching checkered dresses and the ticking sound came from her jump rope slapping against the sidewalk. She carried her doll in one of those front facing baby carriers, so her hands were free to swing the jump rope. The doll bounced up and down with her momentum, its arms and legs flopping lifelessly.

"Aw shit," Pete said, "not her again."

"You know that little girl Pete?" Raven asked nodding in the girl's direction as she kept skipping in place. She was staring directly at Raven, her thin eyebrows drawn together in a glare.

"That's no little girl Raven," Pete corrected as the girl's face broke into a huge grin. The rhythm of her skipping changed to match the cadence of a new rhyme.

"Sad little bird wanted to fly.

Sad little bird didn't know why.

Sad little bird had to try.

Sad little bird is going to die."

The girl stopped skipping on the last word, and drew her index finger across her throat. Raven shuddered and said, "Pete, would you think me any less cool if I said that was creepy?"

"No way. I'm right there with you. She did one of those Manson family nursery rhymes for Grey last night too," Pete said. Shrugging his shoulders he added, "Hell I'm just glad she hasn't done one for me yet."

The girl giggled and started skipping rope again, this time her features were interrupted by that third red eye burning out from directly above her bright blue normal ones. Pete looked down and for a moment he could have sworn that the doll had a little red third eye stitched into its forehead too. He blinked his eyes and looked again but it was gone. She started up her sing song cadence again.

"Eenie Meenie Miney Moe.

Catch a Nig-"

"Oh hell no you don't, you scary little Sesame Street psycho!" Pete yelled and tossed a small globe of blue light right at the girl and her doll. She disappeared before it could reach her. In the empty parking lot her giggles echoed around and Pete and Raven both shuddered.

Chapter 15

"I saw the sky in the north open to the ground and fire poured out." That's supposedly the statement of a local Siberian recalling what they saw when Zeus and I faced off against Legion over a century ago.

That's what they gave as part of an eye witness account. What was it that they really saw? Well now I don't want to be rehashing the question of perception too much, but they saw (what are varying descriptions that are mostly chalked up to a meteorite strike) flashes of fire and destruction. Had they been able to perceive it, they would have witnessed Legion and Zeus spilling a bit of our battle over into the physical world. More specifically Zeus being spiked like a big hairy football in the end zone by Legion, but you didn't hear that from me.

That kind of metaphysical spill over happens quite often. You hear all sorts of tales, yarns, and campfire stories about such things. There are all kinds of names for energy too: heat lighting, corpse candles, Saint Elmo's fire, and...well now I'm sure quite a few of you will balk at this next one, but the auroras too, both borealis and australis. Look up the definitions if y'all don't believe me. Most books will tell you the auroras are "caused by the collision of energetic charged particles with atoms in the high atmosphere." Who do you think energized those particles up north: Santa Claus, or down south penguins? No sir, that's just spilled over energy from my side of things.

Note how those auroras are in places of precarious balance. The tips of the globe have very long periods of continual night or day. They say it can drive a person batty if they live under those conditions for too long. Imagine what it can do to a demon who has been hiding up there for centuries? It ain't pretty, trust me.

Spilled over energy gets excused away by one branch of science or another, swept onto the desks of government workers who aren't respected enough to be given "legitimate" work, or just shrugged off as strange but natural phenomena. Funny how the last is closest to the truth, and it is based on human instinct and intuition, not science.

You can well imagine how hard it is for a person with my experiences to go see a movie (and I can; I get my days off too) based on "real" events. All too often it turns out to be a comedy for me to see how humanity explains away what spills over into their world……

"What the hell was that?" Grey asked stepping out from the pizzeria. "Do I really need to have Harmony call Sep back here to babysit the two of you every time I have to leave you by yourselves?"

"Hey, it was that creepy Romper Room reject from last night," Pete said in indignation. "And besides, you're the one who told me that I'd know when it was time to fry a demon, and when it wasn't. My instincts told me to toast the little bitch."

Raven reached out and placed her hand on Grey's arm saying, "Pete's right. Legion was provoking us. I don't know if it was a Balance tipping moment, but it feels to me like we have crossed that line already. You worked your magic in there I take it." Raven nodded her head toward Giono's pizza. She rolled her eyes when she saw both women giggling and chatting behind the register like a couple of school girls.

"Yeah, no problem for now," Grey said. "I don't know if those girls are going to get a good night's sleep tonight, but I don't think we have to worry about the police getting involved."

He trailed off and watched as two pudgy boys on bicycles started riding through the construction site. One had a swine-like demon sitting on the handlebars of his bike squealing pumping piggy fists in the air with excitement. The other boy had an identical looking pig demon riding behind him with chubby arms wrapped around his waist. They were chasing a raccoon, throwing rocks at it and laughing sadistically whenever they came close to hitting it. The raccoon scampered about trying to find a hiding place. It ran through earthen gullies and troughs but could never find enough cover from its tormentors.

A sharp edged stone struck its mark on the raccoon's haunch. It cried out a piteous scream of pain and hobbled about. The limping animal found sanctuary on the construction site when it buried itself under the treads of a heavy duty front-end loader that the laboring McDougal crews had left to use another day.

Raven had created another gun in her hand, but Grey's touch on her wrist stopped her from raising it. He shook his head at her questioning look and said, "Watch."

"Watch what?" Pete chimed in. "The four little pigs torture that poor raccoon? No thank you Grey. There's Balance on all levels right, so let Raven go show them who the big bad wolf really…oh." Pete stopped because there was an ear shattering roar as a huge demon, similar in structure to a wolf but the size of a grizzly bear, came bounding out from under the front-end loader. The ground and machinery rocked about in the monster's wake.

It launched itself at the oblivious boys and snatched up a pig demon in each massive paw. Landing on top of the lesser demons, the monster held them down with its bulk while they shrieked trying to escape. The huge muzzle darted down in sharp strikes tearing into them, quickly cutting off their squeals. As the wolf-like demon snapped its neck back to swallow down a particularly large piece of shadowed flesh, Pete could see a huge red eye burning out from above and between the demon's smaller eyes.

The two boys started squealing, sounding very similar to their piggy friends to Pete, as the piece of heavy equipment the demon had ambushed them from tipped over. Bulky yellow painted metal crashed down on both boys and bicycles sending dirt, rust, and yelps of anguish into the dusk-laden sky. The newer lights of the plaza had turned on providing more illumination than what was left from the sun.

With its cover missing the raccoon sat in a pool of halogen grooming itself as if it did not have a care in the world. The large wolf devoured the little pigs as the boys whimpered piteously, but the raccoon paid attention to none of it. Instead, it scampered over to a discarded pizza box, lifted open the lid, pulled out a half-eaten crust and started to munch on it, turning it around deftly to nibble on particularly choice sections. It turned its head up in Grey, Raven, and Pete's direction and peered at them with contempt. In the middle of the natural mask-like markings a tiny red eye flashed out from the raccoon's forehead.

"Oh shit," Pete said. "Well I guess you flushed them out, huh Raven?"

*****

The giant grizzly wolf had finished its meal and turned toward them snarling across the empty parking lot. The demon thrummed with dark energy and unconcealed intent to attack as it hunched its shoulders down, slowly stalking toward them. Its three-eyed gaze focused on Grey when Legion's voice escaped from its canine jaws. "You should have left last night when I gave you the chance Grey."

Grey had not taken his hand off of Raven's arm while the tableau unfolded, and she had not dispersed her gun. He did not look in her direction. As an unspoken signal he let go of her arm, and started running to the right side of the demon.

Raven tore off to the left side paralleling Grey's charge with a gun in both hands leaving Pete standing directly in the rampaging demon's path, alone.

"Shit, shit, shit…Alright Pete you can do this," Pete said to himself. "Grace under pressure man. That's you."

Whether it was the demon's own predator instincts or Legion's experience herding it on did not matter. It saw Pete as the weak link to pick off first and charged. The monster would not be swayed from its rush even when Raven and Grey opened fire on its flanks. Raven's bullets chewed holes into the demon's side with surgical precision, and Grey sent huge amounts of energy at it from his side. Through all the harrying the demon kept on charging straight for Pete at a speed so fast it left Raven and Grey far behind in a matter of seconds.

"Fine, come on!" Pete yelled at the demon, balled fists at his sides dripping red sparks. He dug down deep to where he felt the Source pulling on him and threw out a large red shield in a half sphere around himself. The grizzly wolf slammed into it with the impact of a ballistic missile, forcing Pete to stagger back, barely staying on his feet. He looked down to see his feet had ripped a pair of size twelve trenches into the blacktop. The demon rebounded, shook its head from side to side sending red sparks flying from its ink black mane, and squared off against Pete. It swiped a paw the size of a snow shovel at Pete's shield sending more sparks cascading down in a shower.

"Distract it for a moment longer Peter," spoke Harmony's voice from inside his mind. Over the demon's hunched shoulder, Pete could see Raven approaching at a dead sprint.

The demon snarled and bit at Pete's shield. Pete groaned to himself before he said, "Oh what big teeth you have grandma!"

The wolf paused in its dogged determination to tear through the barrier. It tilted its head and Legion's voice came out from the creature's maw, "I am about to devour you fool, and you stand there joking? Perhaps Grey really is slipping if he chose you as an ally. Arrghh!"

The demon's wails were a result of Raven having jumped up onto its back, clamping her legs around its upper shoulders and sending bolt after bolt of azure light directly into the back of its skull. The demon's legs gave out from under it, and Raven rode the hulking form to the ground still shooting light into it. When it stopped thrashing she jumped off and stalked around to face it with Pete. The wolf tried swiping a feeble paw at her when she closed in. Raven kicked the strike away with her left leg, leveled her right hand gun at Legion's center eye and fired point blank.

Pete smirked at her and opened his mouth to speak, but Raven cut him off. "Pete,

I'll slap you if the next words out of your mouth are another little Red Riding Hood joke."

"No," Pete said unconvincingly. "I was just going to ask what we do about those kids? Grey didn't want the cops involved right?" Grey was close enough to have heard Pete's query.

"We don't do anything Pete," Grey said. "That's the harsh truth of what we do. Sometimes we have to sit back and let things unfold. Sometimes the universe only allows people one mistake, and I think those boys just might have used theirs. Maybe the delivery boy for the pizza joint will come back from his run, hear them crying, and call the EMT's in time, but then again maybe he won't. Cruel, but that's life."

A chattering and snappish sound drew all of their attentions back to the construction site. The three eyed raccoon was yelling at them from the top of the overturned front-end loader where the boys were trapped. It was gesticulating wildly at them, and Pete moved closer to see what had the little thing so agitated.

"Grey?" Pete asked.

"Yeah Pete," Grey responded walking up next to him.

"I think that raccoon demon is flipping me the bird. Can they do that?" Pete asked.

Grey looked closer appraisingly and chuckling a bit said, "Apparently they can Pete."

The door chime over Giono's pizza went off, and the raccoon scampered down from the machinery. Julie, the counter girl, had on a light jacket and was turning her head over her shoulder saying, "Thanks Kathy. I'm just too frazzled to concentrate on work. Sam should be back any minute, and it's a slow night anyway." She paused, presumably in response to something Kathy was saying.

"I know, I know, you can handle it. I just feel bad leaving is all. Okay. Okay, I will. Thanks again girl," Julie said and started walking out toward the sidewalk. She paused to pick up a newspaper from the broken dispenser and headed toward the more residential area of town.

She had just turned a corner onto a side street off of the main road when Tommy's truck barreled at high speed into the parking lot. He slammed on the breaks bringing the vehicle to a stop diagonally across several parking spaces. "What makes you think she's still here Tommy?" Kevin asked from his perch behind the driver's seat.

"I don't know where she is dipshit! So we start here," Tommy yelled. "You and Bill get out and start looking. I'll drop Steve and Owen off on the other side of town. Frank and I will drive around, and if anybody sees her use your fucking cell and call me! None of us saw her get in a car, so she has to be around here somewhere. I'm going to go ask Molly over at the *Super 8* if somebody who looks like that crazy bitch is staying there."

One of the remaining panther demons got down from the truck with Kevin and Bill. It growled at Raven, Grey and Pete as it moved around and behind the boys, always making sure that it was mostly hidden behind one of them at all times obscuring Raven's line of fire. Tommy drove his truck out of the parking lot in the direction Julie had gone only moments ago. Pete watched as the rusted bumper and broken taillights vanished down the same side street the young girl had turned down.

"Oh man," Pete said, nodding in the direction the truck had gone. "That cannot be good."

Grey did not have the chance to voice his agreement before the loud squeal of tires on blacktop rang out through the early night. A woman's scream followed in the subsequent quiet but was quickly stifled. Kevin and Bill looked at each other, then shrugging they ran off in the direction the noises came from. Raven stuck out her leg and sent them both sprawling over the unseen obstacle. Sputtering obscenities, both boys climbed to their hands and knees. Before either boy could get back to his feet Grey reached down, pressed a hand to each of their temples, and said, "Sleep."

They slipped into instant coma like states. Leaving them face down on the blacktop Grey stood up saying, "We need to hurry. I don't want these two peckerwoods to be the only human lives I save tonight."

***

The panther demon that had stayed behind shot off in a streak running in the direction the truck had gone. Pete was the first to pursue, but Raven and Grey were right behind him. Pete rounded the corner in time to see the rear end of the demon turn down a side street. He poured on as much speed as he could, tearing through the front yards of houses closing the distance with the demon considerably.

Both the panther demon and Pete stopped short when they reached a tiny parking lot for a small apartment complex where the other three boys from Tommy's crew were clustered around talking. The demon glanced quickly at Pete as it moved around, nose close to the ground like a dog trying to pick up a scent. Grey and Raven caught up to them when the demon found whatever trail it was searching for and ran off into the night again. Pete was poised to follow when Grey grabbed his shoulder and said, "Wait, Pete. I can track Tommy down faster than that overgrown pussycat. I want to hear what these boys have to say, and I want to know why I no longer see any of Legion's corruption on them."

Pete glanced over at them, and realized Grey was right. The boy who was speaking no longer had any of those deep purple and black pulsing veins showing. He was asking the other two, "Should we call the cops do you think?"

"I don't know. Do you think he's really going to hurt her?"

"He'll probably just rough her up some, maybe fuck her."

"I don't know guys," the first one whined. "You seen his eyes too, right? Like where the fuck did they go? They was like all black, and when we wouldn't get back in the truck he yelled at us, but it didn't sound like Tommy, just like in Giono's. It sounded like that girl in that old movie who threw up pea soup you know?"

"Yeah."

"What'll the cops do though? Our fucking luck that douche of an uncle of his will answer it, and he'll want to know why you're holding his shotgun there, Frank."

"Shit Steve! I hadn't thought of that."

"Here's what we do," Steve said. "We head back to Giono's, meet up with Kevin and Bill, tell them what happened, dump the guns in one of those big-ass mud puddles in that construction site, and go get some more pizza. That way that old biddy Kathy or that dipshit delivery guy Sam will see us, and then we have an alibi if Tommy really fucks up this time."

"Yeah, yeah that's a good idea," Frank said.

"Damn right it is!" Steve agreed, "And you dickheads made fun of me for watching those crime shows on TV. I told you it was good shit!"

The three boys started jogging back in the direction of the pizzeria and construction site. Grey watched them go and turned to Pete saying, "Legion lost its influence over them, either through focusing too much on Tommy, or because we destroyed half of the panthers he had hovering around him, maybe both."

"So we let them go?" Pete asked.

"Their actions were minimal, at worst peripheral," Grey said. "If they do what they plan then we no longer have any business with them. We go after Legion and Tommy. See if we can't save that girl Julie too."

"I'll save the girl," Raven said in a tone of voice that brooked no argument. Grey looked over at her, reached out a hand and directed her chin so she would meet his gaze. After a silent moment he nodded his head once.

"Hey," Pete interrupted, looking at each of them lifting his eyebrows questioningly. "I really left you guys in the dust back there huh? I was gone in a flash! You know something, 'Flash' would be a cool name. I was…"

"Not now Pete," Grey cut him off and walked away in the direction the panther demon had gone. Raven sighed, smacked Pete upside the head, and started after Grey muttering, "I should make you wear red tights for that Pete."

Pete yelled after her, "Not '*The Flash*' woman! Just 'Flash,' you know, present tense verb, like Sting. He pulled it off, I think I…oh why do I bother?"

Pete ran to catch up with the two of them.

Chapter 16

It is hard for me to listen to most folk prattle on now-a-days about such…and forgive me if you are one of them, but such inconsequential things. I don't mean to belittle people's problems and such. Life is a fight for everybody. It's only with the passage of time that you can step back and realize if you were fightin' a group of campfire girls or the entire Roman legion.

I know it don't seem like piddly ass shit to the folks worrying about it, but when I see a mother bitchin' at her only kid to 'quiet down and behave' in some ridiculous place where kids are meant to do just the opposite, like a playground, I just shake my head. Piddly ass shit. I've seen riots, actual physical violence over the result of sports. People have died, friends, and not during the game mind you but afterwards because somebody didn't like the outcome. I've also known kids to kill themselves over the stress folks place on them because of those same games. All over there are little league coaches screaming in the faces of boys not yet old enough to play with their peckers, because they didn't hit a ball with a stick, Piddly Ass Shit.

I see folks at their best, and I see them at their worst. It's the nature of my profession; I ain't judging. It only makes a man sad to think on. Y'all don't affect just yourselves with your worrying; that kind of stress floods over onto those around you. It ain't necessary; life is so simple the first time around. We complicate the shit out of it for no good reason.

You can call me a jaded old sinner, but you can never call me a hypocrite. I never worried about piddly ass shit in my life. Maybe it was a result of having to work, and I don't mean forty hours a week in a cubicle either, I mean raw hands working through the daylight without weekends, holidays and vacations to dream about. I slept; I worked. I ate; I worked. I think life and living take on a different mindset when a man don't have porcelain cradling his cheeks when he squats to shit.

I didn't feel so strongly about this in my physical life because most folks didn't have piddly ass shit problems. They had real hardships, not comparin' cell phone plans and bitchin' about bad signals.

And now, well, it's even worse now. Most of my days I spend holding this world together so y'all can go on rioting over soccer scores. It's a little hard to not see most folk's problems as piddly ass shit when if I "drop the ball" everything ends…….

***

They found Tommy's truck in the parking lot of the high school football stadium. The rundown Ford looked out of place among the immaculately tended grounds. The blacktopped parking lot was seamless, the paint delineating parking spaces looked fresh, and the cloying scent of tar hung in the air. The aluminum bleachers for both the home team and visiting sides were set in poured concrete. Well-tended flowerbeds full of late season mums lined the ticket booth and concession stands, with freshly mown grass interspersed between well-trimmed walkways.

"Wow, nice place," Grey said looking about the manicured estate.

"Welcome to the Midwest, Grey," Raven grumbled. "Make sure you genuflect before you enter the sanctuary-"

A woman's muffled cries interrupted them and drew their attention to the field. They quickly passed through the chain linked fence and turnstile entrance. Following her plaintive cries led them to a purple and gold painted archway that tunneled under the home team bleachers. Her distress grew louder as they approached a slightly inclined passage leading up onto the field. "Please Tommy, stop. I'll just go home. I won't say anything to anybody, just please stop."

A loud smack echoed through the empty stadium, and her pleading subsided back into unintelligible whimpers and cries. At the tunnel opening two panther demons were sitting upright on the guardrails, with prehensile tails wrapped around the lower bars, simian-like. The demons smiled widely when they saw them approaching, then did a back flip over the rail onto the rubberized track circling the football field. From the lead Grey turned back to Raven and Pete saying, "This is most definitely a trap, but since I've fought Legion before, many times, and I have years of experience on you both, I want y'all to follow my lead, okay?"

Raven nodded at him and with a thumbs up Pete said, "You got it, boss."

Grey walked up to the recently vacated handrail with Pete and Raven behind and to either side of him. Gripping the rail in both hands he leaned out surveying the dark field. The wrestling movements of two figures out on the centerfield fifty yard line were visible in the starlight. They could hear Julie crying, and Tommy asked, with a hint of Legion's voice creeping into his tone, "What's the matter? You were a cheerleader…I'm sure you always wanted to go out and fuck a football player on the field didn't you?"

Julie's crying had taken on a hysterical edge when Tommy finished speaking. Pete could see that her blouse was ripped opened to the waist, and her bra had been pulled down too, exposing her breasts. Tommy was straddling her hips, grunting and struggling to pull her jeans off one handed because he was holding her arms together above her head restraining them with the other. Julie was kicking and scissoring her legs back and forth, doing what she could to thwart his efforts. Tommy was not a big man, and in her thrashings she pulled her right arm free. Fighting with what she had, Julie raked her nails across Tommy's face. He let go of her other arm with a yelp of pain grabbing at his bleeding cheek.

"Bitch!" he snarled and struck her on the temple with a closed fist, knocking what fight she was showing out of her. Tommy swiped at the blood trickling down his cheek and brought his fingers away covered in night blackened crimson. He growled, "Fucking whore."

He kept his hips straddling hers, effectively pinning her down, and reached around behind his back pulling out the gun he had tucked into the waistline of his jeans. He waved it in her face, turned the safety off, and slapped her with his free hand until she focused on it. With more of Legion coloring his voice Tommy snarled, "See bitch? You're going to stop fighting me right now, or I'll shoot you in the hands so you can't do a damn thing. Then I'll fuck you even harder. Maybe

I'll even fuck you with this gun when I'm done. You got it?"

Julie's eyes were bright with so much fear that all verbalization was beyond her. She could only nod her head. Tommy leered down at her and said, "Good, now take your pants off."

When Julie started fumbling down around her hips to follow Tommy's order Raven hurdled the railing. She strode determinedly toward the assailant and his victim without looking back at either Grey or Pete. Pete turned to Grey, as he watched Raven march off, asking, "I thought we were supposed to follow your lead?"

Grey shrugged his shoulders in response. Both men stood there watching as Raven (still not in a physical shell) hauled off and kicked Tommy in the face so hard that his head snapped back and the gun went flying from his grip. Julie had the presence of mind to scamper out from under him when the opportunity presented itself. She dove for the gun, and had just fastened her fingers around the grip when Tommy retained his wits enough to jump on her back.

"Come on girl," Raven muttered quietly. "You can do this."

Julie and Tommy grappled for the gun. Tommy's lack of bulk provided him little advantage over Julie, but Legion's added influence was lending him strength beyond his physical size. He grabbed her small wrist and squeezed the thin forearm bones until she screamed and dropped the gun. Tommy laughed and crouched over her to take his gun back, but whether by design or accident Julie threw her elbow back and up into his throat. He wretched, gagged and clutched his throat staggering back from the girl. Julie rushed to her hands and knees, scampered over to the gun, and spun around to face Tommy. From a seated position with the firearm shaking in both hands she shrieked, "Get the fuck away from me asshole!"

The football stadium fell into a stilled silence after Julie's screamed order. In the hush, a black form oozed up from the ground behind Tommy. It was tall and lean to the point of emaciation. When it reached down and drug Tommy to his feet it stood nearly twice as tall as the boy. Two narrow red eyes were the only features that could be seen burning out from its long moon-shaped face. There were no nose, no ears, and no hair. The demon's face and body had the appearance of seamless black oil. There was no third eye evident, but the two that were there matched all of the other "third eyes" that Pete had seen previously.

"Here we go," Grey said to Pete from the bleacher railing. Raven retreated from where she had been out on center field to stand back with them. She looked up at Grey from the surrounding track and nodded, a gun appearing in each of her hands. Grey returned the nod and watched as the demon spun Tommy around to face Julie. Her scream let them know that the demon was not hiding its presence from her. It had manifested that hideous shell in both the physical world and the non-corporeal one.

Julie may or may not have been a marksman, but with a full magazine and a target only a few feet away it was hard for her to miss when she opened fire on Tommy and his demonic puppet master. The boy's body twisted and jerked about as bullets tore through his arms and legs. Those that passed through him or missed struck Legion's oily body causing ripples to spread across the black skin where they entered. Tommy was thrown backward from his feet once the shots started hitting his torso. Julie continued to scream and pulled the trigger even though the gun repeatedly clicked empty.

Tommy's body lay supine and unmoving. The tall demon ignored the girl screaming and dry firing her gun in its direction. It stood over the boy's corpse and reached a long hand down shoving it into Tommy's shredded chest cavity. It fished around snarling, "Come here boy! There is no turning back now. You are mine."

Legion yanked its skeletal arm back as it said this, pulling out a squirming black blob that had a vaguely rodent like appearance. It snarled and thrashed in the tall demon's grasp, and it turned trying to bite at Legion's hand. Legion roared, grabbed at what was left of once Tommy McDougal, and with elongated fingers, tipped in sharp black talons, tore Tommy's soul into two pieces. A huge fang-lined maw opened in the previously unbroken face as Legion devoured the pieces in separate bites, licking its fingers to capture any lingering energy like a connoisseur wanting to savor a fine meal.

Julie had screamed herself hoarse and only dry gasps escaped her as she continued to pull the empty gun's trigger. Legion chuckled out a gurgling inhuman laugh, a noise that would make toddlers cry, and moved in her direction. Raven darted toward the terrified woman before Grey could clamber over the rail to land a restraining hand on her. "Damn it," he swore and quickly sped after her with Pete right behind him.

"Back off!" Raven yelled at Legion. "You had your meal and that is all you're entitled to."

"Little bird," Legion cooed, "are you so eager to join me too? I am no longer stuck in that meat suit like before. Do you really want to try yourself against me?"

Legion reached out a long wiry hand in a half-hearted grasping motion toward

Raven. She did not bother to trade pleasantries or banter with the demon. The gun in her right hand went off in a huge flash of red light sending a crimson bullet tearing through Legion's outstretched palm. The demon bellowed an inhuman roar, drawing its hand back just as Grey and Pete had arrived to stand behind Raven.

The noises of pain tapered off and the demon started making an awful attempt at laughter when it spat out, "That was your last chance Jew! Now I will just rape your soul and eat whatever is left!"

If any of this scared Raven she allowed none of it to show when Pete looked over at her. She stared back at Legion with eyes that had started to glow sky blue, twirling her guns on her fingers with the same skill she had shown previously. The moment held the air of a standoff with them standing between Legion and Julie. Pete could see movement in the end zone behind Legion, and when he focused he saw the three remaining panther demons pacing back and forth.

Grey stepped forward and bellowed, "Legion! This is your last and only warning! You have your prize, now leave this town, and I will let you live."

"Oh Grey," the demon thrummed, "I have been fantasizing about this moment for over a hundred years. Please draw out your pathetic warnings just a bit more because I do want to savor this moment. Perhaps call me some vicious names, or tell me how futile my attempts are. You know, classic hero dialogue."

When Grey stared at Legion refusing to humor the demon, it continued, "No? Oh well, one can only dream. I'll have to be satisfied with this." Legion threw back its long head and upper torso, and bellowed an ululating call at the night sky. The sound echoed through the empty stadium, bouncing around the bleachers to fall across Pete from many different angles. He could feel it reverberate up through the plastic grass he was standing on making his legs feel wobbly. At the summons the panther demons dropped onto all fours and prowled in their direction. Pete could see a few other three eyed gazes start to appear in the shadows under bleachers and come out from the tunnels that lead down to the parking lot.

"Grey?" Pete asked

"Easy Pete, easy, just follow my lead," Grey said.

The demons started to take on more definitive shapes as they approached the field. Two that Pete thought looked vaguely like rhinoceroses spliced with dragons grown to the size of school buses came around from behind the visitor's stands, and sent the field goal post swaying when their backs brushed against it. A troop of chimpanzee sized demons had been riding on the rhinos' backs, and they jumped onto the swaying posts shrieking. A flock of vulture bat like things had taken roost on the announcer's box and flapped wings the size of bed sheets. Pete took this all in with rapidly widening eyes.

"Grey," Pete said, worry evident in his voice, "you said never more than a dozen didn't you? I remember that distinctly. You said, 'For we are about a dozen,' right? That's what you said isn't it?"

"Easy Pete," Grey said again.

"Yeah, yeah…but Grey that is way more than a dozen," Pete said. Pointing at a snake-like demon with five heads that was winding itself through the bleachers set out for the marching band, Pete yelled, "And…and what the fuck is that? Does that count as one or five?"

Another flock of aerial demons had taken to roosting on the visitors' bleachers. This group looked more aquatic than something typically seen in the sky. More and more eyes were starting to make their way up from the tunnels and onto the field adding to the press of dark bodies. A large roiling curtain of shadow made of many sized demons drew up behind Legion like a stationary tidal wave poised to crash down around them.

"Just follow my lead, Pete. I have a plan," Grey said under his breath, and then bellowed, "Legion! You leave me no other choice. You will be…"

Grey threw his hands down like a child tossing one of those white wrapped snappers on the fourth of July, but instead of the crack of gunpowder combusting, a giant blinding blue flash shot up. In the ensuing chaos Grey looked to Pete and said, "Run, run really, really fast!"

Grey darted over, scooping up the unconscious Julie (who had passed out from fright) in a fireman's carry, and ran off at a tremendous sprint. Raven followed right after him, and Pete stood wide eyed for a moment as the light started to dissipate. He watched as all of the demons rubbed at their eyes focusing in on him and shrieked in a chorus of evil. "Oh shit," Pete said and started running after Grey.

He blew by Raven when he heard Legion bellow, "Get them! Kill the others, but bring me Grey!"

Pete was about to overtake Grey when he saw another grizzly wolf demon hurdle the concession stand to block their escape. Pete was forming a sphere to throw at it, but he heard Raven yelling behind him, "Down Pete, now!"

He followed her order without hesitation and felt the light touch of her feet tread up his back, right foot, then left, and gone. He looked up to see Raven's form go soaring over Grey and the girl he had slung over his shoulders, firing her guns as she went. Bullet after bullet plowed into the wolf demon's face. It screamed and tried to block her shots with its paws, but the luminous slugs only chewed through its paws as well. It dropped to the ground, and Raven continued to pour her ammunition into it as she landed and darted past its dissolving bulk. Without pausing to turn around Raven yelled, "Come on Flash, move your ass!"

Pete and Grey ran after her as she flew through the turnstile. Grey had to pause momentarily and pull Julie's flesh and blood body through gently. Once they were all in the parking lot they turned back to see a nightmare image rampaging toward them. Hundreds of demons were barreling their way, each with a glowing third eye on their foreheads. The demonic tidal wave had fallen, flowing around the tall form of Legion as it stood mid-field. Grey passed Julie to Pete and said, "Take her and run. I'll slow them down. Legion wants me anyway. Not you two."

"Bullshit!" Raven yelled, firing both guns randomly at the oncoming hoard, which was drawing closer by the second. The mob of adversaries was so thick aim and accuracy were irrelevant. Every shot struck home.

"We can't leave the girl here for them, and we can't take her to Harmony," Grey shouted over the ensuing racket. He turned to Pete specifically placing a hand on his upper arm and said, "Take them both if you have to, kicking and screaming, but run and don't look back."

The squeal of tires on asphalt startled them all as an ice cream truck pulled into the parking lot behind them. Cartoon images of ice cream treats and the happy children eating them decorated the truck's sides. A large megaphone speaker disguised to look like a giant ice cream cone rode on the roof and a yellow happy face complete with pearly white teeth smiling from the bumper was painted on the front. The truck had barely come to a stop when a giant shaggy head popped out of the driver's window. Zeus yelled, "Hey! I hate to break up this whole last stand at the O.K. Corral thing you got going Grey, but how about a ride instead? Bwaaaa!"

Chapter 17

It's said that discretion is the better part of valor. Have you ever noticed how this is reserved for those deemed the "good guys"? When the "bad guys" are the ones doing the runnin' we use language implying cowardice in some form of chicken, yellow, fraidy-cat, and the like. It's the same thing, only our perspective of it is different. Why should the heroes show discretion while the villains are cowards?

What do you call it when a man like me runs for it? I ain't no hero, but I'm hardly a villain either. Well, I like the term "strategic retreat" myself. That has the proper ring to it, because if I retreat it's only to regroup and come at you later from a position of advantage. And trust me, I will come back after you. I never leave an enemy at my back; you can count on that. It may not be tomorrow, or the next day, but if you and I have an issue that comes to blows? You better finish it that first time when you have the advantage, because I'll be waitin' for my fortunes to turn and the chance to seize my moment.

I was never a great chess player. It's a fine game, I mean no insult, but without the opportunity to retreat if you're over-taxed there's no realism, not like poker. If fate deals *you a few shitty hands, and trust me she will, you could try bluffing your way out or recoup your losses when things shuffle your way, bide your time and all.*

Only an obstinate fool stands his ground when it starts to slide out from under him. Sure, if everybody likes that fool then it was his heroic last stand, there ain't nothin' heroic about a last stand. You do it out of respect for the lives of others or out of shear obstinacy. If it's out of respect then you are keeping to the Balance, even unknowingly. If you do so out of obstinacy then you're an ass who gets what he deserves.

I've been accused of being obstinate or contrary a time or two, but that always comes from folk who don't know the difference between being stubborn and being able to see all sides of the argument. Stubbornness has its roots in personalities that cannot let go of a point of view, even when the universe has shown them that view was emphatically wrong. That's the definition of a fool to me......

***

They ran around to the back of the truck. Raven yanked open the doors in time to provide cover as one of the bat vulture demons swooped down slamming into it. Firing around

222

the side of the door Raven punched several holes into the stunned demon's head, while Pete helped Grey load Julie into the back, leaning her against a freezer. When his hands were free he threw a couple of red energy balls at the onrushing hoard before jumping into the back of the truck.

"We're in Zeus! Go!" Raven yelled and closed one door as Pete closed the other. In an instant the ice cream truck went from stationary to what felt like light speed to Pete. The thuds from more airborne kamikaze demons crashed into the truck rocking it from side to side. Zeus squeezed his massive upper body through the driver's side window. Pete could see him leaning out (via the open vending window) firing huge bolts of orange lightning from his hands.

"Bwaaaa!" Zeus bellowed. "Take that you flying pieces of shit! Bwaaa haha!"

The big man continued to laugh and throw bolts of lightning in imitation of the Greek god he was named for. Raven kicked the awning off of the vending window to provide a clearer range to fire from and leaned out to join Zeus in his zeal. Grey had slid into the passenger's seat and reached over grabbing the steering wheel to keep them from plowing into the high school gymnasium.

With all the jostling movement Julie had tumbled from her place by the freezer and

Pete leaned down to check on her. Once she was set back securely he tried to arrange her torn clothing into something approaching modesty. He covered his eyes while he tried to cajole her brassiere back into place, and that was when she woke up, looking down to see some strange black man awkwardly playing with her breasts. When she tried to scream and found her voice to still be gone, Julie slapped Pete hard, gathered her shirt around her and promptly passed back out.

"Aw come on," Pete yelled and touched his face where she had slapped him. "Not cool."

"Hey Pete," Raven said. "If you're done molesting the innocent victim I could really use some help over here. One of those big hulks is catching up to us."

"Bwaaaa hahaha," Zeus' laugh bellowed from outside the window. Pete shook his head muttering, "Just not cool."

The truck rocked hard on its chassis wrenching refrigerator doors open. Popsicles and fudge pops rained down around the passengers as Raven yelled, "Now Pete!"

Pete stood up, but lost his balance as Grey turned a corner too quickly, almost tipping the vehicle without demonic assistance. A box of unopened drumstick novelties struck Pete on the back of the head. Rubbing at the point of impact Pete yelled, "Jesus Christ Grey!"

"Hey, I told you I didn't like these things. If Zeus would get his giant self back in here and drive, I would be more than happy to kill some demons instead," Grey said over his shoulder, yanking the steering wheel back and forth like he was driving a bumper car.

"Move," Pete yelled at Grey, and jumped into the passenger's seat when he did. "I'll drive. The people with more experience at demon hunting can attack the oncoming army from hell, and the man who actually lived in a time that people drove cars and not rode horses will drive." Pete stood precariously behind the driver's seat as Grey retreated.

"Hey, you too jumbo," Pete slapped Zeus on his copious rump which was blocking Pete from actually getting into the driver's seat.

Zeus pulled himself out the window up onto the roof and leaned back down to the window so his long braided beard and hair were upside down making him look like a giant rag mop with eyes. He tweaked Pete on the nose and said, "No time for love *Dr. Jones*. Bwaa hahaha"

Pete swiped a hand at Zeus and said, "Let me drive. Hey, Grey? Where the hell am I going?"

Grey had broken the small square windows out of the back doors, and he was throwing ball after ball of light out of them. He turned to look at Pete, still tossing energy over his shoulder without aiming, and said, "Just head out of town. Get us away from homes, and onto a highway where we can lose these things."

Pete was looking at Grey in the rearview mirror while he gave him directions. With each word Grey uttered Pete could see three huge glowing eyes getting closer to the rear of the truck. The instant Grey finished speaking, Pete jammed on the accelerator to escape what was now a single glowing eye in the mirror because it had gained so much ground so quickly. He heard Zeus stumble and yell, "Hey Pete what are you…oh shit! Big rhino looking thing with pesky little chimp demons riding side saddle coming up fast! Ha!" The last was punctuated by another flash of orange lightning.

Defensive driving took on a whole new meaning for Pete as he dodged on-rushing demons and attempted to navigate down unfamiliar city streets. He ignored decades of ingrained adherence to traffic laws and sped through stop signs and blinking red lights. Pete flinched when a squirrel darted out in front of the on rushing ice cream truck. One loud crunch told Pete that the first innocent bystander had been claimed in this skirmish.

Pete spun the steering wheel in his hands and turned onto a larger road. A rotund swine-like demon had managed through luck or skill to anticipate the route Pete would take. It was standing in the middle of the road that Pete had turned onto and was speeding down. The demon had large tusks like a wild boar and it lowered them, bellowing out a challenge to Pete. Flooring the truck Pete yelled, "Fine, you want to play chicken Porky?"

The ice cream truck ate up the distance between them and the demon. Pete did not slow down or swerve while the demon stood its ground squealing as the truck's smiling bumper plowed right into it. When there was no subsequent thump or bump like there had been with the squirrel, Pete swore and leaned forward to look out over the hood. When he was stretched as far over as the steering wheel would allow, a twisted porcine face roared up over the hood and pressed against the windshield. The demon screamed loudly; Pete screamed even louder and in reflex turned on the windshield wipers.

"Duck," Raven shouted from directly behind Pete's right shoulder. Having learned to trust her taciturn orders Pete did as she commanded instantly and felt a tingling sensation on the top of his head as the light from her guns shot over his stooped shoulders. The verdant bullets spilled energy over into the physical world plowing through both windshield and demon, sending them flying out ahead of the truck into the night. This time Pete felt the appropriate thumping as the truck ran over the pig demon.

"Christ Pete!" he yelled at himself. "You really got yourself mixed up in it this time. Driving around in a Good Humor knock off, violating every traffic law while dodging demons, rescuing damsels in distress, your friends are shooting balls of light around, and there is a giant on the roof laughing his ass off at the peril. Looking for adventure, Pete? Come join us, we'll save the world starting in…Hey! Where the fuck are we? I don't even know the name of the damn town! And where the hell is the goddamn highway!"

"Turn right up here Peter," Harmony's voice said inside Pete's mind.

"Jesus Christ!" Pete shrieked. Then in a calmer tone of voice he apologized. "Oh yeah, sorry ma'am. I sort of forgot about you. Can you get me to the highway? Everybody is kind of busy at the moment, and I don't know where I'm going. I never thought about using you like built in OnStar. Hey, can you dial my sister in Albany? Let her know I'm doing well?"

"Peter," Harmony sighed, "shut up, and drive."

"Yes ma'am."

Harmony guided Pete through the unfamiliar neighborhoods and streets until they reached a sparsely lit onramp. Raven was firing her guns in concentration while Grey was doing much the same with his light globes, and Zeus was tossing lightning bolts around indiscriminately as Pete drove the ice cream truck up the highway entrance ramp. Pete could see in the side view mirrors that their pursuit had dropped down to just the super-sized rhino demon with its accompanying three chimp riders chattering and shaking their fists from its back.

"Hey Pete," bellowed Zeus' voice from the roof. "You see that bright red button? Give it a push would you?"

Pete looked down at the dashboard and found what he assumed was the button that Zeus was talking about. Fingers hovering over it he tentatively asked, "What is it? Warp speed or something?"

"Just push it man!"

Pete sighed, braced himself and did what he was told. No jet-boosted rocketing forward or cool Acme-made booby traps fell from the truck when he pressed it, but Zeus' raucous laughter rang out as soon as the megaphone speaker on top of the truck started playing *Pop Goes the Weasel* in a calliope ice cream truck chime. Pete looked up at the roof, pounded on it a couple of times with his fist and yelled, "You need help Zeus! You hear me?"

"Bwaaa Hahaha!" was the only response he received. Glancing back into the side mirrors Pete noticed that he was not the only one who was able to accelerate out on the open stretch of highway. The rhino demon had gained on them without the city detritus of park benches and parked cars to impede its progress. He could hear Grey laughing from the rear of the truck. Pete asked, "What's so funny now? It can't be Zeus' choice in music."

"No," Grey said, "seeing your face in the mirror just now reminded me of the look you had back in that stadium when I said, 'Run!' It was priceless."

"Hey! You were the one who kept saying, 'Follow my lead, blah blah blah, easy Pete, easy,' and all that. 'I have a plan,' all that experience and the best you could do is run?" Pete asked.

"Yep," Grey said still laughing. "You'd be laughing too if you saw your face. It was too damn comical. You looked like that wide-eyed black boy, Buckwheat, from those old "Little Rascals" shorts…Say, Buckwheat would be a good nickname."

"Hell no! Grey, do you hear me? If you start calling me 'Buckwheat' you can kiss your metaphysical retirement good bye! My proud African spiritual ass will be running to the Source faster than you can say 'Move toward the light!' Do you hear me back there?"

Raven was now laughing with Grey, and they had both stopped firing. Neither of them was sure if the joke was all that funny, or if it was the high emotions of the moment that had to find a release through humor. Pete was ready to scold them some more when he saw running lights up ahead, and he realized that they were catching up to a semi-truck. It was then that Pete realized how few living people had been out and about in the town. *Were the demons' actions keeping the town's residents indoors at night or was that just the Midwest way?* Pete thought to himself. Growing up and living most of his life in metropolises Pete simply was not sure. Couple that with his new vocation and he wanted some clarification, but he would have to wait for a more opportune moment. He yelled, "Grey! There's a semi up here! What do I do? Is this one of those 'spill over' moments?"

"Well," Grey said blandly, "I don't have my driver's license mind you, but I believe the law says you should put on your turn signal and pass at a reasonable speed."

"Bwaaa! Ha!" Zeus laughed.

"Assholes," Pete groused, pounding one fist against the roof as he did.

***

Jim had been driving trucks long haul across country since he was twenty four, and now thirty years later he was still doing so. His wife had been nagging him to stop and retire from the long sleep-deprived routes for the past few years. "You're too old Jim Donovan!" Jim said to himself, imitating his wife's voice. "And you're too fat! You can't keep that up much longer and still keep your health."

Jim was thinking about how easy these drives were for him, how they were his form of therapy and meditation, an opportunity to get away from nagging women and whining children when he started hearing *Pop Goes the Weasel*. "What the hell?"

He looked in his left side mirror and saw an ice cream truck come barreling up from behind. He glanced over when it pulled up next to him. There was a Viking on the roof laughing loudly and sitting astride a giant ice cream cone as the young black man behind the wheel smiled sheepishly and waved. Jim waved back out of habit, and the truck flew past blaring *Pop Goes the Weasel* into the night. He shook his head to clear it and reached down to turn up the radio in case the police were looking for that ice cream truck.

When he looked back up, something out of a horror movie was staring back at him.

232

Its three glowing red eyes were the size of trash cans, and it had horns sprouting up from its elongated face. There were scampering figures dancing about the monster's head and shoulders as it ate up the highway, leaving Jim and his semi in its wake. Jim closed his eyes for a moment and reopened them; both monster and ice cream truck were gone.

"Damn it woman, I think you're right," Jim said to himself.

***

Once the highway was clear again the demon pushed itself to its top speed and pulled up parallel to the ice cream truck. The chimp-sized demons jumped from the hulk's back onto the roof where Zeus fried the first one mid-leap before it landed. The second lost its head to a lightning bolt as it stood to gather its bearings, but the last one closed in enough to take a swipe at him with its serrated claws. The demon wailed, dancing and capering about with delight when it saw the deep black furrows it had left in Zeus' massive shoulder.

"Oh no you don't, you little shithead!" Zeus said and grabbed the last demon with his massive hand. He lifted it up off the roof by its throat, sending a jolt of orange lighting down his arm into the demon. It jerked and thrashed as the light flooded through its shadowed body. When it could no longer hold the current racing through it the demon's body exploded in a flash of light coupled with dark chunks of shadow flesh. Zeus shook his hand to fling free the globs of blackened glop that clung to his fingers, muttering an "urrgghh," of distaste.

Zeus looked over at the hulking rhino demon still keeping pace with them. The beast had started nudging the side of the truck with its massive horns sending the roof rocking under his feet. Raven jumped out from the vending window and onto its heaving shoulders. She started firing lavender tinted bullets into the back of the demon's skull, climbing up to balance her body precariously between its horns, and concentrated her fire around Legion's center eye. Grey followed in her tracks, diving out of the vending window. Not one to miss out on the action, Zeus jumped from the swaying roof landing next to Grey who nodded once at him in an unspoken agreement. Then both men dropped to their knees placing hands flat against the behemoths skin and started sending jolts of light through the beast.

The creature faltered and started to slow. Raven dexterously ran down its spine toward the rear end and tapped both Grey and Zeus on the shoulder as she past them to get their attention that the job was done. They jumped off into the grassy median and rolled with the force of impact. The hulking demon lost control of its bulk and that much mass traveling at that high rate of speed made for a spectacular mess. Its front end collapsed, sending its rear up and over, flipping heels over head like an SUV attempting gymnastics. The demon somersaulted end over end half a dozen times before it came to rest on the highway and dissolved into a lake of oily black matter that sunk into the blacktop. The leftover negative energy that had once been the demon oozed across the highway killing whatever plants were struggling for life along the sides of the road.

The three of them stood in the grassy median watching the demon dissolve. They could just make out the taillights of the ice cream truck miles down the road. Then a dip in the highway made it vanish all together but for the tinkling calliope music.

"Huh," Zeus said. "Does anybody think Pete noticed we aren't in the truck anymore?"

Chapter 18

Religion is a funny thing ain't it? People have fought and died by the millions, all over their religious beliefs. Families feud over it, countries go to war, and certain profiteers make fortunes all over those beliefs. I think I've made it clear that I believe in the Balance of things, always shifting in one direction or the other, but balancing out. That is my belief, mine. I got no right to tell you to make it yours, and you got no right to force yours on to another person. So what if folks don't believe what you do? Convert or kill? Can't ya'll just be content to save yourself, as it were? What's the rationale behind that I wonder? Does a crusader think, "Oh well, this fellow doesn't believe in my god, so that doesn't make him a person according to that god, and I can now kill him?"

Seems to me like folks tend to place little addendums onto their god's strictures: thou shall not kill……..only those people who believe in me, the rest are fair game!

You can feel sympathetic and empathetic without it leadin' to enmity; it is possible folks. You want to know something else about my belief? It's who I am, I live it, and so few people actually follow the same strictures and dogma that they are willin' to kill another man over.

All the beliefs floating around out there among the physical world have only gotten pieces of the truth. They get all caught up in human failings and lose what truth they do know. Good and evil are what they are. You can't convert or kill everyone who ain't on your side. Sooner or later there'll be nobody left.

I say, take what pieces you feel are right for you from any religion. It don't hurt to learn one lesson from one source, and learn a different lesson from another. Take reincarnation for instance. For those folk who believe in Karma and Samsara they say you're buildin' up a kind of cosmic scoreboard of good and bad deeds. The concept of Karma holds close to the Balance, I can see that, and Samsara is the endless cycle of suffering that life is. To stop that all you need to do is go back to the Source. I think reincarnation as a punishment for folks who done wrong, returning as lesser animals than human, was just some holy man who was close to death seeing things from my world. He saw people being "reborn" into demons, twisted animalistic versions of themselves, and he said, "Ah, those must be the evil ones being punished." And then folks moving back to the Source are breaking that cycle of Samsara, ending their suffering, but that is only a guess mind you.

See what I mean about getting pieces of the truth and then tellin' their story as a belief. That holy man saw a bit of things and his mental conditioning turned it into a story he could comprehend. Always remember that the universe is infinite and the human mind is finite. None of us can know it all. A rat-like person may die and grow into a rodent-like demon, but then again he may just have had a bad life and he turns things around in this one. It's change folks, you are what you are, only as long as you want to be. Change is always coming, whether it is the end or just the beginning, that ain't for the likes of us to know……….

***

Pete drove down the ink black highway in silence. The silence did not carry over into his mind where he was screaming and carrying on. *Where the hell is everybody? One minute everyone is yelling, cracking jokes, and blowing up demons. And the next it's just poor old Pete, all by himself (except for a half-naked white girl) driving a damn ice cream truck blasting "Pop Goes the Weasel" into the great American heartland!*

"Calm down Peter," Harmony said, her voice interrupting his mental diatribe. "There is a rest stop a few miles ahead on your right. You can pull over in there and wait for the others to catch up. I will bring them to you shortly."

"Oh," Pete said, and after a moment's reflection he asked, "Is everybody alright?"

"Yes," Harmony said. "Zeus sustained a minor wound, but it has all but healed already."

"Good," Pete answered, "so what's next?"

"I assume you mean after I bring the others to you?" Harmony stated. "That will be up to Grey. He knows this business better than anyone. I am sure he already has a plan, and two back up plans, plus an ace in the hole."

Noticing what appeared to be the lights of a highway rest stop fast approaching Pete asked, "Here? Lord, I haven't seen a pit toilet rest stop in years! I don't suppose I could just keep on driving until I found a nicer less urine scented one?"

Harmony laughed saying, "No Peter, this will do for the moment. The girl is safe, and so are you. Take a minute and rest. You have earned it." After she said the last, her presence faded back into Pete's mental closet.

Pete turned into the rest stop and was not surprised to see that his ice cream truck was the only vehicle there. He shut off the ignition, rested his head back against the seat, and drew in a few deep breaths. Pete turned to check on Julie. The girl was still passed out against the Rocket Pop freezer chest. The crickets and katydids chirruping were the only sounds to accompany Pete's breathing and he started to think: *I did earn it didn't I? I helped the cowboy save the girl, and we all got away safe. Pretty damn heroic if I do say so myself.*

A scratching sound interrupted the insect symphony and drew Pete's attention away from his self-aggrandizing. The noise kept skittering around the truck, making it hard to pinpoint its location. Looking about the truck's interior Pete said, "What the hell is that?"

He had started to stand up, twisting and climbing into the cargo area to see if the noise was coming from back there. Before he completely vacated the seat Pete felt a presence over his shoulder looking at him from the open driver's side window. He slowly turned back to see what was there and found a small squirrel-like demon, jet black fur with glowing blue eyes. There was no Legion's red third eye staring from above the creature's typical orbs. Pete held back his reflex to launch a sphere of energy at the demon on sight. Not sure how to proceed Pete said, "Um…hello there. Can I help you?"

The squirrel demon did not respond. It stared silently at Pete with unblinking eyes flicking its tail agitatedly. "Okay," Pete muttered, "so…nice night? Hmmm, what's it like spending your afterlife as a squirrel? Bet you didn't expect that huh? You see…"

In a deep cultured baritone the squirrel demon interrupted Pete, "You ran over me."

"Beg pardon?" Pete asked.

"Back in town," the diminutive demon continued. "You ran over me with this gaudy…" The demon trailed off and looked around the ice cream truck before finishing "thing."

"Oh, that was you?" Pete asked conversationally. "Sorry, I was sort of busy you know? Running for my life and all, you know what I mean?"

"Quite," the demon snipped, "I was doing much the same when out of nowhere this buffoon driving a truck with a happy face on its bumper attempts to turn me into a road kill pancake."

"Yeah…look, again I'm sorry," Pete said shifting nervously in his seat. "You know, I just can't get over James Earl Jones' voice coming out of a Warner Brother's Tiny Toon."

"You're new at this, aren't you?" the demon asked with another flick of its tail.

Pete flinched and said, "It's that obvious, huh?"

"Transparently," the demon drawled. "Look, I only stopped by as a courtesy. Accident though it may have been, you saved my life by dragging me away from Legion's hoard. I do not wish to spend eternity in slavery to that creature. So I felt obliged to notify you that I was not the only unintentional passenger you were dragging. Good evening." The demon jumped down from the open window and scampered into the night.

"Wait," Pete called after it. "What do you mean unintentional passenger?" He opened the door and started to chase after the squirrel demon but stopped when he heard a rumbling snort. Pete turned to look in the direction the noise had come from and saw the boar demon he had run over with the truck back in town. Pete realized the creature was much larger than it had looked from his previous point of view up behind the steering wheel of the truck. It stood somewhere between seven and eight feet tall, the reverse articulated legs ending in enormous hooves made it difficult for Pete to judge its exact height. Snorting again, the demon dropped to all fours, humped back and massive shoulders still making it the size of a Volkswagen Beetle. It scraped its front hoof against the concrete sending sparks into the air, and prepared to charge.

"Shit," Pete said, then repeated it over and over in a litany of profanity as he ran in the direction the squirrel demon had gone. He ran past the pit toilet, past the solitary picnic table, past the rusted out barrel that served as a trash can, and past the mown area that delincated the boundary between rest stop and the adjoining farmer's field. Once his feet hit the dried soybean stumps Pete ventured a glance over his shoulder. The pig demon was sitting on the picnic table, shaking and holding its stomach.

What the fuck? Pete thought. *That son of a bitch is laughing at me. Hell no Pete! This is your show damn it! You taught for a living, so let's teach in the afterlife. No overgrown pork chop is going to laugh at me!*

Pete turned fully around and started to march off back in the direction of the rest stop. Red light was pouring from his fists as he stepped back onto the mown grass of the park proper. The demon noticed him coming and snorted, shaking its porcine head. It said, "Leave now, and I will let you go. I owe it to you for the laugh."

Pete did not bother speaking with the demon. When he was close enough to be sure of his aim Pete let fly a comet of energy the size of a basketball. The sphere struck the picnic table and exploded in a shower of sparks and wood. The demon had jumped off the table right before impact, landing a few feet from Pete. The demon roared a challenge, and Pete struck it across the face with a hand coated in flame. It rocked back from the blow reaching a hoof up to touch its cheek where the shadowy flesh was sizzling. The demon spat, "You will die for that rookie!"

Pete did not back down when confronted by his larger opponent. He had not had any martial arts or hand to hand combat training in his physical life, but Pete did have anger on his side. Anger and determination fueled his swings as he struck the demon again and again across the face and in the abdomen like a boxer. Each blow landed with the added weight of light on his fists, acting as brass knuckles of positive energy. The demon was quickly losing strength, and it stumbled, squealing under Pete's barrage. At some point, Pete was not aware of when, but as the last blows landed he realized he was chanting, "Th-th-," as each punch struck. When the demon swayed and started to topple over, Pete swung with an upper cut that landed on the thing's chin, knocking its head completely from its body. He said, "Th-th-that's all folks!"

Pete stood there with his hands on his hips, quite pleased with himself as the demon dissolved into a black glop of negative energy sinking into the soil, killing any plant matter it touched. The self-satisfied smiled he wore vanished when he heard the squirrel demon say, "Amateur," from somewhere in the night.

Chapter 19

It's the aftermath of battle that I dread. Most folks get worked up and stressed out over the calm before the storm or the chaos of the actual fightin', but for me it's always hardest at the end. You stand back, lick your wounds, care for the injured, and count the dead. A warrior, no matter how skilled, can't be aware of all the skirmishes occurring around him. He won't always know who of his brethren have fallen until the idea of avenging them is a moot point anyway.

There is rarely a bright shinin' sign proclaiming the victor or the concured. Most times, if you were able to speak to soldiers right after battle and ask them who won, you'd get one of two responses either a dazed "I don't know" or a cynical "No one." Legends and history will fill children's heads with the boisterous camaraderie and supportive fellowship of who was deemed the "victor". Sure, to the victor go the spoils, those spoils being the chance to write history the way they want it to be remembered. They need to keep those children all bright eyed over the battles won, because those tiny faces beggin' to make their name, earn daddy's respect, and write their own version of history will be the next generation's fodder afterall. Got to keep those dreams of glory coming somehow.

Pessimistic you might think? No, more like sadly realistic, and if you don't agree with me, fine, that's your prerogative. But I suggest when you've lost as many friends as I have, seen the peripheral damage, had the power to change things but were impotent in using it, then come back and talk to me. Walk a mile in my boots and all.

I didn't get to Normandy until it was over, being occupied elsewhere, yet there were so many lost souls still wandering about in the aftermath that it looked like the battle could start back up at any moment. Demons scampered about prodding and cajoling those dead young men into followin' their cause. There are damn few angels that hang about battlefields let me tell you. War is strictly the purview of evil. Sure, good understands the necessity but that don't mean they enjoy it. In war somebody always stands to gain something. Angels for their part don't want much. Kind of goes with the territory of giving to others, you know? Since war is always about taking they tend to shy away from battle.

Dying in a blaze of glory huh? You tell me which is more glorious: a phone call or, if they're lucky, maybe a visit to your spouse or parents by men who never met you saying you'd died, or raisin' a family, strugglin' through the years to make ends meet, holding your first child, holding your first grandchild, letting the years take their toll? Glory to you friends, wherever you think you can find it.

There were other warriors at Tunguska with Zeus and me. Note the past tense. Their names aren't important to this story, but don't you worry none. There ain't a day goes by that I don't think of them. I say their names to myself like a mantra during battle, over and over. It ain't exactly vengeance, but it ain't exactly what you would call letting things go either. It can be hard to mourn a friend who doesn't leave a body. One who is gone forever, just swallowed up and incorporated into something else, (that something usually being what they were fightin'). It's enough to drive a sane man crazy. Good thing I ain't never been mistaken for sane………..

***

As the trio of Grey, Raven and Zeus stood on the dark Illinois highway, Harmony's presence came forth in their minds and said, "There is a rest stop a few miles in the direction Peter is traveling. I am directing him there now. Please, come to me, and I will take you there so you can be waiting for him when he arrives."

Zeus moved forward toward the glowing doorway that had opened in front of them without checking to see if the other two followed him or not and disappeared into a flash of illumination. Grey moved to pursue, but stopped when he noticed Raven was not moving along too and said, "You coming darlin'?"

"No," she sighed and shook her head. "I'd rather walk. I have two legs and my own power still. I'll be along shortly. Go check on Pete. I'm sure he'll be a bit frazzled. Probably having a one-sided argument with himself."

Grey put a hand on each of Raven's shoulders and turned her to face him. He stared into her indigo eyes with his gunmetal gray ones. They stood there like that in silence for a time taking the measure of each other. Grey could read another's mind just like Harmony, but it was an invasive violent process if the person did not want to be read. He gently tried to open Raven's mind to his and every time she flinched away. Without wanting to violate his friend's spirit Grey stopped his mental prodding, closed his eyes, shook his head and said, "Alright, you know what you're doing. You're a big girl and I know you'll do what you think is right."

He leaned in and kissed her on the cheek, then turned around. He vanished through the same doorway Zeus had moments earlier, leaving Raven alone in the night. Grey walked into his prairie meadow version of Harmony to find her and Zeus waiting for him only a few paces from where he appeared.

Harmony had her arms folded across her chest and said, "She is not coming, is she?"

Grey leaned forward and kissed Harmony on the cheek, mimicking what he had just done with Raven, (a gesture of imitation that the voice of the Balance chose to ignore). "No, no she ain't," Grey confirmed, "but shouldn't you know that already, darlin'?"

"When I tried to ask her, she slammed our connection down! Just like a spoiled child slamming a door when it does not get its way," Harmony said.

Zeus was shuffling around uncomfortably behind Harmony when Grey smirked, chuckled to himself and said, "Well it's an awful nice night out there, honey. Maybe she just wanted to walk with a little privacy and sort of cool down from the heat of battle and all. Can't say I blame her none." He started to walk by Harmony, kissed her on the top of her head, moseyed a dozen steps but stopped when she roared.

"Jasper Reynolds!" Harmony's voice thundered from every corner of the pasture, echoing around the open field, and rumbling up from the soil. "Do not try that charming 'Awe sucks ma'am' cowboy nonsense with me! I know you are both dodging me, and I will not tolerate it."

Grey did not turn around to acknowledge her ire face to face. He kept his back straight, his hands at his sides, but his head drooped when he quietly said, "Yes Harmony, you will."

Harmony's head rocked back as if Grey had slapped her. Her freckled features morphed to the cold visage of a statue depicting a Roman goddess, her eyes disappeared into black voids, and her voice dropped to temperatures only measurable on the Kelvin scale. She said, "Excuse me?"

Zeus shuffled a bit faster from foot to foot like a child looking for a bathroom and muttered, "Hey…um this looks like it should be a private conversation. I'll…ah…I'll just go check on Pete." He darted past Grey and vanished in a flash of light.

The sunny skies of the prairie meadow vanished under a roiling storm front of cumulonimbus clouds as lighting flashed and thunder boomed. The waist high grasses whipped about under gale force winds. Rolling fields started to literally roll as the earth shook beneath Grey's feet. He turned around to face Harmony. He watched the storm reflect in her black depthless eyes and stood his shaking ground, laughing. "You are many things darlin', but subtle ain't one of them."

"Explain yourself!" she demanded, in what could only vaguely be called Harmony's voice. It seeped up from the ground, blew through the wind, and drove down from the sky. The energy crackled, buffeting Grey's hair about like he was standing in the midst of a hurricane.

"You'll tolerate it darlin' because you don't have a choice," Grey said into the storm. "You've given us your power, but allowed us to keep our autonomy. Was that a mistake? Yes or no, don't matter now does it? You dealt the hand my dear, and we're playing the cards. You want to raise the stakes, or should I call?"

"I could wipe the slate clean, and take all my power back," the voice warned. "I have done it before, and I could do so again. I could deal with things as I did before I enlisted aid from your kind."

"Point of fact, I don't think you could," Grey said quietly, never breaking his gaze from her bottomless well eyes. "You've been neigh omnipresent for so long darlin' I don't think you realize the limits of your own power. Ain't nothing permanent, you know that better than anyone. I ain't challenging you, but you should take a moment to look at things from Raven's perspective, or Zeus', or Pete's. You claim to know them because of what your 'Power' can give you, but how would you feel if the Source or whatever might be stronger than you were constantly whisperin' in your ear, as it were?"

The lightning, thunder, and violent winds tapered down, but the bruise colored clouds still obscured the sky, giving Grey the impression of standing in the eye of a cyclone. Things were calm for now but could disintegrate back into chaos at any moment. Harmony unfolded her arms and closed the distance between her and Grey. The top of her head coming to just below his rough shaven chin, she looked up to meet his gray eyes, and blinked her lids once transforming the black pools back to her typical soft brown.

"Grey," she said, "how do you do it? The emotions, I felt them before humanity had crawled out of the muck, and I still become carried away, but not you. Even when you defy me you still keep your wits."

"I'm just better at hiding it than most is all," Grey said giving her a lopsided grin. "You know that sweetheart; I have my moments. I've been known to cause a storm or two. I just like to think a bit before I act is all."

"Yes," her eyes flashed letting him know this was still shaking ground to be treading, "but it never seems that way."

The sun started to break through, and when she leaned in to rest her head against his chest there was not a cloud in the sky, just a mild spring scented breeze stirring the field. The meadow Harmony and Grey stood in was a picture of American frontier life once again when she told him, "Just be careful, Jasper, and watch out for her…Raven is more fragile than you think."

Grey looked down at Harmony, nodded his head once and turned around. After a half dozen strides he disappeared in a flash at the same spot Zeus had. Harmony stood there watching long after he had gone; godlike power and lack of an actual physiology did not stop a tear from running down her cheek.

***

Grey walked out onto the old pit toilet rest stop. A single whiff of the night breeze told him that only the very desperate traveler was willing to stop here, and even then judging by the smell most just headed over and used the surrounding tree line instead. Grey noticed that Pete had parked the ice cream truck as far from the pit toilets as he could. Zeus was standing outside munching on a Drumstick talking with Pete when Grey drew close enough for them to notice. Zeus sighed audibly and wiped an arm across his face clearing away the melted vanilla ice cream and bits of chopped nuts that were stuck in his mustache. With his face temporarily clear of debris Zeus asked, "Everything okay Grey?"

"Just fine Zeus, and how you doin' Pete?"

"Oh I'm just dandy Grey," Pete said. "There's nothing like driving an ice cream truck into an open sewer on a clear autumn night. Plus I had to fight that giant pig demon I ran over earlier. Oh and I was called an amateur by a little squirrel demon that sounded like *Darth Vader*."

"Good, glad to hear it," Grey said ignoring Pete completely. "Zeus, you mind tossin' me one of tho-"

Grey stopped midsentence because Zeus was already tossing him a Drumstick underhand out of the box he had pilfered from the truck. The big man motioned to Pete and raised his bushy eyebrows questioningly. When Pete shook his head to decline, Zeus just shrugged his massive shoulders and pulled another one out for himself. He unwrapped the frozen novelty and asked around a massive mouthful, "So now what?"

"Regroup, see if Harmony can scrape up any extra help, and then go in guerilla warfare style, hit and run, pick Legion apart by pieces. We start now, but when the sun rises we double the pace," Grey instructed while taking a bite from his cone.

Zeus grunted and nodded dislodging the chucks of nuts and chocolate glaze that had accumulated in his beard. Pete sighed, then reached into what was left of the vending window, rooted around knocking over a piece of charred, and passed Zeus a handful of napkins. The big man took the proffered handful but tossed them over his shoulder, sticking his tongue out at Pete. Rolling his eyes, Pete turned to Grey. "What about the girl in the truck? That kid is going to need some serious therapy man."

"She's safest where she is Pete," Grey said, and explained further when Pete's face contorted into a look of dubiety. "That's as far as our responsibility to her goes. Legion only wanted her to draw me out, but that's a moot point now. She'll wake up confused, but as long as Zeus didn't steal this truck, she'll be fine. She'll call a friend to come out here and pick her up. They'll assume somebody slipped her a roofie, and over time she'll convince herself she imagined most if not all of it."

"No," Zeus corrected in a solemn voice. "I paid cash for it boss. It made the owner real happy too. He owed money to a loan shark over some gambling debts or something."

"Okay," Pete said shaking his head as if to clear it. "So we just leave her out here? In the middle of nowhere? What if more demons come along?"

"They won't," Grey said. "Legion has claimed this town. Hell, Pete, you saw what it did to those two demons at that construction site. Most demons won't venture this close with Legion being so aggressive lately, and even if they did, they wouldn't risk doing anything to her and drawin Harmony's attention their way, meaning 'my' attention. You may not have noticed Pete, but with a few notable exceptions like Legion or Malign, most demons are scared of me. I'm the boogie man, the guy the monsters fear."

"No shit, really? You hide it so well Grey," Pete said sarcastically, then bringing his hand up to his forehead, opening and closing his fist trying to make it look like a third eye asked, "So all those demons we saw in town today among the shadows were under Legion's sway? Darth squirrel wasn't."

"Yeah, most of them probably were, with a few exceptions like that little fello-" Grey was interrupted by Zeus who blurted, "Hey, shouldn't Raven have been here by now?"

"Wait, why isn't she with you guys?" Pete asked looking around as if he expected her to jump out at him from the pit toilets.

"She's playing a gambit," Grey said, not meeting the questioning expressions on the other men's faces.

"What?" both Pete and Zeus asked simultaneously. Grey took a deep breath, looked up to the night sky and said, "Raven let herself be taken hostage by Legion. She felt she would be able to trick it into thinkin' it had control of her, and that it could use her as leverage to draw me out. That's the opening we need. We'll split up, divide and conquer, and when I'm in place Raven will spring her trap. She didn't let Harmony know because she knew that Harmony would never risk Legion converting Raven to its purposes, so I distracted Harmony while Raven made her move. She may not be happy about it but it's too late now. At least that was what I was able to read off of the girl; she was blockin' me for some damn fool reason. For better or worse the pieces are in motion boys…Game on."

***

The dried out bases of this year's harvested corn stalks brushed against Raven's feet as she ran cross country. She did not want to go back through town via the highway and risk tipping Legion off to where Grey and the boys had gone to ground. Many demons were dim-witted fools, easily convinced of their own superiority, but Legion had been around too long to be taken so lightly. If she waltzed back into town the way they had gone Legion was bound to smell a rat and send more troops out past where they had destroyed that behemoth. Her best chance of tricking Legion into believing it had trapped her legitimately, proving to it that she did not want to be captured, was to circle round and approach from a different direction.

She only hoped that Legion would not be in a rage after Grey had escaped its trap, that it was thinking clearly enough to use her as leverage and not kill her outright. The trick would be to make her capture look convincing enough without making it a last stand or giving up too easily. Grey knew what she was planning; the man could read people, living or dead, angel or demon, better than anyone she had ever known. It was one of the skills she had hoped he would be able to teach her someday, but perhaps it would become another of those abilities only he could manifest. Raven regretted that she had to block him as she had, but if he had seen exactly what she was thinking and how she was feeling he never would have let her go. She did not want him to see her as weak, ever.

She knew he was tired (if anybody deserved a rest it was Grey) but she was not ready to let him go. *It is always hardest to let go of our heroes, admitting they are just as human as we are, faults and all*, she thought to herself, *but damn it! I lost one family in this world. I don't want to lose another, not him.*

"If he reads people so well you stupid girl, then he knows how you feel about him," she said, giving voice to her thoughts instead of letting them run around inside. "He only sees you as a daughter, and loves you like any parent would. Hell he doesn't even love Harmony the way you want him to love you! It's his weakness, because it requires giving too much of himself, and you always go running off trying to prove yourself to him like a fucking love struck puppy dog!"

She stopped her one sided dialogue as the night-darkened houses started appearing in clusters, letting her know she was getting closer to town. Along with the homes, Raven started to see the occasional three-eyed gaze coming from the concealment of shrubs, porches, or under cars, wherever the cover was deepest. Doing her best to ignore them and not give away that she was alert to their presence, she waited until the demons started trailing her in groups before reacting to them. Stealth was a skill some evil creatures had a plethora of experience with, but Legion had spent so much time hiding that it seemed not to care how well its minions concealed themselves. When the demons following her had amassed to the size of a small parade Raven said, "Might as well thin the herd a bit for Grey."

When she stopped running, Raven stood frozen in the middle of the rural road where the first street lights into town were visible a few miles in front of her, a lone figure with a demonic mob trailing out behind her. The more courageous demons started closing in, but most stayed at a safe distance. Either Legion was testing the waters for a trap, or the individual intelligences that the controlling demon allowed them to retain had seen her in action before and were leery of what she could do. Raven turned and started shooting before any of the demons made their move. The closest few paid for their courage with their lives, dissolving into pools of negative energy before the other demons had even registered that they were under attack.

Raven, by going on the offensive, had triggered the start of the chaos. Some of the smaller demons ran off into the night, others charged her only to be destroyed, and a few just stood frozen in place watching their doom approach in tight black leather pants. For a time it looked like Raven would wipe them all out and go strolling into town without a scratch. Each of her bullets found their mark, piercing Legion's third eye. There was no energy wasted or spilled over into the physical world as she mowed down the demon hoard that had had the temerity to stand against her. Then the small demons that had fled at the battle's onslaught returned riding the vulture bat creatures like hang gliders. Raven started firing into the air when she heard the demons' wails closing in. Had the creatures been subject strictly to the laws of the physical world she still may have prevailed, but punching holes through the wings of monsters made more of shadow than substance did not impede their aerodynamics one bit.

The tiny demons shrieked high pitched battle cries as they let go of their winged mounts, and dropped onto Raven like ferocious living warheads. The smaller demons clung to her, barbing her flesh and digging in like ticks. She shot off the ones she could reach, but more and more started to cling on, driving her down to her knees forming a dog pile of writhing black bodies. The guns disappeared from her hands as she started to send off imprecise energy bolts like Zeus preferred. She exploded the diminutive bodies with the infusion of energy like overcooked popcorn kernels, and peeled off the shadow remnants of their dead deflated corpses when they continued to cling to her.

The larger winged demons hovered over her undeterred by the blasts. Then they swooped down and succeeded with their bulk where their smaller brethren had failed, covering her in a cloak of their bodies as they latched on. With a final scream of expelled power, aided by a blue wave of concussive force, Raven sent all of the demons smoking and screaming from her body out into the night.

She sat kneeling on the scorched asphalt in the center of an open ring. Quickly becoming surrounded by snarling demonic bodies, chin resting on her chest, panting heavily, Raven was trying to regain her strength when she heard footsteps that made her raise her head. The dark sea of creatures parted as the tall two eyed form of Legion strode over to tower above her. Raven could see the pigtailed girl skipping around behind him, twirling her doll by one patchwork arm in a halting jerky dance.

"Well, well, well," said Legion crouching down to Raven's level, "Look what we have here, the cowboy's little pet bird. Tell me little bird, how long do you think it will take before your screams cease to entertain me?"

Things started going dark for Raven as Legion struck with the speed of a serpent, its long fingered hand wrapped tightly around her throat lifting her from the ground. It shook her body much the same way the little girl was shaking her dolly. Then Legion turned around, dragging her back into town in the fashion of a cartoon caveman towing his would be bride. She could feel some of Legion's energy seeping into her, black tendrils seeking to violate her spirit, grasping at the core of her being. Before it could infiltrate too deeply into her, she slammed a defensive wall around what portions of her psyche that she could. The last thought she had before the darkness claimed her consciousness was, *At least that part was easy.*

Chapter 20

Pride, man oh man that is one bitter bitch of a pill to swallow ain't it? I've seen stubborn toddlers, not yet out of diapers, jam a square peg into a round hole just to make it fit. Grown men and women will die before they admit to an error, all because of pride. Empires have fallen, monarchies toppled, and dictatorships destroyed all over that single obstinate mindset, pride.

It seems silly to me. No error in judgment or personality trait is worth destruction my friends. We all fall to something at some point; why would you let the end come over pride? It's no fun to admit you were wrong, but damnation how could it be more painful than oblivion for you to shrug your shoulders and say, "Shit, I guess I was wrong on this or that."

Some folks are more prideful than others. It saddens me to think how it's usually the most prideful who affect things on a large scale, often instigating catastrophic changes for mankind. I stood there in 1961 watching them build that Berlin Wall. Twenty-eight years later standin' in the same damn spot I watched that symbol of pride fall. You can argue the politics behind it if you like, but pride was the root. Pride is a deep runnin' taproot that will slowly erode the strongest wall.

Pride can make a person do foolish things, say hurtful curses, and commit any manner of silly acts.

This here example may offend some of you folks, but I don't mean it to. I just want to illustrate what pride can do, from a certain point of view.

Christians use the story of poor old Job as a lesson in how faith in God don't depend on what a man is given in his livin' days. I ain't arguing that mind you, but let's take a look at that story from a different perspective. The devil is our instigator and he goes to God saying, "Hast not thou made a hedge about him, and about his house, and about all that he hath on every side? Thou hast blessed the work of his hands, and his substance is increased in the land. But put forth thine hand now, and touch all that he hath, and he will curse thee to thy face."

....Alright, Grey's Cliffs Notes version, "God, you gave Job everything, take it away and he's going to call you an ass.".....

So long story short God takes everything from Job in a fit of pride to show that old agitator Satan that his man Job loves him no matter what God does or does not do to him. Either way you look at it God tortured a man because Satan challenged Him, prickin'

264

his pride, or the devil manipulated God into torturing that man Job to satisfy his pride. This is the omnipotent all knowin' God folks, and he gave into his pride. What are a bunch of regular everyday folk to do with theirs?

I never heard a good answer to that one friend, just roll with it I guess, that's all we can do.

I've swallowed more than my fair share of pride over the years, believe you me. The hardest morsels to choke down, the ones that lodge in your throat like a burr are the times you are trying to help others. It don't seem right that your pride should trip you up when all you're doing is helping, but there's what we think is right, and then there's what is. Better to choke your pride down than to let it choke you…….

***

When Raven regained awareness there were demonic faces leering and laughing down at her. She screamed, sitting up in a crouch, flailing her arms about for meager cover thinking she was back in Poland. With all that had happened to her since having been a hallucination to escape those horrific creatures, Legion's cruel chuckle was actually a welcome sound. It meant that she had not dreamed up an escape. It meant she could defend herself unlike before. It meant that Grey was out there and he would be coming for her. Legion's voice interrupted her thoughts, "Oh I count on that little bird, but if you want to fight me too much we can certainly go back to 1942 for a visit. All those memories are still locked inside you, waiting for the right touch to help them escape. I was not personally involved in that little bit of genocidal mayhem, so I am quite interested to see what nightmares you have roiling around in there." It caressed a shadowed talon along her temple as it said the last.

Legion reasserted its mental control to stop her flailing, forcing her to lie down prone on her back. She could feel Legion's restraining claws piercing into her left arm, dark roots digging into her, seeking dominion over thought and action. Her right side and lower half were completely under her control still. Not wanting Legion to realize that she had more control than it thought, she lay there enduring the jeers and prodding of Legion's pets as the master demon invaded her mind.

It was difficult to shut out the vial things they were doing since it was her spirit and mind that they were ransacking and not a physical body. Needing to gather her bearings she escaped to that section of her mind she had secured for herself before Legion's torture began, a mental retreat to run for like many victims of violent crimes create. The method of loci was one of the first lessons Grey had insisted she learn when she started her tutelage under him. He had said, "A mental palace is a mnemonic tool darlin', and like any tool it can be used as a weapon or as a defense. Since you ain't nothing but mind now, having a stronghold to run to in an emergency could save what's left of you."

Well Grey, I'm here, now what? she thought as she looked out from behind the windows of her memory palace. Those windows provided her with a vista of whatever her mental body's eyes were focused on. "Thoughts within thoughts," Grey's voice echoed around the walls of her defensive mental bunker. She had created a literal war bunker of poured concrete and its windows were reinforced with metal mesh. "Master those thoughts darlin'. Marshal them, and keep them from runnin' around. As long as you got control, ain't nobody else going to take it from you. Focus."

With a flick of her wrist Raven shut the blinds on the bunker's windows. Standing in the middle of her retreat she breathed in and out. Time meant nothing. She breathed, she focused, and when she had control of her thoughts again, she opened her vision. The black leering faces were still violating her exterior, but when she focused past them she was able to reconnoiter her surroundings. That gave her something to concentrate on. She was under a roof and not outside. The echoing of

267

Legion's voice told her she was in a smallish room. *Was it still the same night? How long had she been away from herself? Was it the next day and Legion was hiding from the light?* More and more questions cropped up for Raven without the comfort of answers. Frustration started to slip in, and she lost control of her focus when a particularly grotesque demon ran its tongue up her right thigh. Sensation bled into her memory bunker as the demon's tongue lingered momentarily at her hips then trailed up her torso to hover grinning directly over her face. Its tongue lolled from its slavering jaws and all three of its eyes twinkled in malicious glee until Raven threw open the door to her mental bunker and brought a gun up in her right hand, blowing the demon's head completely off of its body in a shower of black tarry ichor and sparks of light, both of which melted into Raven's skin as they cascaded down.

The other hovering demons scattered to the edges of the room screeching and gesticulating obscenely at her. Legion chuckled and said, "Very good little bird...I knew there was still some fire in there. Now, show me where you are hiding it."

Raven could feel Legion sending its energy further into her, seeking out the area it had not taken control of and corrupted yet. The gun she had manifested in her hand disappeared, and she screamed out in pain as Legion's presence tore through her like shards of glass in a tornado, ripping open thousands of tiny holes and digging into them, seeking a way to gain control. The hardest part was to fight back just enough to let it know she was still resisting, but not give away how much she had held in reserve until the moment was right. *Come on Grey*, she thought in that walled off bunker she was barely holding together. *I don't know how long I can do this.*

Legion started laughing out loud. The hideous sound shook the concrete slabs of her bunker dislodging tiny pebbles to scatter and roll about the room. Raven did not know if the laughter was out of enjoyment in its labors or if some of what she had been thinking had leaked through. She hoped it was the former but was terrified that it was the latter. More laughter raced through her mind, chasing her consciousness like a predator running down its prey, and Raven could only reinforce her walls with screams.

***

"Grey! Hey Grey, you alright man?" Pete asked. Grey was staring off into the distance as the sun rose. The remnants of the demon he had just destroyed melted around his boots as Pete tried to get his attention.

"I'm fine Pete," Grey said, not looking away from the rapidly lightening deep russet and burgundy colored horizon. "But I don't know if Raven will be able to hold out much longer. She's strong, but so is a diamond. If that demon finds her fracture lines she'll crumble apart in pretty little pieces just like a precious gem. We have to thin out Legion's hoard as much as we can while the sun provides us cover. I just hope that bastard leaves enough of her to come back to us when we need her."

"Bwaa Ha! Got you, you slippery son of a bitch," Zeus bellowed interrupting their conversation. Both Pete and Grey turned away from the dawn's light to see him dragging the tail of the five-headed snake demon over his left shoulder. He was several blocks away from them on the town's main street. The serpent demon thrashed and hissed as Zeus pulled its entire length out of a dark alley into the first rays of the sun. Laid out in full the monster was nearly half as long as a city block. Once it realized its thrashing was not going to deter the large man, the demon switched tactics, arched its body up and struck down at Zeus with all five sets of fangs open.

"Oh! The grumpy little snake wants to play, does it?" Zeus yelled and dodged to the right with a shoulder roll as the demon struck, crushing its maws into the sidewalk with the force of a locomotive, but he never let go of the thing's tail. Once he had bounded back to his feet Zeus grinned and said, "My turn."

The burly giant grabbed a hold of the demon's tail with both hands. He wrapped the tip of the serpent's tail around his forearms and started to rotate his shoulders up and around his body like an Olympian hammer thrower. The demon fought the first few rotations, but soon it became subject to Zeus' inertia and left the ground. Zeus roared with laughter as he swung the huge Naga demon over his head around and around, and with a grunt of effort he brought his arms forward slamming it into the ground. Another grunt of effort and heave of shoulders brought the snake demon up and over Zeus' head to land flat out on the other side. Zeus continued to slam the monster back and forth until all five heads stopped hissing, and with a hearty "Bwaaa!" he stopped and sent a jolt of light up the limp creature's back. The five heads exploded out the end in a firework force of gore, and the rest of the body dissolved in the sunlight.

Zeus turned to his friends grinning seeking their approval. Grey chuckled, and gave the big man thumbs up. Pete clapped his hands but quietly said to Grey, "Why am I reminded of *Bamm-Bamm* from the old *Flintstones* cartoons?"

Grey smiled and said, "Me too, but you're closer to the truth there than you know my friend." He walked away from Pete over to

Zeus without elaboration. Pete watched as Zeus made hand gestures to describe what he had done in case Grey had missed any of it, and Pete was struck again by how much everyone sought out Grey's approval. Even this hulking Viking of a man wanted Grey to toss him a colloquial western comment of affirmation.

"And he wants you to replace him Pete?" Pete said to himself. "Yeah right." "Give yourself time Peter," Harmony's voice echoed in his mind. "You do not have to take his place tomorrow. An eternity can pass in an eye blink as you are now, and you are already learning. You see what a leader he is, but many of the others like Zeus over there do not see past his presence. You see the approval they seek even if they do not, so watch how Grey handles things and emulate him."

"Alright darlin'," Pete said imitating Grey's drawl.

"Not that much emulation Peter," Harmony said with humor evident in her voice.

***

The angels and beings of light that Pete had seen in such abundance the previous morning were not out in the same force today as they went about their task of dragging Legion's demons out and exterminating them. The few luminous entities that did show themselves kept to watching from a distance like dour compassionate gargoyles perched atop buildings or scared neon deer peeking out from behind trees and bushes. Pete sent a flock of pixie-like lights soaring up into the sky as he pursued a panther demon through the evergreen hedge the lights were perched upon.

The demon gained speed whenever it hit a shadow from a house or car but slowed tremendously when it was exposed to the sun. The creature's mass eroded slowly as the energy from the sun ate into it; according to Grey all Pete had to do to destroy it was prolong that exposure indefinitely and the demon would eventually disappear altogether. *Easier said than done*, Pete thought. *If the damn thing isn't doing its Carl Lewis impersonation through the city streets, then it just sinks into the ground.*

Pete could hear Zeus one street over calling, "Here kitty, kitty, kitty," and knew he was on the hunt for the last remaining panther demon. Grey had said that Legion's panthers were not like the other demons it took possession of. The panthers had been strong demons that Legion allowed to have more autonomy. Grey had likened them to mob enforcers that Legion sent out to collect owed debts. That was why they had been around Tommy and his friends. If Grey had not forced its hand, eventually Legion's panthers would have brought Tommy and all of his friends to their master.

The other demons Legion controlled were mostly mindless drones or complete extensions of Legion itself, so unless Legion had more panthers hidden somewhere in reserve, these two were the last. Grey had added though that if Raven had overplayed her hand there was a chance that Legion would convert her into another panther to face them, although her power would never allow the monster to fully subvert her. That thought provided Pete with the terrifying image of a demon enhanced by Legion's power coupled with Raven's skills. It would be a reckoning force.

Distracted by these thoughts Pete almost ran directly into Zeus when they rounded their corners, chasing their respective panthers down as the slim light eroded creatures slipped down the same storm drain. "Damn!" Zeus yelled. "Quick little buggers huh?"

"Yeah," Pete agreed distractedly. "Hey Zeus, I was wondering, do you think Legion will be able to turn Raven into one of those panther things? Grey's worried that might happen."

Without hesitation Zeus shook his head and said, "Not a chance. And even if it did, that bitch is so stubborn she'd just turn on her new master, and claw its three eyes out! Bwaa!...Oh hey when we get her back don't tell her I called her a name, okay, please?"

Zeus said that last with such an earnest look on his face and pleading seriousness in his voice that any sarcastic or teasing remarks Pete had been planning died before he could say them. He nodded his head with as much gravity as he could. Zeus let out a huge sigh saying, "Thanks buddy. Oh hey look! I see another one under that delivery truck!" He took off at a sprint, dove head first under one side of the truck, somersaulting out the other with a squirming two faced rodent demon the size of a basketball in one huge fist. It was trying to bite him but both heads were turning in opposite directs, and Zeus held tightly on to its scruff.

He lifted it up out to his side and started sending jolts of yellow light into its trashing body. The barrage of light swelled the demon to the size of a balloon, and with a resounding bang the demon exploded. Zeus smiled, waved at Pete, and started skipping away. It took Pete a few moments to realize that the big man was whistling *Pop Goes the Weasel*.

***

"I need any extra hands you can spare," Grey said to Harmony. He had not gone back to her fully, but chose to speak to her while going about the business of exterminating any demons he could find. To Grey's way of thinking there was no point wasting valuable time performing one job at a time when a man could multitask.

"Now you would like my assistance?" Harmony asked. "I was under the impression that you and Raven could handle this without my help."

"Spiteful doesn't suit you darlin'," Grey said. "We have a job to do here, and any aid you can send our way would make it that much easier."

"Since when have you ever done things the easy way, Jasper?" Harmony asked.

Grey sighed and said, "Since I started to believe you were right, okay? I don't know for sure if Raven can hold out against Legion long enough for me to finish this, and if I had a few more folks out there thinning the herd with Zeus and Pete, I may be able to save her before it's too late."

"I cannot argue with the truth. This discussion is on hold for another time, but do not think for a moment I will let it go permanently, Jasper Reynolds. But in all honesty I do not have that many agents to spare. Things have been more turbulent than normal lately, but I do believe I can send Ronin, Wandjina, and Awha. Their corners-"

"Ronin's going to be pissed having to play back up," Grey interrupted.

"Perhaps this is your personality rubbing off on me, Jasper," Harmony said, "but when isn't he? As I was saying their corners of the world are the most serene at the moment; look for them soon. To save you time I will let them know what is transpiring and set them loose on the hunt so you will have no need to bring them up to speed. Good luck Grey."

"Thank you darlin'," Grey said. He reached down and pulled a piglet-sized creature out from behind a dumpster and crushed it under the heel of his boot in a shower of sparks.

***

"Reinforcements are on the way boys!" Grey shouted to Zeus and Pete from across the park, the same park where they had originally set foot in this town. The two of them had run something to ground in the rafters of the picnic shelter. They were taking turns jumping up and swiping at it, looking to Grey like a pair of drunks swinging at a piñata.

Whatever it was it avoided the men deftly, even when Pete climbed up on the stacked picnic tables to close the distance. He fell back down on his rear after a single swing slid the precariously balanced tables out from under his physical shell body.

Behind Grey a cultured voice spoke into the aftermath of the clatters and clanks from the toppling tables, "On the contrary, reinforcements are here."

"How you doin' Ronin?" Grey asked without turning around. A very slender and very tall Japanese man in a three piece business suit complete with pinstriped fedora cocked at a jaunty angle stepped into Grey's peripheral vision. He said, "I was just fine, enjoying a bit of peace actually, pursuing some of the more physical and cerebral pleasures we are so rarely allowed the time for. Then Harmony comes calling saying the great cowboy Grey needs a hand exterminating a demon that he was supposed to have destroyed before I was even born."

"Good to see you too Ronin," Grey said as if the man had greeted him warmly after years spent apart. "Don't be sore over havin' to play SWAT for me. I've done it for you more than a time or two. Are the ladies with you?"

"No, they are out doing your job hunting out this infestation," Ronin corrected, and looking over at Zeus and Pete he added, "unlike your boys goofing around down there. What are they doing? Playing keep away?"

"I doubt that. Hey guys! What's going on down there?" Grey yelled. Zeus and Pete looked up and walked to the edge of the shelter. Pete rubbing at his backside yelled, "We stopped for lunch and that damn raccoon snuck up on us and stole our French fries. We can't get them back."

A greasy wrinkled paper bag was launched from the rafters smacking into the back of Pete's head when he finished speaking, and a chattering sound that was very close to laughter followed as the raccoon jumped down from the rafters onto a picnic table and sprinted off at a speed no animal could naturally attain. Pete swore and shouted, "Oh hell no! Zeus, grab the fries! I'm getting that little bastard," and he ran off in the raccoon's wake.

"Well Ronin," Grey said, chuckling, and rubbing the back of his neck. "I'll be damned; you were right after all."

The tall Japanese man did not reciprocate Grey's chagrined smile as he turned, sighing, and walked away.

"Yep," Grey said to himself, "good to see you too."

***

The day wore on in one big game of "hide and seek" with Legion's hoard and Harmony's soldiers of the Balance. Monsters were pulled from under cars, yanked out of the ground, fished out of storm drains, evicted from houses, garages, sheds and buildings. Zeus was forced to drag a chimp-like demon out of a port-o-potty, kicking and thrashing so wildly the pair shattered the fiberglass outhouse in a thunderous clamor.

Introductions between the foreign warriors and Pete were made on the run because Grey was unwilling to stop the hunt for pleasantries. Pete decided he liked the diminutive Awha. She had the complexion of a South Asian or Pacific Islander and wore a simple white one piece garment with a pair of oversized novelty sunglasses. It also helped endear her to him when she laughed at the resulting mess of Zeus' and in lilting high pitched voice said, "Explosive diarrhea."

The androgynous Wandjina was a different story. Pete was not sure how to take her. Grey had said it was a she, but the constant blurring of her skin and lack of speech made her difficult to understand; she was not rude, just distant, and almost alien or ghost like. *Ironic*, he thought, *I guess we're all ghosts, but she's more ghost than most.*

Ronin on the other hand was an uptight pretentious prick, but with decades of teaching at an Ivy League school Pete had plenty of experience interacting with his type. Pete did what he could to keep things "strictly business" in his interactions with Ronin without the run-on dialogue and elaborations he was prone to. Ronin was not impressed. He was not a man to be impressed by much, be it taciturn conversation or running dialogue.

His lack of impression was only exacerbated when Ronin saved Pete's life. Pete chased what he thought was only a small rodent-like demon too far into an alley as the afternoon gave the shadows depth. One of the hulking rhinoceros dragon demons that had survived the previous night's battle was lurking behind a dumpster, and it snatched Pete off the ground with claws the size of Buicks. Pete thrashed about, throwing energy wildly around, but he could not drive enough power into the brute to even slow it down. He was able to break free of its grip but only by grabbing a hold of one of the huge horns that sprouted from the monster's forehead and wiggling his lower half out. The demon pawed at its face a few times and tried to ram Pete into a wall, but the demon was either too slow or stupid to realize the solid matter would do little to dislodge its unwanted passenger in their current condition.

Pete screamed as the demon charged into the adjoining brick wall, passing through it like a spoon through Jell-O, only to find himself in the women's shower room of the local gym. No energy had spilled over into the physical world, and several young women were going about their post workout ablutions without the slightest inkling that there was a man holding on to a demon's horns right next to them. Pete screamed again as the demon yanked him back out, but in disappointment not terror.

When it had pulled clear of the wall the beast tried changing tactics and it shook its massive head from side to side like a waterlogged canine. Pete held on under the wild gyrations but spun around on the horn he was hugging so he faced the monster's rear end affording him a front row seat as a tall Japanese man soared down from the roof of the nearest building driving a coalesced blade of energy into the back of the demon's skull. The behemoth gave one feeble groan, shuddered, and then dissolved underneath both men.

"Wow," Pete said dusting himself off. "Thanks man, I owe you one."

"Why don't we just start a tab, Buckwheat?" Ronin answered primly and stalked back off into the waning daylight.

"Hey! Wait! Did Grey tell you to call me that?" Pete called after him. "Or Zeus? It was Zeus wasn't it?"

"Bwaaa Hahahaha!" Zeus' raucous laugh echoed around the alley, and a shaggy head quickly darted back from the rooftop rim that Ronin had so recently dropped down from.

"Asshole!" Pete shouted up after him.

Chapter 21

I think the worst type of fool is the man who fools himself. Self-delusion folks, it's the saddest thing ain't it? Lie to your friends, lie to your family, definitely lie to your enemies, but don't you ever lie to yourself. But if you feel that you must, at least respect your own cognition enough to not believe your lies. A great poet once said,

"How do you sate a shadow

Adding light makes it grow

Extinguish the light, and darkness will consume

Fear the perpetual night and gloom

Rationality breeds hope from despair

For without light, darkness cannot compare

One will not exist without the other

A balance of both is the truth to uncover"

Well I don't know about great or not. I just made that verse up, but see what I mean about self-delusion? It's an easy trap to fall into because it's one we lay for ourselves. The

Ego and Id love to mess with a man's mind. They're his own inner demons if you will.

It's a sad shitty truth how often we can be our own worst enemy.

Alexander the Great once told me, "Grey, I thought I should rule the world. Not that I could, that I should. Do you see my folly? And did I learn from my self-delusion? Of course not. I carried that same mentality into the afterlife as well."

That's from a man who had created such a myth for himself in life that most of you folks think his last name was "the Great!" If great men can be self-deluded and foolish, then I say we should just try to be men and leave greatness alone……..

***

"He doesn't love you," purred a new voice inside Raven's mental bunker. It was neither Harmony nor Grey nor Legion speaking to her. It was strange she mused, how quickly she accepted oddities like someone speaking within her thoughts, an occurrence that would have been cause for cataclysmic concerns in her physical life. The voices just seemed to be a common practice now. The voice continued seeping from the windows and oozing from the walls, "He isn't coming for you, is he? He'd have been here by now if he was."

"He's coming," Raven answered. She shouted her response to the invisible presence behind the voice wherever it was. "I've just lost my ability to measure the passage of time, but he's coming. He came for me once when he didn't have to. He'll come."

"Maybe, maybe not," the purring voice continued. "He has to have trimmed Legion down by now. It's been at the minimum a day, maybe more. He could cause some serious damage in a day couldn't he?"

"Who's to say he hasn't?" Raven snapped in retort.

"Do you honestly think Legion would just sit back and let Grey dismantle the army it took a century to assemble and not try using you as bait to stop him?" the voice cooed.

"If it's still daylight Legion wouldn't risk taking on Grey with such a handicap," Raven insisted. "Besides Grey escaped it in the pitch of night. Legion would be no match for him in the sunlight."

"Maybe, maybe not," the voice purred again. "He could just be chalking you up to a lost cause. He could train Pete and just move on. He is planning on leaving us anyway, isn't he? Why bother with the likes of you?"

"Shut up!" Raven screamed at the voice. "Just shut up and leave me alone! He's coming for me…please Grey… Come for me."

The voice laughed but held any other comments or opinions in check for the moment.

***

Pete had had trouble all day long going about exterminating demons in full view of the physical world around them. Cars passed and people walked by while Harmony's soldiers fought to keep the Balance, slaughtering demons in front of real estate agents showing houses, children riding bikes, and old men playing chess. *There is so much more to the universe,* Pete thought. *People have no idea how little of it they can see.* He had this point driven home as a car drove through him as he chased down a demon in the middle of the street. The Kia passed through him without slowing, and Pete felt a small tug on his legs, but otherwise the world and its physical passengers spun on none the wiser.

With night's fall the town shut down once again. In most suburban towns the businesses would have stayed open past six p.m., but Legion had been insinuating itself into the local's world slowly. Shops that once stayed open late into the evening started keeping daylight hours only. The business owner's blamed it on the unhealthy influence of the urban sprawl edging into their neighborhoods, yet all the problems they referred to were caused by locals who barely ventured past the cornfield boundaries of their city.

The leaders of the various church congregations in the small town preached about hellfire, and guided their parishioners to embrace a "hardworking family values type" of living, up with the dawn and to bed with the dusk. Only the reckless, unfortunate, or demonically influenced ventured out after dark. With Legion's army depleted by their day's labor the city was giving off the feel of an abandoned ghost town. It would be some time before the inhabitants started to venture out of doors again when the sunset.

"This town is tainted," Ronin said to Grey as they stood watching the lights in homes turn off before the dusk had turned to full night. "The people attempt to disguise their fear as piety."

"Ain't that often the case wherever we go?" Grey asked arms folded across his chest, breathing in the cool night air. A front had blown through as the day passed, the clear nights they had been afforded previously were gone, and the sky threatened to dump heavy, chilling rain.

"Touché," Ronin said. "So how big of a dent do you think we made?"

"Enough," Grey answered. "At least it will have to be."

"Ah, it is always so encouraging to work with you Grey. I will go gather the troops for your no doubt inspiring speech so we may present a united front." Ronin suited action to words, and soon all six of them were gathered around a small corner park on the downtown main street. Grey surveyed those who would stand with him against the darkness. They sat or stood in various poses of relaxation, from Ronin's straight backed samurai at ease to Zeus who was lying down on the edge of a small fountain playing in the water. They were an eclectic but honorable crew to Grey's mind.

"Well?" blurted Zeus, "now what?"

"We wait," Grey said. "We've done what we could with the daylight, and now we wait and see what Legion has left to throw at us. Stay together, watch each other's backs, and wait. Something tells me it won't be long."

As it turned out Grey was right, but instead of a roaring army of three-eyed nightmarish creatures using the cover of darkness to barrel down the street toward them, they heard a rhythmic ticking. In the small puddles of illumination cast down by the few working streetlights a pigtailed auburn-haired head could be seen skipping in their direction, her dolly snuggled securely once again in its front facing baby carrier. The girl stopped in the shadows cast by the last streetlight before the corner park where they were waiting. She was almost within reach of Grey when she cleared her throat dramatically and piped up in her sing song voice:

"The cowboy wants to save the day

If he's quick enough he just may

There's a score to settle, a debt to pay

So listen to what Dolly has to say"

The Raggedy Anne doll sat up in its carrier, and the third eye Pete had seen stitched there before opened wide. The doll moved its stubby arms about in a stretch and cleared its throat. It was Legion's deep bestial voice that came from the tiny thread lined lips to finish the rhyme, "If you have the balls, walk this way."

The girl and her doll turned around and started skipping slowly back in the direction they had come from. Grey followed without comment and the others fell in behind him. Ronin watched the girl's back from over Grey's shoulder and said to no one in particular, "Now that was just downright disturbing."

"Do you think he loves her?" Raven asked the voice. In a place where time had no meaning she could not tell if she had been speaking to it long or for only a short while. It hardly mattered in any event because the voice had become her only companion, a shred of sanity in an insane existence.

"Loves who my dear?" the voice inquired back.

"Harmony. Does Grey love her, do you think? Everyone says he's her favorite, but what does that mean? She wasn't human like we were, right? What does she know of love? She's no more human than the Source." Raven gave voice to these questions that had long plagued her.

"Maybe, maybe not," the voice responded. "She has power, yes? Or is she power? Is it power he loves? He does, doesn't he? All men do, you know that."

"Maybe, but who doesn't love power?" she asked. "Gender has nothing to do with it. He could still love me. He does love me. Harmony could just be his dealer, the way he gets his fix."

"Junkies would do nearly anything to get a fix, you know that too."

"Shut up, he loves me."

"Maybe… maybe not," the voice purred.

***

The odd assortment of troopers for the Balance followed the little girl and her doll as she skipped down dark, deadly quiet streets. Traveling through neighborhoods, the group retraced routes they had been on earlier that day while clearing out the demonic infestation, all the while moving forward to the rhythmic ticking of the girl's jump rope. When they passed the shopping plaza with Giono's pizzeria and started winding back along Main Street Pete could no longer hold his tongue.

"Hey! Creepy Longstocking," Pete shouted. "Where are you taking us? We've gone in one big ass circle and we're almost back to where we started. What gives?"

She giggled but just kept on skipping without turning around.

"Shit!" Grey yelled smacking himself on the forehead with an open palm. "I can't believe I was so stupid! That son of a bitch is delaying us. It must be close to turning her. Why destroy me when he can send whatever is left of Raven to do it for him! Break me before it takes me."

"Damn, what do we do?" Pete asked stopping their now fruitless journey.

"You're with me, Pete. The rest of you run interference for us. That bastard has to still be at the football stadium somewhere. It's the furthest from where we are now. We've just been circling the damn thing. Let's go Pete," Grey said and took off in the direction that would take him to the stadium by the most direct route. He stumbled to a stop when the last two panther demons dropped down from nearby rooftops to block his progress. With an indecipherable ululating noise Wandjina flung herself onto the closest one. Awha started shooting bolts of azure lightning at the other before it could pounce on either Grey or Pete. Over the crackle of energy she said, "Go, now."

Grey and Pete sped off without hesitation into the night. When their backs were no longer visible Ronin turned to Zeus. "Are you disappointed he did not ask you along, big fellow?"

"A little…I guess we did too good of job earlier huh?" Zeus said shrugging. "Nobody left to fight?"

A loud thunderous bellow was issued from behind them. Both men turned their tall frames around, one slim, the other broad, to see who their challenger was. The pigtailed girl bellowed again at them, a noise suited more to prehistory when large lizards roamed the earth than modern suburbia. She doubled over a bit like she had a stomach cramp, cradling her arms around the doll at her midsection. Her pigtails swayed around her as she shook with what seemed to be pain. When she moved her hands back they could see the doll had turned around in its carrier and was burying itself into the girl's stomach, parting black tinted flesh as it dug a large hole into the demon child's abdomen. The noise that came from her this time held equal parts anguish and rage as the wound resealed itself.

Ronin had created another blade tinted with energy in his hand, and he turned to Zeus lifting his eyebrows in an unspoken question. Zeus just shook his shaggy mane and shrugged his bulking shoulders. Their attention was drawn back to the girl when her screams stopped. She stood, stooped over like a marionette without someone to tug on the strings. Her arms hung limply from her sides, and her neck sagged so far that her chin was resting on her thin chest.

In a rush of shadows a gigantic figure ripped out from the child's back. Pieces of blackened flesh and gore showered the asphalt and splattered, making hissing sounds where they landed on the streetlights. When the monster had cleared the small body that it had been contained in, it threw its black limbs wide; arms spilled over into the physical world and knocked lampposts over. It stood on reverse articulated legs that raised its height to over three times that of the already tall men. A pair of large bat-like wings unfurled from its back, the span of which scraped the sides of buildings on either side of the four lane street breaking windows on the upper stories.

Broken glass raining down around it, the monster bellowed another roar and slammed massive fists into the road sending a shock wave in the men's direction, nearly toppling them.

Zeus gained his balance first, and turned to Ronin bellowing, "Never mind! This is more like it. Bwaaa!"

He charged the monster, light dropping in sparks from his pumping fists, with the lean Asian warrior close behind. The demon swung a massive arm at Zeus when he was in range, but the large man moved his metaphysical bulk whip quick like a dancer and dodged the creature's strike. He used his momentum to carry himself around behind the demon where he grabbed a hold of a gigantic wing in one hand and swung himself up clinging to the creature's neck, belting out a battle laugh as he held on. The she-devil's head was large and saurian in appearance, but its neck was thin and bird like, giving the big man an easy place to grapple onto.

Where Zeus was graceful with his bulk, Ronin moved in an embodiment of the phrase "faster than thought". He held a static blade of light in each hand, chiseled katanas of focused energy crackling with sparks along their razor-sharp edges, as he harried the giant demon form from the front. The monster wailed in pain as the two men flooded it with energy, eating away at it. With a jump and rush of air from its wings the demon took flight to escape the blades of the dexterous soldier, at the same time reaching back to grab onto Zeus.

The Viking double had embedded himself like a huge hairy tick on the demon's neck. The monster managed to dislodge him by digging into its own "flesh" and tearing the surrounding area off its back. It cocked an arm back dripping with its own gore and threw Zeus at Ronin who had scaled the closest lamp post to strike at the demon while it was airborne. The two warriors connected with a shower of sparks and rolled end over end down the deserted city street.

When they came to a stop Zeus was lying atop Ronin in a very compromising position. Ronin said primly, "Would you please remove yourself?"

"Ha! You love it skinny and you know it." Zeus leaned down and kissed Ronin on the cheek before he got to his feet and reached a hand down to help Ronin up. The other man took the proffered hand sending sparks flying, but he said, "I have half a mind to just lie here and let that she-devil eat you, you uncouth barbarian."

"Nah, you'd miss out on all the fun." Zeus responded with a wink and threw a lightning bolt over his shoulder without looking. It crashed into the flying she-devil's torso and sent her falling back to the ground with a resounding thud. Several car alarms started wailing when she landed. Zeus grinned and turned, running after the fallen monster.

***

"Why doesn't he come? Why doesn't he love me?" Raven asked.

"Because he can't love. Grey doesn't love anyone," the voice instructed. "That is why he is so powerful. His lack of love allows him to make the hard choices, choices that a person who could feel love would never willingly make."

"But if he doesn't love," Raven reasoned, "then why stay and do what he does?"

"He isn't staying, remember?" the voice said harshly. "He's leaving. Love isn't enough to keep him here. You're not enough to keep him here. He isn't coming for us. He does not love us. We need to accept it, and survive how ever we can, right?"

"Maybe, maybe not," Raven returned the voice's favorite response back on it and retreated as far as she could into her small mental bunker. The bunker had shrunk down to the size of a club house. As the walls crumbled she braced them up. The windows had long since been cracked and mortared over with whatever she could imagine, blocking her view from the inside. Her bunker was damaged and rundown but it was still there, still hers, for now.

Chapter 22

Y'all want to know what the hardest part of my job is? It ain't destroying demons, suffering the righteous looks from angels, or standin' back and watching humanity screw itself over year after year without lifting a finger until the very last instance. No, those things ain't so bad once a man gets used to them. Even regret don't get on my nerves so much as the job itself does.

Ask any stay at home parent, garbage man, factory worker, or mailman. They can tell you the worst part of my job, because it is the worst part of theirs too. It never fucking ends. It's just like the laundry, the dishes, the trash, the mail, or the parts on the assembly line. You save the universe today and you have to save it tomorrow, and the next day, and the next. It keeps going on, and the real bitch of it is that the only way to stop it is to let everything fall apart into chaos. That sounds melodramatic I know, I'm sorry, but look how often those other folks that do redundant jobs sort of lose their minds. Now imagine the shit storm that would come about if I went, as I believe the term is, postal?

Most of the time folks don't want to hear about that. No, they want everything in this life or afterlife wrapped up in neat little packages of task A done, now task B, and once those are done we never have to do them again. Bullshit! Come on, nothing works like that. What, do you really believe that life is a nice tidy package?

People hold on to that concept so tightly it is a form of fanaticism. Cultures carry it over into their mythos and entertainment. Do you honestly think after all the short folks with hairy feet were done with their epic pilgrimage to melt a piece of jewelry that some other evil creature didn't craft a magic necklace the very next day? Or do you think that the dark side or light side wins? No, the story never ends. The battles always continue on and on. We indoctrinate children from birth with the story of "the hero wins and the evil villain fails." Sure that happens sometimes, but other times the villain eats the heroes face and stir fries his balls in olive oil and garlic. It has to happen from time to time. We can't tell the little ones that, I agree. But look around, go on I got time, what do you see? The world is now full of little ones who never grew up past those stories. They are adults in every sense of the word, but they never had to learn that the story never ends. They run about livin' in a fairy tale world thinking good guys win and bad guys lose. Ha, I've met several presidents and dictators who were breathing examples that that ain't the case.

I bet you've been wondering, "What about angels, Grey? You're always talking about fighting demons, but what about

300

angels?" It happens of course, less often than demons, but angels get carried away at times too. Woodstock, yeah you heard me, the original Woodstock back in '69 out in New York State. I had to step in and stop what was going on, not with a bang or flash of light and thunder like I do with demons; angels wouldn't respond to that. So I slowly walked among those dancin' and swayin' bodies and planted the suggestions that material possessions and hedonism weren't so bad after all, and those young hippies eventually grew into middle aged men driving Beamers. I had to do it. Some dreams are wonderful, but the repercussions if those dreams were realized would be catastrophic. Those angels were so caught up in the moment they did not see how they were changing the focus of an entire generation of Americans. If I'd let them go on, who knows? Maybe we would have had peace, and that pretty dream would have ended the world.

For every happy ending there has to be a shitty one too. The real ending to the universe will just be an ending, neither happy nor sad. Everything would be gone, without a single entity or soul stirring about to mourn it. I don't want that, and I think it's safe to assume you don't either, so for now I'll just keep on doing the same thing day after day after day……

***

The cloud-laden sky started to drop cold, almost sleet-like rain as Pete and Grey made their way to the football stadium. They encountered no resistance on their trek even when they drew to within a few blocks of their destination. Pete commentated on this, "Nothing trying to stop us? That's a good thing right? I mean the creepy kid and the pussycats tried, so was that all Legion had left to throw at us? It's just tall, dark and ugly now, right?"

"No, Pete, it isn't a good sign," Grey corrected him as they slowed to a walk when the bleachers hovered into view, looming over the nearby houses creating an eerily gothic scene a reminder to Grey that humanity only padded their gladiators now but had not abolished the practice. Grey stopped completely and pulled Pete down under the cover of a hedge when the shadowy form of a winged demon playing sentinel soared around to their side of the stadium. Pete, to his credit, did not blurt out a question but looked questioningly at Grey who pointed to his eyes then to the demon that had roosted on the press box watching the road they had just been approaching on.

In a voice so quiet that Pete had to strain to hear him, Grey said, "It's a bad sign Pete. Legion is playing the last pieces he has

302

closely. That either means he's desperate and down to his last resources, or he wants to prolong this last bit of torture with Raven and use her against me."

"What, like clichéd bad guy monologue-ing?" Pete asked.

"Yeah, pretty much," Grey said nodding his head in agreement.

"Bullshit!" Pete whisper yelled as loudly as he dared. "Why would a super powered mega demon bother with banter? That crap only happens in movies and usually shitty movies at that."

"It's not that farfetched, Pete," Grey said. "Think about it. We're talking 'demons' basically creatures that are obsessed with power. What's the point in having power if you can't hold it over someone? Legion is worse about it than any other demon I've faced. It's one of the reasons it takes control over other demons; that way it always has an audience to bask in awe over the power it has. Legion is a bully, and bullies love to gloat. Hell that's probably why that Tommy kid was attracted to it. Like attracts like, right?"

"So you're saying all those over-the-top Bond bad guys were actually realistic?" Pete asked.

"In our world, psychologically speaking? Yes," Grey said. "There is always an exception, but not many demons will just take a life without gloating. Maybe that's the Source's way of giving us a chance to keep the Balance, a few moments of monologue to readjust the scales? I don't rightly know, but if you ever come across a demon that just kills without pausing to savor it, remember what I taught you."

"Yeah, what's that?" Pete asked.

"Run, really fast."

"Right…thanks," Pete said sarcastically.

"Seriously Pete, you don't mess with a killing machine like that. They're rare, but they are out there. Legion ain't one of them, so just remember it when the time comes." Grey said turning his eyes to the sentinel demon. He debated their next course of action. If the lookout demon stayed there much longer he would have to forget whatever element of surprise he had hoped to gain and go after Raven. The longer he waited the worse off he feared she would be.

Grey had started to shift his feet to stand when the vulture demon jumped down from its perch and swung out over the parking lot soaring like a stingray given flight. Without Legion's early warning system to call out an alarm Grey and Pete started walking toward the bleachers. Grey spoke out of the side of his mouth as they strolled, "Pete I'm going to call

Legion out once we're in there. Whatever he throws at us, I need you to keep it off my back until I can get to Raven. Are you with me?"

"There may be some screaming that sounds a lot like a little girl," Pete said, "but that's just my war cry. Don't let it distract you."

"Fair enough," Grey said ruefully and slapped Pete on the shoulder. They were walking down the same path they were the previous night, ending at a tunnel leading up to the field. Grey and Pete stood for a minute at the same handrail overlooking the field. Before Grey announced their presence he turned to Pete, his gray eyes starting to glow with a white blue light. He smiled at Pete and said, "Let's go."

***

The giant winged she-devil thrashed in pain swiping huge hands about its face and head trying to dislodge the phantasmic Wandjina who wove in and out of the creatures head like a swarm of angry hornets. Wandjina's amorphous body momentarily hovered in front of the demon's face. When the monster opened its mouth to bellow a challenge Wandjina flew down its gullet disappearing completely into the monster's head. The she-devil shrieked pressing clawed hands the size of couches to her temples.

"Quickly now," Ronin ordered as he and Awha sprinted out from behind the cover of an alley dumpster. Ronin started striking at the monster's lower body once again while it was distracted, carving smoking lines of light on its legs. He twirled his blades about like a dervish as Awha (having destroyed the last of the panthers) created a small star in her hands. The she-devil screamed louder as the light started to eat at her form. When it swiped a talon-tipped hand down at the diminutive Awha, the miniature star burned two of the demon's claws off. The palm-sized star reflected off the Asian women's oversized shades as a tiny smile spread out from the only exposed portion of her face.

Energy began spilling over into the physical world in large sloppy bursts. With that much power being thrown about it came as no surprise to any of the warriors when they heard the hissing sound of the sleet hitting Awha's handheld star. The she-devil staggered back from the small woman, trying to escape into an alley and the deeper cover of darkness within, and attempted to remove the vicious amoeba that was tearing her apart from the inside too. Ronin circled around behind her literally cutting off the demon's retreat with his flashing blades. The demon swung its damaged hand at him and lost its remaining digits, but the force of the blow knocked Ronin from his feet and sent him crashing into the side of a nearby building.

Ronin staggered to his feet shaking off the blow. He looked down at his now soiled suit, and sighing ran a hand across the worst sections. When he finished he was nattily attired once more. Before wading back into the fray he looked up to the top of the nearby courthouse. It was the tallest building on Main Street at six stories high, and from the tip of the clock tower he could see the burly shape of Zeus getting to his feet. Zeus threw both arms up toward the storm-choked sky, and lightening poured down into his outstretched hands. His body jerked around a bit but then steadied and seemed to be pulling the power right out of the storm. He started glowing and pulsing with contained light, yet he called more down from the sky.

When the large man bellowed out, "Move now!" All three warriors stopped their harassment and fled. Wandjina swooped out of the she-devil's nostrils and scooped Awha up in her arms as she passed. Ronin ducked back into the alley the demon had been trying to hide in and watched the creature stagger around after all its antagonists stopped at once. It turned its massive head from side to side trying to figure out where they had gone, so it did not see the enormous bolt of lightning Zeus threw at it until it was pierced through the chest like an insect in an entomologist's display case. The demon flailed about on the ground trying to escape from the light burrowing into its chest. Zeus started throwing storm charged bolt after bolt into the she-devil. Its wails were barely audible over the barrage of power Zeus was sending its way. Chunks of asphalt were showering up from the impact, and the tar used to seal cracks was running into the gutters.

The monstrous demon stopped thrashing and started to dissolve like a shadow at high noon. Zeus stopped his light show and yelled down, "Is the fucking thing dead yet?"

"I do believe so…wait," Ronin answered when he saw a small shape scampering away from the downed bulk. He sped over toward it and skewered the evil patchwork doll on one of his blades, raising the small form, now dissolving too, up to eye level. Shaking his head he whispered, "Downright disturbing."

***

Stepping out onto the center of the field Grey threw back arms and yelled, "Legion! Show yourself, demon!"

Light bulbs in the scoreboard burst into a shower of sparks at the sound of Grey's voice, and the glass windows of the press box, concession stand, and nearby gymnasium burst out in cascades. Pete muttered a quiet, "Impressive."

"Thanks Pete. I was worried it may be a bit melodramatic," Grey said turning to face his friend.

"No, no it was just right. Not too much - Oh Shit!" Pete said the last in his war cry because the tall two-eyed form of Legion had appeared behind Grey. No slowly melting up from the ground tonight, just nothing there one second and nightmare given form the next. Before Grey could turn around Legion had one skeletal arm cocked to strike. Pete tackled Grey out of the way as Legion struck. Black talons ripped down Pete's back sending spikes of ice cold fire through his core as he fell to the ground.

Legion did not hesitate as it drove its advantage home with slashing claws and snapping fangs. Grey rolled with the momentum of Pete's tackle and put forth a shield of energy to protect them from the surprise strike. As Legion pummeled the luminous gray dome that was keeping it from getting at its downed prey, gunmetal sparks flew from the demon's ink black fists. The barrier held under the onslaught providing Grey with a chance to touch Pete's back, sending healing warm light into his wounds. "Come on Pete. You alright buddy?"

Pete groaned as he started to turn over saying, "Damn it man. You said he'd monologue!"

"Eh, so I was wrong," Grey said shrugging his shoulders. "It's got to happen to everybody sometime right? Nobody's perfect I'll try and keep it to these once in a blue moon type occasions."

"Whatever man," Pete said staring up at the night sky. He stirred, rolling over into a crouch facing the side of the shield that Legion was attacking like a rabid gorilla on steroids. "Shit! Fuck!" Pete yelled scurrying away from the demon and sat as close to Grey as he could before continuing, "Okay…okay it looks really, really pissed man. What do we do now, Grey?"

Legion had summoned what was left of its army as it raged against Grey's shield. They had charged onto the football field surrounding the two men. Scampering about around the protective circle in a wave of black bodies and flashing red eyes, the demons poked at the barrier checking it for weaknesses. Pete looked around wide-eyed with another war cry perched to escape his lips as he surveyed the creatures pounding on Grey's shield. Grey answered, "I could probably hold them off until dawn when they would retreat, but I doubt Raven would last another day. I have a plan, we could…"

Grey trailed off as all of the demons stopped attacking and stood gargoyle still as a purring voice spoke from behind Legion's tall spare frame. "Let me talk to him, hmm, lover? It could be fun."

A decidedly female form rounded into view trailing a clawed finger down Legion's arm. What was left of Raven looked like she had been dipped in tar and stretched out into feline proportions only her features gave away her identity. Her eyes smoldered out at them as she said, "You should have left me, Grey. Now you've gotten Pete killed as well."

She prowled around Grey's dome in a circular route. The other demons shied away from her, parting like a living curtain whenever her path brought her near them, always providing Grey and Pete with an uninterrupted view. There was a thin onyx colored leash that started around her throat and ended in one of Legion's boney hands. Grey noticed that the hallmark third eye had yet to make a visible appearance on Raven's forehead. She halted her pace and crouched down to be at face level with them saying, "Such a shame. He had great potential too."

Grey could read no sign in her words, body language or aura if there was any of the woman he knew still in there ready to strike, or not, as she had planned. He evaluated the distance the other demons were giving her and judged by the leash that Legion did not quite have full control yet, but as the thing wearing Raven's face had said he was not just gambling with his life now. He had brought Pete into this too. Grey looked over at Pete, and the young featured black man met his eyes with jolts of red light firing in his irises. Pete nodded; Grey hoped it was in support, because the time for deliberation was over. He had to act.

Without turning around or moving at all from where he kneeled to keep from warning Legion's tools, Grey threw his shield out in an explosion of light. Monsters tumbled end over end as the wave of energy struck them. Some were launched so far back from the blast that their bodies landed in smoking lumps on the bleachers. Others who were not strong enough vanished completely in the wave of power as Grey slowly stood from his crouch. Legion screamed in impotent frustration clearing the light from its eyes.

Pete was tossing out globes of red light before the creatures had had a chance to recover. Two of them dissolved in a blinding flash as they attempted to strike back. A few smoldering bodies had scampered back to the field from the bleachers, and Grey ripped through them in a burst of illuminated violence tearing the demons limb from limb with incandescent fists. A smaller version of wolf demon jumped at Pete with its jaws open to rend and tear, but Pete threw a ball of crimson light down its throat that exploded in a

312

firecracker fashion ripping it apart from the inside out.

"Ha! That's right! I'm just burning doing the *Neutron Dance*! Who else wants a piece?" Pete yelled, thumping a fist on his chest.

"I do," Legion's snarling voice said directly behind him. Pete turned around wide-eyed just as a large shadowed fist stuck him full in the stomach. Pete flew backward the length of the football field to smack into the goal post. Sliding down he whispered, "Ow."

Landing in a heap, Pete looked around for Grey. All that was left of Legion's vast demonic army was the panther demon formerly known as Raven and the skeletal puppet master himself. Gray was fighting with his back to Legion fending off Raven's newly added black tipped claws. She would swipe; he would dodge or block with an open palmed strike encased in light. It was obvious to Pete that Grey was holding back to keep from injuring her if some of his friend was still there. Legion, not caring how it gained its victory, kicked a spurred heel at the back of Grey's knees causing him to falter, and Raven snarled in rapturous joy as she drove into Grey's torso knocking him over onto his back where she perched on his chest. Legion screamed its joy into the night as Pete tried to get back to his feet and help his friend.

***

"See how easy he crumples before us!" the purring voice snarled. "He was never that strong. He was more myth than substance. He never deserved our love did he? He is fragile, weak, and soft. More bark than bite."

"He was holding back; he does love us," Raven argued from her bunker that was now no larger than a closet. "No, wait. Me. He loves me. There is no 'us'."

"Too late for that now, sweetie. There isn't enough of you left to fight off a fly," the voice said appearing in front of Raven for the first time. The shape the voice had taken looked like her, but it was not her. All her soft lines were contorted into harsh angles on the voice's face. It continued to mock her, "I'm going to tear his throat out, and you can watch from this tiny mental coffin of yours. Then I'll use the power I gain from devouring him to aid my efforts in rooting out what's left of you."

"No, no you can't. This is me; I have control," Raven screamed into the twisted mirror image of the voice.

"Please, I am you too," the voice said dismissively. "You pathetic little child I am what you kept hidden all those years. I am

314

what those men made you into in that hellish prison as they raped your body and licked at your tears! I am what Grey stopped you from becoming you stupid whiny whore! Now shut up! I want to enjoy this."

***

Grey did his best to keep his friend from shredding his body with darkness and devouring him. Legion was sending as much energy as it could down the dark leash it held in its fist, lending its newest pet power as it tried to destroy one of Legion's oldest adversaries. The tall demon danced and capered about, ululating in its terrifying imitation of laughter at the struggling companions. It could feel the fear and anger radiating off of them like a bonfire as it basked in the glory of the moment. Grey held the presence of mind to think to himself, *Oh sure, now you're gloating, you piece of shit.*

He had held back as long as he dared, and between grunts of effort Grey said, "Raven, darlin', if you can hear me in there, don't do this. I can't choose you over the Balance, you know that. If Legion takes me now I don't know if the Balance will hold. I refuse to be the linchpin that destroys everything. Can you hear me? I'm sorry, darlin'. I love you, but I am sorry."

The master demon was not the only one to gain in skill during their century apart. A Balance warrior could not keep the energy he used, what Grey had told Pete was true, but that did not stop him from learning how to draw as much power as he could use at one time and directing where it went. Grey started to gather in a huge amount of power from the Source, Harmony, and the world around him. It would be one big shove with enough energy to destroy both Raven and Legion. It would hurt. He would have a gaping emotional wound for some time, but better to be merciful and do it as quickly as possible.

I'll grant what piece of mercy I can, Grey thought, *for a loved one.* At the very last second before he sent the torrent of light he had built up barreling into the demons, a small voice escaped from the panther as it was close to sinking its jaws into his face, "I love you too."

A gun appeared in the demon's left paw. She smiled sadly, and then winked one eye at Grey. Before he could stop her, Raven lifted the gun to the side of her head and pulled the trigger. Light flashed from the muzzle, and a glob of black tore from the woman's face. Grey and Legion screamed simultaneously, both in a rage over loss but out of two entirely different mindsets and perspectives.

When the body on top of him sagged to the side no longer pinning him down, Grey rose to his feet with power crackling uncontrolled all around him. The artificial grass of the field melted and bubbled from the heat of the energy Grey had gathered. Legion had stopped dancing and laughing. It stood emotionlessly facing the warrior blazing with light in front of it. The moment held an air of finality as man faced demon, opposite polarities of power incarnate, and they acknowledged each other with simple eye contact. There was no sound as Grey charged Legion; black void met bright light. He surrounded the demon with his power, trapping the monster as it thrashed about in the center of a giant sphere of rage fueled energy. The globe swelled out to a diameter equal to the width of the field before exploding in a supernova wave, sending energy rippling out in three hundred and sixty degrees of direction.

A quiet settled over the stadium. Pete was the only thing capable of movement as he sat blinking. He stirred about and looked around noticing that the stadium had suffered major collateral damage, or spill over as Grey called it. The plastic grass had melted into odd patterns of swirled colors; the aluminum bleacher seats were standing out at buckled and twisted angles in their concrete foundations. Add that to Grey's earlier entrance, and Pete figured the school board and athletic boosters were going to be ticked off at whatever vandals took the rap.

In the ensuing silence Pete managed enough strength to crawl over to the limp form of Raven laying on her side in the fetal position. The woman had returned to the body she used when Pete had first met her. He held her close to his chest, but he could feel no energy pulsing out from her, no spark of life or whisper of the vitality that this woman had once possessed. Pete could see no sign of Grey or Legion anywhere among the wreckage. There was nobody with him on the field as dawn started to peek over the edges of the bleachers. Pete began to cry and shake as he sat there, mumbling through his tears, "I'm sorry I wasn't fast enough to help, either of you. I'm sorry."

Then he felt Harmony open her door inside his mind, "Peter, Peter it is alright. She is still there, or else she would have dissolved or dispersed in Grey's storm. Look closer, look here."

Harmony guided Pete's hand over to Raven's core where a warm sensation pulsed up his hand. A small spark jumped from his fingertips. He started to laugh and cry again at the same time. Raven murmured something he could not make out. Pete brought his ear down closer to her and asked her to speak up. She repeated herself, and Pete could just make out a very weak voice piece together the phrase, "Crazy ass white woman."

Pete stopped crying altogether and started laughing hysterically instead. "Damn right girl, damn right." He rocked her back and forth in his arms.

Harmony guided Pete's head up toward the rising sun as it illuminated the field and before she retreated she said, "Watch."

The light that had not so long ago torn through the stadium came seeping back in around the bleachers, field, and scoreboard. As the sun cleared the concrete risers fully, the light formed into a glowing ball at center field a few feet from where Pete held Raven. A rangy and thin figure started to take shape within the sphere. It stepped forward as the light faded, and as one dusty broken boot followed the other out onto the melted turf the light disappeared.

Grey crouched down and touched Raven on the cheek smiling. When he looked up at Pete his eyebrows drew together in a frown and he said, "Pete, are you crying? You are, aren't you? Man what a sissy."

Pete started laughing again, but around gasps he managed to say, "Asshole."

Chapter 23

Convalescence, a word that brings to mind old folk's homes now-a-days, but that is not the only meaning it has. It means to recover strength and heal over time. Soldiers from any war you care to name know the meaning of convalescence. Some say time heals all wounds, get busy livin' or get busy dyin', but they all mean the same thing really, at least to men like me.

Some wounds run deeper than others. There are hurts and pains that no physician can get to. Injuries to the spirit are harsh; those pains typically run Marianas trench-like deep, with self-inflicted ones being the worst kind. I've seen mothers tear themselves to spiritual shreds over their children, devastated lovers who rip pieces of themselves out tryin' to bring back what they lost, if only for a moment, inflicting more harm by not letting go than if they had just let time do its job.

I hear folks say a man digs his own grave in life. You always think of that as a task done all at once, but really it's done a spoonful here and shovelful there. The heartache from a friend's death will take a big ass scoop out of the hole, but a newborn baby adds a couple handfuls back in. People seem to forget that, and to me it only seems reasonable that if you can dig your own grave, then given the *opportunity, you could start to fill that fucker back in too.*

It's up to you and how you view it of course, but why should we not be allowed to right our wrongs? You break a bone and it heals, most times teachin' you a lesson in the process. Sometimes fate really screws you over and that broken bone don't heal right, at best giving you a gimp, at worst turnin' gangrenous and killing you. I don't get along too well with fate. No sir, I say fuck that cruel sadistic bitch. She don't care none what she does, so grab a hold and fix the things you can, friends.

When you no longer have a physical body all injuries drive right through to the core of your being. The broken bones are a lot harder to mend when they're no longer there. Spirit flesh or energy can still burn given the right conditions, but maybe instead of burning that soul can turn it into a kind of tempering instead. A hard craft to learn when it comes to tangible steel, so imagine the skill it takes to apply that to metaphysics instead. Boggles the mind a bit, but I know a few out there who have done it, and I firmly believe that what one man can do, another can do.

Remember, you can lick a wound too much and infect what you were trying to heal. It's all a matter of, dare I say it, Balance.......

***

Don's Eats diner was a more appealing and busy establishment in the light of day. Pete, Grey, and Raven had all squeezed into one side of the booth the men had occupied previously. Zeus with his tremendous bulk had filled the entire opposite bench seat. The same tired waitress now swooped about with a carafe of coffee in one hand all but bouncing from foot to foot as she filled orders. She had tied her hair back in a braid and tiny lavender lights held on to it emitting small squeaks and giggles as the hair bounced along with its owner.

Raven sat huddled in the far corner of the booth, pressed up against the wall sipping a glass of orange juice, absorbing the warm morning sun as it filtered in from the window. Grey was sandwiched between her and Pete, eating a cheeseburger and fries while Pete poked at his omelet and glared daggers at him.

Zeus had an entire buffet of breakfast foods spread out before him. Plates devoted to single foods: bacon piled three layers thick, sausage patties, hash browns, French toast, and pancakes stacked by the dozen. He had managed to cajole the waitress into leaving him an entire carafe of coffee as his personal mug, and it would send muddy brown trickles down the sides of his beard when he gulped from it.

A newspaper slapped down onto the outside edge of the table because it was the only space clear enough for it. All four heads turned up when Septemsab'aa nudged Zeus in the ribs with an elbow as he tried to free up enough room to sit. "Move over, young man."

"Sorry sir," Zeus said and sent the old bench seat to creaking as he wiggled his massive cheeks to make room.

"That is better, thank you," Sep said as he sat. "I thought you may find this newspaper interesting. This is the local herald from a certain small town in Illinois you all have visited recently. Where is Ronin? I thought he was helping you?"

"He did," Grey answered, "but you know him. When I suggested he get some breakfast with us he asked if we were eating real food or cheeseburgers. So he and the ladies went back east." Grey picked up his cheeseburger and took a huge bite.

Sep raised his eyebrows derisively but unfolded the newspaper and started to read aloud, "The first article, I am unsure of its pertinence, but I thought it merited mentioning. 'Two hundred year old clock tower struck by massive lightning storm melts beyond repair.' Did any of you have anything to do with that?"

He said this while staring directly at Zeus. The big man shrugged his shoulders

323

sheepishly but kept looking at his plate and stuffed an entire pancake into his mouth making it hard to decipher his response, but it sounded like, "Mmmphbe, bfft if lmmed coppml."

"Be that as it may," Sep continued, "but looking cool is hardly a justifiable excuse for being so sloppy. I spoke with Harmony, and she agrees with me. Please be more careful in the future. Another article of interest reads *Local teens, heroes*. A group of young men saved two boys who were trapped under heavy machinery at a construction site on the edge of town. I found that to be a rather touching tale of redemption myself."

"Luck," Grey grunted.

"Perhaps," Sep agreed, "but change comes about in strange ways. We both know that. One man's luck is another man's redemption."

Grey only nodded his head and took another sip of Coke. He reached out his free hand and laced his fingers through Raven's. She turned away from the window to give him a tired smile, but it was still a smile. Sep watched the interaction speculatively but was respectful enough not to comment on it in front of everyone.

Pete reached across grabbing the paper out of Sep's hands and said, "No shit! Check this out. *Local man missing, the search for*

Thomas McDougal continues, he has been missing for three days and friends and family fear the worst. I kept wondering what happened to his body. I just figured so much shit was going on none of us noticed if the local police were up to anything around the football field or not. Huh, what do you think happened?"

Sep responded, "No way to know Peter. There are just some answers even we are not privy to. I must say I am surprised to see you so quiet, Grey…well, more so than typical I mean. Is this a last meal among compatriots? Or are you planning to stay around a bit longer? You know my opinion on the subject. I feel there is no sense overdoing it."

"For the moment I'm stayin'," Grey said. "Pete here ain't ready yet, plus he might start crying if I left."

"Bwa…" Zeus' laugh was cut off by a dirty look from Pete and punctuated with a zap of red lightening sent into his foot under the table. Sep looked at them in disapproval and sighed, saying to Grey, "For the moment?"

"Yeah, Sep, for the moment," Grey agreed, squeezing Raven's hand, sending orange light dancing around their intertwined fingers. "That's all anybody can guarantee ain't it, just for the moment?"

Sep nodded, "Very true, Ramadi. Anything other than that is more than we have the right to ask." He stood, bowed slightly at the waist, walked away from the table and out of the diner.

"Grey, did you ask him not to teleport?" Pete asked.

"Yep."

"That's what I thought," Pete said. "Hey look…Um…I'm glad you're staying."

"Yeah, me too," piped in Zeus, but with a mouthful of sausage it sounded more like "Ymm, mff ooo!"

"Me too," Raven said, fully looking at her friends for the first time since they had sat down. She tightened her grip on Grey's hand, "For the moment."

"Um," Pete added staring down at his coffee. He swirled in another packet of sugar and said, "I hate to bring this up now, but for the life of me I can't think of a good time to do so…um, did anybody ever catch that raccoon?"

***

A human body is a heavy thing, but it is even heavier when it is dead weight. It may take a grown man a long time to drag a dead body from one place to another; for example, it might take a grown man a full day to drag a dead body from a football field in the center of a small town out to the surrounding farmland.

Using that example, it stands to reason that it would take something smaller than a grown man a longer time to pull or drag the same load, no matter if that something smaller had demonic assistance. It could take days, maybe three or more if the one doing the dragging were about the size of, perhaps, a raccoon.

Epilogue

I've lived a long time. I died a long time ago. How much longer will I live? Even now I don't have an answer for that one. Honestly, I don't reckon I want one either. It would take the wind out of my sails so to speak. People always say, "Oh, but I could make my peace with it and tell those I love how much they mean to me." Truly, is that what you'd do?

Wake up! Do it now if they mean something to you. Don't let things go unsaid. The clock is tickin' friends. Tomorrow ain't a guarantee; it's only a hope. Each individual person's story ends. It may be that your story is only a few tragic chapters long, or then again maybe your story will run on ad nauseam thick as a Biblical tome. Who knows? Maybe tomorrow morning on your way to work there'll be an accident, and Wham! Your story is over. Or maybe it ain't over. Maybe somebody will be standing there waiting for you, and they'll tell you about your choices.

Stay there hanging around, maybe turn into an angel or demon depending on the type of person you were, move on back to the Source, or just maybe y'all will come work with me, Jasper Reynolds, but you may as well just call me Grey.